D0364459

A NOTE FROM
CHRIS RYAN
SAS HERO

When I came up with the idea for *Battleground*, I drew on all my experiences of the first Gulf War.

Back in 1991, I was a member of an SAS patrol that was inserted deep behind enemy lines in Iraq. We flew in 200 miles by helicopter and were dropped off to look for missiles. Unfortunately, we were compromised by an Iraqi force. There was a large firefight and the patrol was split up. I ended up by myself, and the only way to escape was to walk to Syria (west of Iraq). It took 7 days and 8 nights in freezing conditions – I can't tell you how cold it was. Two of my colleagues actually froze to death. Every day I would lie up in a hollow and wait till nightfall before walking 40 kilometres every night. It was probably one of the worst experiences of my life. I eventually got to Syria, where I crossed the border to safety.

What you'll get in *Battleground* is a realistic account of how Ben survives being dragged into Afghanistan along the Pakistan border. Not only is this area inhospitable and very difficult to survive in, there's a war going on and Ben finds himself stuck right in the middle of this dangerous place.

When you put all these elements together you've got the start of a great novel, which will hopefully keep you turning those pages. If you do enjoy *Battleground*, don't forget to try some of my other Code Red novels which also feature Ben.

What are you waiting for? Read on!

Chris Ryan

CHRIS RYAN
SAS HERO

- Joined the SAS in 1984, serving
in military hot zones across the world.

- Expert in overt and covert operations in war
zones, including Northern Ireland, Africa, the
Middle East and other classified territories.

- Commander of the Sniper squad
within the anti-terrorist team.

- Part of an 8 man patrol on the
Bravo Two Zero Gulf War mission in Iraq.

- The mission was compromised. 3 fellow
soldiers died, and 4 more were captured as
POWs. Ryan was the only person to defy the
enemy, evading capture and escaping to Syria
on foot over a distance of 300 kilometres.

- His ordeal made history as the longest escape
and evasion by an SAS trooper, for which
he was awarded the Military Medal.

- His books are dedicated to the men
and women who risk their lives fighting
for the armed forces.

CHARACTER FILE

NAME: Ben Tracey

NICKNAME: Big Ben (known as this at school)

AGE: 14

HOMETOWN: Macclesfield, Cheshire

CURRENT STATUS: Schoolboy with a knack for being in the wrong place at the wrong time

HAIR: Dark blond

EYES: Blue

SKIN: White

HEIGHT: 1.74 metres

WEIGHT: 61 kilograms

BUILD: Slim. Athletic

BACKGROUND: Mother – Dr Bel Kelland, an active environmentalist. Father – Russell Tracey, a chemist

SKILLS: Basic pilot skills. Horse riding. Strong swimmer. Computer wiz. Quick instincts. Calm under pressure. Some orienteering and navigational technique

INTERESTS: Music. Film. Keeping fit

LIKES: Pizza

DISLIKES: Termites

FEARS: Enclosed spaces. Snakes. Rats

BATTLEGROUND

FACT

On 7 September 1997, former Soviet military commander Alexander Lebev claimed that 100 Russian-made suitcase-sized nuclear bombs were currently 'not under Russian control'. The Russian Federation denied these claims, but they were backed up by Stanislav Lunev, the highest-ranking Soviet officer ever to defect from Russia. Lunev believed that some of these nuclear weapons had already been deployed. What was beyond doubt was that the Russians no longer knew where they were . . .

*Also by Chris Ryan, and published by
Random House Children's Books:*

The Code Red Adventures
FLASH FLOOD
WILDFIRE
OUTBREAK
VORTEX
TWISTER

The Alpha Force Series
SURVIVAL
RAT-CATCHER
DESERT PURSUIT
HOSTAGE
RED CENTRE
HUNTED
BLOOD MONEY
FAULT LINE
BLACK GOLD
UNTOUCHABLE

*Published by the Random House Group
for adult readers:*

Non-fiction
The One That Got Away
Chris Ryan's SAS Fitness Book
Chris Ryan's Ultimate Survival Guide

Fiction
Stand By, Stand By
Zero Option
The Kremlin Device
Tenth Man Down
The Hit List
The Watchman
Land of Fire
Greed
The Increment
Blackout
Ultimate Weapon
Strike Back
Firefight
Who Dares Wins

One Good Turn
Adult Quick Read for World Book Day 2008

LOCATION:
AFGHANISTAN

NOT FOR RESALE

AFGHANISTAN FACT SHEET

Location:
Between Iran in the west and Pakistan in the east

Current status:
War zone

Recent history:
The Soviet Union invaded in 1979 and fought a long war with Afghan tribal warriors, known as the Mujahideen. The Soviets withdrew in 1989 and Afghanistan descended into civil war, before coming under the rule of the repressive Taliban regime. The Taliban allowed the Al-Qaeda terrorist Osama bin Laden to hide in their country after his organization destroyed New York's World Trade Center on 11 September 2001. This led to a coalition invasion of Afghanistan, led by the British and the Americans, who overthrew the Taliban. But there is still a determined Taliban resistance, especially in the south of the country, and the coalition is engaged in a bloody, devastating war with these determined insurgents.

Prologue

The mountains of Afghanistan, 1986.

'Ambush!'

Dmitri Kirov, the Soviet soldier, barked the word in Russian. He was in the middle of the convoy, which came to a sudden halt. There were ten of them in three vehicles, all heavily armed because they carried a precious cargo: the case at his feet in the rear of this open-backed truck.

They'd been going slowly. The road up into the mountains was narrow. The pale, wintry sun failed to melt the patches of ice on the road, and with the wind it felt like it was several degrees below zero. Worse than that, their own army had littered this place with anti-personnel mines as part of their long war against the Mujahideen of Afghanistan. These mines were an

1

effective way of killing people. The trouble with them was that they didn't mind which people they killed: Mujahideen, innocent children, or Soviet soldiers.

To drive through this part of the world was to take your life in your hands.

'*Ambush!*'

Kirov was a tough man. A fierce soldier. They all were. That's why they'd been chosen for this job – a job where they could expect random attacks from a determined enemy. But even he knew, as he stood exposed in the open air with his AK-47 pointing straight ahead, that the situation was bad. To his right, on the slope leading up into the mountains, three men in black robes and head-dresses had appeared from nowhere. They each knelt on one knee and pointed their rifles in the direction of the convoy. Four more men appeared, two at the front of the convoy and two at the back, at a distance of about twenty metres. They were dressed the same way, but instead of rifles they carried rocket-propelled grenade launchers. RPG-7s. Dmitri Kirov would recognize them anywhere.

There was a still, horrible silence, then one of the men at the front barked an order.

The thumping sound of the grenades being launched went right through Kirov. But it was nothing compared to the sound they made when they hit the front and rear trucks in the convoy. It was a massive explosion that echoed across the mountains. The truck ahead of him was a sudden flash of orange fire and black smoke. He thought he heard the sound of one of his comrades screaming inside it.

The scream didn't last long.

Kirov felt his skin scorching; he could smell burning diesel and his own singed hair. Smoke surrounded him and he started firing blindly towards the slope. There was an immediate return of fire. Bullets started zipping over his head, but by some miracle they didn't hit him. He had to duck down into the back of the truck for cover, his head in his hands as fear overtook him.

He heard the sound of shouting and made a quick calculation. There had been four men in the front truck and three in the back, which meant that of the ten of them who had set out that morning, seven were already dead. Kirov expected to join them any second.

The comrades in the front of his truck started shouting, and then there was the sound of two shots.

Then silence. He knew what that meant.

With a cold, creeping feeling, Kirov realized he was the only one left.

The two trucks were still burning and crackling. He looked up from his crouching position, and through the wobbly heat haze he saw three of the black-robed men approach, their rifles pointing in his direction. Kirov knew there was no way he could fight his way out of this situation, so he left his AK-47 on the floor of the truck and raised his hands in the air. Perhaps the Mujahideen would show him mercy. Just perhaps . . .

A harsh voice, speaking Russian with an accent. 'Get down!'

Kirov hesitated.

'Get down! *Now!*'

He did as he was told, wincing from the heat of the burning metal on either side. Once he was down from the truck, one of his attackers grabbed him by the arm and pulled him to the edge of the road before forcing him to his knees and pointing a gun at his head. The rest of the ambushers swarmed over the truck like black wasps.

Kirov was shaking with fear. 'P-please,' he stuttered. 'Please, do not—'

'Silence!'

A second ambusher approached and the two black-robed men spoke in what Kirov supposed was the Afghan language of Pashtun. Then the man who held him at gunpoint spoke to him once more.

'What are you carrying in the back of the truck?' he demanded.

'N-nothing,' Kirov stuttered. 'It is nothing.'

'Kill him,' the second man said.

'*No! Wait!*' Kirov's breath came in sharp, frightened gasps. 'I will tell you.'

'You should do it quickly, if you don't want a bullet in your brain.'

Kirov could hardly get the words out. 'It is a weapon,' he said.

The two Mujahideen looked at each other. 'What sort of weapon?'

'A bomb,' Kirov replied. 'A suitcase bomb. Nuclear. If you destroy that truck, it will take out half this mountainside.'

Behind him, he heard the flickering sound of the two burning vehicles. His attacker slowly lowered his rifle and started unwinding the black cloth that was wound round his head. He had dark, sweaty skin and a long beard. His eyes glowed. Kirov couldn't tell if that was because of the reflection of the flames or for some other reason.

'A nuclear suitcase bomb,' the bearded man repeated. 'I have heard of such things.' He shouted an instruction, then watched as the Mujahideen on the truck carefully lifted the case and gently laid it on the side of the road two metres from where Kirov was kneeling.

Shaped like a cylinder, it was khaki-brown in colour and held together with canvas straps. It was rather battered and old – to look at it, you would think it was a soldier's trunk from an earlier war. The bearded man crouched down to inspect it. He stroked the case, rather like someone petting a cat. His face was sweating profusely, but a smile played on his lips.

He looked directly at Kirov. 'We will take it with us,' he said quietly. 'The day may come, God willing, when this weapon will change all our fortunes.' He said something again in Pashtun, and Kirov watched as two of the others picked the case up once more and started carrying it up the mountainside.

The bearded man stood up and for a moment he looked as if he was going to leave Kirov there on the roadside. *What will I tell my superiors?* the Russian thought to himself. The idea was almost as terrifying as being left here with the Afghans.

He didn't get a chance to think on it any further because he realized he was being spoken to. 'Get back into the truck,' the bearded man told him, nudging him once more with the butt of his rifle.

Kirov could only do what he was told. The two other trucks were burning less angrily now, but they still let off a lot of heat as he stumbled back towards his vehicle.

'Get into the back,' the Mujahideen instructed.

Kirov did so. His AK-47 was still lying on the floor of the truck. He wondered if he should bend down, pick it up and try to fire at his attackers. But he didn't have the time, because just then he realized what was happening. From the slope above him, one of the ambushers was raising his RPG launcher and pointing it in Kirov's direction.

'No!' the Russian shouted. '*No!*'

But too late.

He heard the sound of the RPG being launched. For a split second he saw it thundering towards him.

It was the last thing Dmitri Kirov ever saw. His truck exploded into a fireball just as the group of Afghan Mujahideen disappeared up the hillside, carrying the suitcase bomb and shouting in triumph as they went.

Chapter One

Twenty-three years later.

'Ladies and gentlemen, we will shortly be arriving in Islamabad, where it's a very hot Sunday morning. Please ensure your seatbelts are fastened and that any luggage is safely stowed under your seat or in the overhead lockers.' The pilot's voice was as calm and reassuring as pilots always are.

Ben Tracey's mum, Dr Bel Kelland, looked at him. 'Do your seatbelt up, love.'

'All right, Mum,' Ben replied. 'I heard.' And if Ben had heard, his school friends sitting in the seats around them probably had too.

'*Do your seatbelt up, love!*' a mocking voice said from behind.

Bel raised an eyebrow, but Ben shot her a warning

glance and she kept quiet.

Ben was nervous – on his mum's account, not his own. And not because of the flight – though he had reason enough to be, after his previous experiences in aeroplanes – but because of what she would be doing over the next couple of weeks. They would have an hour at Islamabad airport before Bel, Ben, his school friends and the teachers who were accompanying them took an internal flight to Quetta. Near there, Ben would be staying with a Pakistani family as part of a two-week exchange programme that his school regularly organized with a charity that promoted links between the two countries.

'Awareness!' Mr Knight had said to them weeks ago back at Ben's school. It was during a meeting with the six youngsters who were going on the exchange, and their parents. Mr Knight was a rather dull teacher with half-moon specs, long strands of grey hair combed over to hide his bald patch, and a fondness for the sound of his own voice. 'Awareness! That's what it's all about, ladies and gentlemen. Pakistan will be very different to Macclesfield. There'll be no' – he had waved his hands about in a fuddy-duddy way – 'no Nintendos out there. That's what you call them, isn't it? Anyway, you'll be living with real Pakistani families, eating with them, going to school with them and basically experiencing what life is like in a very different part of the world. It'll be a strange world to you, but believe me – when the Pakistani students come back here, your lives will seem equally strange to them. We've run the exchange for a number of years now, and although not all the students have found it easy, I believe they've all found it a richly rewarding experience . . .'

Ben had been one of the six students who, after two interviews – one with the school and one with the charity – had been selected to go on the exchange. Three boys – Ben, Jez Thompson and Ed Hughes; three girls – Rebecca Simpson, Nazindah Hasan and Amelia Roberts. Apart from the teachers, they would be his only British companions for the next two weeks. His mum's work, in the meantime, was going to take her over the border into Afghanistan. A rather different kettle of fish and Ben could tell that she was nervous too, even though she did her best not to show it.

His ears popped as the plane lost height.

'I still don't see why I can't come with *you*, Mum.' Ben was looking out of the window at the sun rising above the vast mountain ranges below. 'Someone could have taken my place on the exchange. Loads of people wanted to do it.'

'I've told you, Ben,' she said, gently putting one hand on his knee. 'It's too dangerous.'

'If it's too dangerous for me,' he replied, 'it's too dangerous for you.' He turned to look at her. 'There's a war going on in Afghanistan, Mum. People die there.'

'And that's why *you're* not going,' his mum replied. 'Look, Ben, Pakistan isn't exactly the soft option. I know you're going to have your friends around you, but it's not like going to summer camp. You need to be careful.'

Ben looked down. 'I know,' he said.

'I'm very proud of you, Ben,' she continued in that tone of voice she *knew* embarrassed him, but which she used anyway. 'Most kids your age spend their holidays playing on their computers. For you to come out here is very . . .' For a moment she appeared lost for words. 'I'm just proud of you, OK?'

Ben silently looked out of the window again. 'I just don't want you to get into trouble. I've read about Afghanistan in the papers. About the Taliban and everything. They're . . . they're vicious. And Helmand Province, where you're going, that's the worst place of all.'

'I'll be fine, Ben. My work is important. The people in Afghanistan are very poor. They need to be taught how to farm—'

'Yeah, yeah,' Ben interrupted, 'I know. Corn, pomegranates, soybeans, anything but poppies.'

Ben understood why she was going to such a dangerous part of the world. The main crop of the Afghan farmers was the poppy. Poppies meant heroin.

Almost all the heroin that hit the streets of Britain came from Afghanistan. The poppy fields had to be eradicated, but nobody could do that without showing the farmers how they could make a proper living by growing different crops. And so the British and Americans had invited scientists and environmental campaigners to the region to try and educate the locals in new farming methods. The scientists would be given heavy military escorts. But even so, not many people felt inclined to go to Afghanistan. Ben's mum was one of the few who were willing.

His dad had tried to persuade her not to go, but she had overruled him. That was just the way she was. 'And anyway,' she had said, 'the school will welcome volunteers to help with the exchange. I'll be able to go out and come back with Ben. Then we'll both feel better, won't we?'

Russell hadn't been able to argue with *that*, especially as Ben didn't exactly have a spotless record when it came to staying out of trouble.

'I'll be all right, Ben,' Bel said. 'I want to make sure you're settled in your village first. When I leave, I'll have a military escort and they'll take very, very good care of me.'

Ben didn't reply. He just continued to look out of the window as the plane descended towards their destination.

* * *

It was much later that day when they stepped out of the terminal of Quetta International Airport. There were ten of them: three boys, three girls, three teachers and Bel. The heat of the sun was like a slap on the face. Ben squinted, then pulled his shades out of his pocket and put them on. People swarmed around them. They were a strange mix. Some wore clothes that wouldn't be out of place on Oxford Street; others wore robes and sandals and looked to Ben like they were from another century. He noticed quite a lot of the locals staring at them.

Ahead of them was a large car park. The vehicles were all very old, but one of them looked less elderly than the others. It was a minibus that had once been cream but was now a dirty grey-brown because of the dust. A man leaned against it, the only other white face around. He looked about fifty, with grey, slicked-back hair, old jeans and a beige shirt. His tanned face spread into a smile when he saw them, and he waved.

'I can carry my own luggage, Ben,' Bel said lightly.

Ben shook his head. 'It's all right,' he said, and he struggled with both his mum's rucksack and his own as they walked towards the van.

He heard a noise from behind: a coughing sound that badly disguised the word, 'Creep!' Ben looked over his shoulder to see a class mate with blond, floppy hair. It was Ed Hughes and it was no secret that he and Ben didn't like each other much. In fact, when Ben had heard that Ed had successfully applied to go on the exchange, his heart had sunk. Before he could reply, however, he heard a sharp reprimand. 'That will do, Ed. Ben's just trying to be helpful. Maybe you could take a leaf or two out of *his* book.'

Ben cringed. Miss Messenger standing up for him would only add fuel to the fire. Sure enough, Ed continued leering at him, though he didn't say anything else. Ben was glad when they reached the minibus and he could dump the two bags on the ground.

The guy waiting for them held his arms out. 'Welcome, everybody,' he boomed. 'Welcome. *Welcome!*' Ben heard Ed snigger, but the man obviously didn't. 'Great to see you. Good flight? Hot today. Still, you'll have to get used to it. I'm Carl, by the way. I'll be taking you to Kampur. Not far, but it could take a while. Bad roads—'

Bel interrupted him by holding out her hand. 'Pleased to meet you, Carl,' she said with a smile. 'I'm Bel. This is Ben.'

'Of course, of course, pleased to meet you.' And as he spoke he was surrounded by the three teachers, who all shook his hand in turn. 'Everyone's looking forward to seeing you all,' Carl announced, 'and hearing all about life in England. Our charity doesn't get many people willing to come out this way, to be honest.

Plenty of people happy to sponsor children, but not to actually come out here. And awareness is everything, wouldn't you say? Shall we, ah . . .'

He opened the doors of the minibus and there was a moment of bustling. Miss Messenger and the other teachers – Mr Sawyer and Mr Knight – started organizing everyone, bellowing instructions about where the boys should go and where everyone should sit. Ed's voice rose above the hubbub – he didn't want to sit by a teacher – but most people seemed to ignore him. Miss Messenger approached Ben and Bel, a kind, concerned look on her face. 'Why don't the two of you sit in the front with Carl?' she said. 'If you want to, that is, Ben.'

'All right,' Ben said, quiet but secretly grateful. Miss Messenger obviously knew how worried he was about his mum.

The seats were scorching hot. Bel sat in the middle and Ben by the passenger window. It took a couple of goes for Carl to start the engine, but they were soon off, driving out of the car park and onto a busy main road. Behind them, everyone was chatting excitedly, but up front they sat in silence.

They passed cars, motorbikes and the occasional rickshaw. There were fruit stalls along the side of the road, and children playing. There were also, Ben couldn't help noticing, a lot of policemen armed with rifles.

The air was hot, dry and dusty and he was already sweating. He rolled the window down, but it didn't make much difference.

'Busy around the city,' Carl explained in a loud voice. When it was clear that nobody in the back was listening to him, he continued to address only Ben and Bel. 'But it'll quieten down as we head west.' As he drove, he grabbed a clipboard that was resting on the dashboard. 'Ben . . .' he murmured, one eye on the clipboard and one on the road. 'Ben Tracey?'

'That's right,' Bel answered for him. Ben *hated* it when she did that.

'We've put you with a lovely family. Just three of them – mother, father and daughter. Quite western in the way they live their lives.' He smiled. 'Shouldn't be too much of a culture shock for you.'

Ben thought of telling him that shocks were the one thing he was used to, but he didn't. They drove in silence.

'Been to Pakistan before, Ben?' Carl ventured after a while. 'Know much about it?'

'A bit,' Ben murmured, but before he could say any more, Carl was gabbling away again.

'Beautiful country. *Beautiful.* But poor, in places. You shouldn't expect luxuries where you're going, Ben. The people there live hand to mouth. Good people, Ben. *Good* people. A few rotten apples, but you get the same anywhere, don't you.' As he spoke, he cast a sidelong glance at Ben. 'You're staying with a lovely family, Ben. A *lovely* family. They don't have much, but are happy to share what they have. And they're looking forward to seeing you, Ben. Really looking forward to seeing you.'

They passed a bus. It was multicoloured and packed as tightly as a tin of sardines. Then more policemen, four or five of them on a street corner, all armed. Ben couldn't help staring at them.

'You're aware of the security situation in this part of the world, I suppose.' Carl looked in the rear-view mirror as he spoke.

Bel shot him a quick look. 'We've been led to understand that Kampur is relatively peaceful.'

'Oh, of course,' Carl said quickly. 'Of course, of course. Lovely people. *Lovely* people. Ignore the rumours.'

'What rumours?' Ben demanded.

'Nothing. Nothing. But you know how people will talk. Village gossip, nothing more.'

'*What rumours?*'

'Nothing. Really, nothing. This is going to be a great experience for you, Ben. A *grand* experience.'

Ben didn't feel particularly reassured and Carl seemed to sense that. 'Honestly,' he said, 'it's true that there are other places in the region – to the north and south and closer to the Afghan border – where I would not recommend you to go. But Kampur is a safe place. Safe as houses. We wouldn't let a group of school kids stay there otherwise – can you imagine the sort of publicity the charity would get if something went wrong?' He smiled – a broad, almost cheeky grin. 'And after all, it's not exactly Helmand Province.'

Ben felt a twisting in his stomach. He looked at his mum, but Bel was staring firmly at the road ahead. Carl seemed to realize he'd said something wrong. He opened his mouth, thought better of it and clamped it shut again.

They continued to drive on in silence.

Chapter Two

SAS Headquarters, Hereford, UK.

There were four of them in the unit. Ricki was the leader, but Toby, Matt and Jack were equally skilled. They had all been in the SAS for five years and they worked together like cogs in a watch, each man practically knowing what the other was thinking.

They sat in the briefing room. No windows, no pictures on the wall. Just an overhead projector beaming a map of southern Afghanistan onto a whiteboard and the ops sergeant standing next to it, giving them their instructions. He was a tall, thin man with hollow cheeks and a scar across his forehead. He didn't look like someone you'd want to mess with; but then again, nor did any of them.

'Here's your schedule,' he announced. 'Leave here

tomorrow at oh-six-hundred hours. Regular green army flight from Brize Norton to Kandahar, arrival twelve-hundred hours. Overnight at Kandahar, then on to Camp Bastion the following morning. You'll be inserted into the town of Sangin by Chinook under cover of dark.'

He turned to the map and pointed out Sangin. It lay right on the Helmand River in the northern part of Helmand Province. He didn't really need to point it out to the unit. They'd been on ops in this part of the world so many times that they knew the geography well.

'Good old Sangin,' Ricki said. 'Sometimes I think I should buy a house there. It seems to be where I spend all my time.'

'Last time I looked,' Matt rumbled, 'all the houses had been flattened. I'd stick with Hereford if I were you.'

'Yeah,' Ricki replied with a wink. 'Good point.'

'All right,' the ops sergeant interrupted their banter, 'listen up. As you know, we've got intelligence guys on the ground in Helmand. They're all reporting the same thing. The Taliban in the area are preparing something big. It could be anything. All we know is it's hush-hush. They won't refer to it on their radio transmissions, and the low-level Taliban recruits we've managed to capture know nothing about it. Whatever it is, the commanders are keeping it to themselves.'

'Let me guess,' Matt piped up. 'That's where we come in.'

The ops sergeant nodded. 'The American special forces are spread thin on the ground. We're sending you in to help gather information. You need to get as close to the Taliban commanders as you can. By whatever means necessary, gentlemen. Whatever it is the enemy have got planned, they're excited about it. That's enough to make our own commanders very nervous indeed. As things stand, we've got the enemy on the back foot. If they manage to do anything to upset that, it would be a disaster for the war effort and for the people of Afghanistan.'

He looked at them all with a serious expression, and this time there were no jokey comments.

'All right, gentlemen. You'll receive more instructions when you're in country. You can check out your weapons and spend the rest of the day putting your packs together. RV back here at oh-five-hundred tomorrow.'

The four men in the unit nodded, then stood up, left the briefing room and went to make their preparations.

The minibus of exchange students hadn't driven far before the outskirts of Quetta started to melt away and the scenery changed dramatically. As Carl had promised, the road was bad – stony and bumpy. It took them alongside a vast lake, in the middle of which was a small island only ten or twenty metres wide. Perched in the centre of that island was some kind of shrine. It looked ancient and very beautiful. And in the distance, the ever-present mountains. Even though the van rumbled and chugged, there was a sense of peace about this place. The others in the back seemed to notice it too. They were quiet and a few of them had even nodded off.

'I've heard that some of the Taliban in Afghanistan come over the border from Pakistan,' Ben said suddenly. 'Is that true? And are the Taliban really that dangerous?' The question had been rather on his mind.

Carl glanced at him as he drove. 'There's Taliban,' he said, 'and then there's Taliban.'

'What's that supposed to mean?'

'*Ben*,' his mum admonished.

'It's OK,' Carl said. 'It's an important question.' He paused for thought before speaking again. 'Have you heard of the Ku Klux Klan, Ben?'

He nodded. 'Yeah.'

'Well, the Taliban are to Muslims what the Ku Klux Klan are to Christians – a horrible perversion of the way things are supposed to be. Islam is a very peaceful religion, but the Taliban give it a bad name. They used to be in charge of Afghanistan and they were very brutal, especially to women. They were deposed in two thousand and one by the British and Americans because they allowed the terrorist leader Osama bin Laden to hide in Afghanistan after nine/eleven. There are still some Taliban who want to take back the country. Most of them are very vicious fighters who don't mind if they die, because they think they are fighting a holy war.'

Ben glanced at his mum, who was looking straight ahead.

'You said "most of them" . . .'

'That's right, Ben.' Carl nodded. 'You see, some people join the Taliban for other reasons. Because they don't like the government; because they're poor; because they're misguided. They're not radical or evil. It's just possible, Ben, that you will hear people claim to be Taliban sympathizers. Avoid them, but don't fall into the trap of assuming that they're all bad. They're not. They're just poor. The Taliban commanders take advantage of them. But not in Kampur, Ben. These things are very localized.'

They passed an old man by the side of the road. He wore ragged robes and carried a staff which he was using to direct two rather thin-looking sheep. The old man stared at them as they passed. His face was leathery and wrinkled, his eyes piercing.

'What about the ones in Helmand Province?' Ben asked. 'Are *they* all bad?'

'Stop asking Carl so many questions, Ben,' his mum said a bit peevishly.

Ben opened his mouth to argue, but one look from her told him that probably wasn't a good idea. He shut it again and went back to looking out of the window and watching the strange, unfamiliar, beautiful landscape slip slowly past.

The day was almost done by the time they trundled into Kampur. Ben was sweaty, dirty and tired from the long journey.

It was called a village, but to Ben's eyes it was bigger than that. A small town, ramshackle and sprawling. Some of the buildings were made of brick, others of mud baked hard by the fierce sun. The grander places had tiles on the roofs, but most of the dwellings were covered with sheets of corrugated iron. They reminded Ben of the huts he had seen in the Democratic Republic of the Congo, and were none the more welcoming for that.

Even though the sun was sinking in the sky, there were still food stalls by the side of the road and plenty of children playing in the dusty streets. As Carl drove the minibus slowly through the town, the vehicle attracted a lot of attention from these kids. Some of them waved; others chased along behind. Ben thought he knew why: it wasn't much of a vehicle, but it was a lot classier than the few rusty, beaten-up cars he saw parked around the place.

'Here we are,' Carl announced suddenly with a smile. They came to a halt.

It was a subdued group that dismounted from the bus. Ben sensed that everyone was feeling a bit nervous. He certainly felt like they were a million miles from home. It was good to stretch his legs, though, and he did a couple of circuits of the minibus before looking around properly. They had parked on the edge of a square. Surrounding it were what Ben could only describe as shacks – rickety stalls with iron grilles in front of them. He supposed they were shops, but they were closed at the moment.

In the middle of the square was a large group of people – young and old. They watched the new arrivals expectantly. Mr Knight and Mr Sawyer, who knew Kampur from exchange programmes in previous years, saw a couple of faces they recognized and strode towards them, smiling and with hands outstretched.

'Come on, everyone,' Carl boomed, clipboard in hand. 'I'll introduce you to your families. There'll be some group activities organized later in the week – spectacular countryside nearby, *spectacular* – but for now it's important that you get to know your exchange partners and settle into your families. Come along! Don't be shy!'

Ben and the rest of them followed. There was a moment of awkwardness as the two groups refused to mingle, but as Carl started reading off names and introducing Ben's school mates to their new families, the awkwardness disappeared. For all of them, that is, except Ed, who looked at the small Pakistani boy who was to be his exchange partner with his usual sneer. Ben wondered why he had even wanted to come in the first place.

'Ben Tracey? Ah, Ben. Come with me and meet Saleem and Harata.' A man and a woman approached. Their clothes were western in style, but old; they each had a big smile on their face as they shook Ben's hand. 'And this,' Carl continued, 'is Aarya.'

Aarya was standing quietly behind her parents. She had long, shining black hair, clear brown skin and deep-brown eyes. She looked shyly at the ground.

Ben held out his hand. 'Hi,' he said. 'I'm Ben.' Her fingers felt very small in his.

And then his mum was there, introducing herself. Before he knew it they had picked up their bags and were walking away from the square: Saleem, Bel and Harata chatting freely, Ben and Aarya in silence.

They had only been walking a couple of minutes before they stopped by a low wall in which there was a wooden gate. Behind it there was a compound, the walls built from pale, sandy bricks. In the front was a courtyard with two fruit trees – Ben couldn't tell what kind. And beyond the fruit trees was a simple, red-painted door which glowed in the reflection of the setting sun. It did not look especially lavish, but it wasn't the poorest place Ben had seen since arriving in Kampur.

'*Allahu Akbar*,' Saleem said. And then, in very good English, 'Welcome to our home!'

He ushered them in. 'You must be very hungry,' he announced as they walked past the fruit trees. 'Harata and Aarya have prepared food for you. Come in, come in!'

At the main entrance to the house, the family removed their shoes. Ben and Bel did the same before stepping inside. It was dark here, but cooler, which was a relief. They were led through an empty hallway into a room with a low round table no more than knee height. 'Please,' Saleem told them, 'sit.' And as if showing them what to do, he sat on the floor at the table. Ben and Bel copied him.

The three of them chatted politely about the journey while Aarya and her mother brought bowls of food to the table. Delicious smells filled the room and Ben realized he was ravenous. Still without looking him fully in the eye, Aarya handed him a plate of spiced lamb and a huge, warm flatbread. Ben looked around for some cutlery, but there was none and Saleem smiled at him. 'We eat with our right hand, Ben,' he said, before tearing off a piece of his bread and using it to scoop up the lamb. Ben did the same and crammed the food into his mouth. It was delicious.

'We are sorry,' Saleem said politely to Bel, 'that you cannot stay with us longer than one night.'

Bel inclined her head. 'My work . . .' she explained between mouthfuls of food.

'I understand that you are going to Afghanistan.'

She nodded.

Saleem's face grew serious. 'It is a troubled country,' he said mildly.

'I hope what I am going there to do will help to heal it,' Bel replied. As she started to explain the reasons for her visit, Ben's mind began to wander. He supposed he should be feeling nervous; but the family with whom he would be staying had been so welcoming that he almost felt at home. He looked at Aarya and smiled. For the first time, she smiled back.

His ears tuned in once more to what his mum was saying. '. . . and as the Taliban use money from the poppy trade to finance the war, it's important that we do something to stamp it out.'

The Taliban. With those two words, a sense of unease returned to Ben's stomach. He remembered everything Carl had said in the car, and he found himself wanting to know more.

'Are there Taliban here?' he asked.

There was a silence. Aarya and her mother bowed their heads and looked down at their food. Saleem cleared his throat uncomfortably. Somebody shouted out in the street, and for a moment it was the only sound. He blushed.

It was Saleem who broke the silence. 'Aarya is looking forward to showing you her school tomorrow,' he said. The girl's head remained bowed. 'We do not get many young people travelling to our village.'

Ben hardly heard him. His skin was still hot with embarrassment and his mind was ticking over. He had asked about the Taliban and the mood had changed. Now he had just one question in his head.

Why?

Chapter Three

Ben and his mother slept on rolled-up mattresses that had been unfurled on the hard floor of a plain room which contained nothing but a religious text on the wall in Arabic. They were woken just before sunrise by the call to prayer. As Ben drowsily sat up he listened to the lone voice of the *muezzin* – the mosque official – wailing into the early morning. A bit different from the annoying beep of his alarm clock back home, he thought. And then he saw that his mum was already packing her rucksack by the light of a torch. He watched her for a while before she realized he was awake.

Bel smiled at him. A sad smile. 'I'm leaving at sunrise,' she said. 'I've got an army escort picking me up and then . . .'

'You will be careful, won't you, Mum?'

She sat on his mattress and ran her hand through his hair. 'Course I will, love. Don't worry. They'll take good care of me. And Aarya and her family will take good care of you.'

He nodded.

'I have to go,' Bel said. 'I'll see you in two weeks, OK?'

'OK, Mum,' Ben said quietly. He kissed her, then continued to watch as Bel finished her packing and quietly left the room.

Ben suddenly felt very alone. He wished he could lose himself in sleep, but there was no way that was going to happen now. As the wailing of the call to prayer faded away, he hauled himself from his bed, got dressed and ventured out of the room. Aarya and her mother were already up. The small house smelled of fresh bread and the women were placing tea and small, sweet pastries on the table.

'Good morning, Ben,' Aarya said. Her English was surprisingly good.

'Morning.' Ben yawned. He looked around. 'Where's your dad?'

'He has gone to the mosque to pray. My mother and I made our prayers at home when we awoke.' She gestured towards the table. 'Please. Eat.'

Saleem returned just as Ben was finishing his breakfast. His face glistened: it was already hot outside. Any of the awkwardness that Ben had caused last night had disappeared and his smile was as broad as ever. 'Your mother has left?' he asked.

Ben nodded. He didn't want to show that he missed her already.

Saleem looked genuinely upset. 'I had hoped to say goodbye,' he announced. Then he rubbed his hands together. 'Never mind, never mind. You and Aarya should leave. School starts early here, Ben, before the day becomes too hot.'

Moments later, Aarya was beside him, a small canvas bag of books slung over her shoulder. She smiled at him and led the way to the door.

The early morning sun was bright. It shone through the fruit trees in the courtyard and made Ben's skin feel warm. 'How far to the school?' he asked Aarya.

'It is close,' she said. 'Only ten minutes to walk there.'

'Your English is very good.'

She looked away modestly. 'I try to study hard,' she said. 'And I talk to any English people who come here. They help me.' She smiled. 'I am looking forward to coming to your country in the future.'

Ben nodded. They were in the main street now and it was surprisingly crowded. They passed shops that were little more than open-fronted stalls selling all kinds of things: brightly patterned material for clothes, fruit, records, engine parts. All the shopkeepers smiled at him as if they were trying to persuade him to come into their store. Ben, of course, just kept walking and looking around. Many people wore traditional dress: women in brightly coloured robes, many with head-scarves wrapped around their heads and covering their hair, men with long beards and turbans. But there were just as many, like Aarya, in jeans. He noticed that she received some disapproving looks from a few of the older people, even though to Ben's eyes she was dressed rather modestly – unfashionably, even. Ben himself attracted attention too, but more because of his white skin than anything else.

For a minute or so, they walked in silence as Ben absorbed the sights, sounds and smells of this strange place. But he couldn't stay quiet for long. The con-versation they'd had at last night's meal had stayed with him and he wasn't the kind of person to keep quiet about these things.

'Aarya?' he asked.

'Yes?'

'Last night at the table, I mentioned the Taliban and everyone went quiet. Why?'

For a moment he thought she wasn't going to answer. She slowed her pace slightly and looked away.

'I had an aunt,' she said. 'My mother's sister.' Aarya's face had stiffened, and Ben realized that this was an effort for her. 'She met a man, very religious. We are all practising Muslims, but some people would like things to be as they were hundreds of years ago. He was one of those people. They married. This was when I was still very small, but I remember her well. She was a kind lady.' Aarya smiled. 'She used to bring me sweets and play games with me whenever I wanted. But she did not stay in the village. In Afghanistan, the Taliban were in power. My aunt's new husband insisted that they move there. To Kabul, the capital. He wanted to live in that very strict place.'

Ben was listening carefully. He felt as though all the sounds of the street had disappeared into the background. 'What do you mean, strict?' he asked. Aarya appeared not to hear him.

'I remember the day she went,' the girl continued. Her eyes were lost in thought. 'I wept. I begged her not to go. I said to her: *If he loves you, he would not make you*. She just held me and promised that she would visit often. I wept for a week after she left and every day after that I asked my mother when she would come back to see us. Mother could never give me an answer, so soon I learned to stop asking.'

'Why didn't she come?' Ben asked.

Aarya shrugged. They walked round a rickshaw that was parked by the side of the road. 'In Afghanistan,' she said darkly, 'under the Taliban, women were not free to do as they wished. My aunt sometimes sent letters, but they told us nothing. My father says this is because her husband would have read everything first.'

Ben continued to listen in silence.

'About a year after she left,' Aarya continued, 'we received word that she was going to have a baby. My mother was very excited. And so was I. In Pakistan, Ben, families are big. Everyone has cousins. But not me. I was looking forward to it.'

Her voice was quieter now. Ben didn't know how, but he could tell she was about to reveal something terrible. 'What happened?' he asked.

'The baby was born. A little boy. But my aunt—' Aarya drew a deep breath, as if she was summoning the strength to continue. 'She died. Under the Taliban, women were not allowed to receive proper medical care. My aunt was banned from seeing a doctor. She was banned from having medicine. She died a painful death.'

There were tears in Aarya's eyes now.

'We have never heard from her husband and we have never seen the child. We were happy when the Taliban were removed from power in Afghanistan, but even now my mother will not have their name mentioned in our house.'

Ben found himself blushing again at the memory of his insensitive question the previous night.

'I didn't realize the Taliban were as bad as that,' he said.

'They were worse,' Aarya replied hotly. 'You would not believe the things they did. Women were not allowed to go to school. They were not allowed to speak in public. They would be beaten with sticks by the religious police if they broke the rules, or even stoned in the street. To death, sometimes. People were executed in public in horrible ways, or had parts of their bodies cut off as punishment. Hands, ears . . . The Americans and the British did a good thing, removing them from power.'

Aarya was walking quickly now, as if the thought of it had filled her with angry energy.

'Only they're still there, aren't they?' Ben said, thinking of his mother. 'In places, I mean.'

Aarya nodded. 'There are people,' she said, 'even in this country, who still support them.'

'Why?'

A frown creased Aarya's forehead. She looked like this was a question that had troubled her too.

'For different reasons, I think. Some people really believe that the Taliban were right; other people are just' – she searched for the word – 'just thugs. They try to force us to agree with them, but my family and I will not be bullied, even if it means trouble for us.'

'Why would it mean trouble for you?'

'There are families in this village—' she started to say. But then she thought better of it. 'God willing, the Taliban will be defeated in Afghanistan. Maybe then they will fade away from this part of Pakistan too.'

She gestured ahead. They were in front of a concrete building, blocky and ugly. Ben had been listening so hard to what Aarya said that he hadn't noticed their surroundings. Now, though, he recognized the building from a photo the charity had sent him before he left. 'School,' the girl said proudly, raising one arm like a tour guide presenting a wonder of the world. 'We are here.'

Ben was the last of the English people to arrive at the school: the others were all waiting for him out the front. Even though it was hot, the three girls wore long sleeves, which they had been told was the custom.

'Morning, Ben,' Mr Knight said as he approached. 'Probably the earliest you've been up since Christmas Day, eh?' Mr Knight was the kind of teacher who liked saying things that weren't very funny. 'All right, everyone,' he continued when he realized he wasn't going to get a laugh, 'we're going to sit in on an English lesson this morning. Best behaviour from you all. That includes you, Ed.'

'Yes, *sir*,' Ed replied sarcastically, but he fell quiet when Mr Knight gave him a dangerous look.

They spent the morning in classes full of sixty or seventy young Pakistani students, all crowded into basic rooms far too small for that number of people. They'd been warned that it would be very different to back home. 'It's the only school in Kampur,' Miss Messenger had explained to them all. 'That's why it's so crowded, and there's not enough money to make it bigger.' The English students were clearly a novelty – Ben was not the only one who drew curious looks and the occasional giggle. He supposed that would die away once they'd been around for a bit.

By the time midday arrived and they were all dismissed to return to their families, Ben was exhausted. He was hot too. The sun beat down as he walked back out of the concrete building to the front of the school where he had arranged to meet Aarya. Crowds of children spilled out, the air filled with their chattering voices – mostly in the Pakistani language of Urdu, of course, which Ben could not understand – while he scanned the area trying to find his new friend.

There she was, about thirty metres away against a low wall. And something was wrong. She was surrounded by several boys and Ben could tell they weren't trying to chat her up. Her chin was jutting out, but even from this distance he could tell she was scared.

Just then he heard a voice. His heart sank. Ed.

He was alone, without his exchange student. 'What's

the matter, Ben?' he taunted. 'Your girlfriend in trouble or something?'

'Shut up, Ed,' Ben replied.

Ed snorted with laughter, then turned away. Ben kept his attention on Aarya.

He hesitated. He was a stranger here. It wasn't his place to get involved in schoolyard fights that he didn't understand. Maybe he should hold back. See how things panned out. Aarya was pretty feisty, wasn't she? She could take care of things . . .

But as these thoughts went through his head, he knew he couldn't stand by and watch his new friend being bullied. Aarya was all by herself and the boys were closing on her.

Ben shut his eyes.

He cursed under his breath.

And then he ran towards her.

Chapter Four

There were four of them. Ben counted them while he ran. And as he approached, it became clear that they were all broad-shouldered and quite a bit bigger than him. He stopped just a few metres behind them. 'What's going on?' he demanded.

Aarya looked at him. Her eyes widened and she shook her head. 'Please, Ben. Don't . . .'

But it was too late. As one, the four boys turned to stare at him.

They all looked very alike, with dark hair and thick, bushy eyebrows. They each had their own distinguishing characteristics, however. One had a large, hooked nose; another wore a gold-coloured chain around his neck; the third had a bruise on the side of his face; and the fourth wore an embroidered but dirty hat. The lad with the hook nose looked like the leader and he spat something out in a harsh-sounding language. The others laughed. It wasn't a good sound.

Ben wasn't going to be intimidated. He pushed past them and approached Aarya. 'Are you OK?' he asked.

'Yes,' she replied. She didn't look like she was very pleased to see Ben. Suddenly she shouted in alarm. Ben felt hands grabbing him on either side. He struggled, but they were too strong for him. All he could do was watch as the hook-nosed boy strode up to Aarya and with a forceful yank pulled her school bag from her shoulder. Aarya shouted out again. She tried to grab it back, but he just pushed her away then turned to Ben. His dark eyes were full of contempt. The boy smiled an ugly smile and then, without any warning, punched Ben hard in the stomach.

Ben gasped for breath. He tried to double over, but the others were still holding him upright. Until, that is, they threw him onto the ground and the four of them walked away, laughing harshly.

Aarya bent down and placed one hand lightly on his shoulder. 'Ben, are you all right?'

'On top of the world,' Ben replied in a hoarse whisper as he pushed himself back up to his feet. 'Who were the ugly brothers, then?'

He noticed that there were tears welling up in Aarya's eyes. 'They are *thugs*,' she said. 'Just thugs.

They do not think I should be allowed in the school.'

'Why not?'

'Because I am a girl.'

Ben frowned. 'Well, we have to get your books back.'

'No, Ben. Just leave it. It's best to stay away from them, all right?'

'No,' Ben replied. 'It's not all right. What's so great about that lot that makes them untouchable?'

'There's nothing great about them, OK, Ben?' Aarya said waspishly. 'They're just not very nice and they come from bad families.'

Ben blinked. 'You said they didn't think you should be allowed to come to school because you're a girl,' he said. 'They're not, you know, Taliban . . . ?'

'Of course they're not Taliban.' The way she spoke, Ben wondered if she had forgotten he'd just tried to help her out. 'The Taliban are not strong in Kampur. They're just . . .' She looked like she was struggling to find the word.

'What?' Ben demanded. 'Sympathizers?'

Aarya shrugged. 'Maybe. Something like that.' She scowled. 'I have never seen them at the mosque, though.'

Ben felt angry. 'Do you know where they live?' he asked.

She nodded. 'On the outskirts of the village. Away from other people.'

'Come on, then.'

'What?'

'We're going to get your bag back.'

Aarya shook her head. 'It doesn't matter,' she said, turning and starting to walk away.

'It *does* matter,' Ben called after her. As he spoke, he saw Ed, watching him from a distance, that unpleasant sneer still on his face.

'Hey, Aarya,' Ben shouted. 'I thought you told me earlier today that you weren't going to be bullied.'

That got her attention. She spun round and there was a fire in her eyes. 'I won't,' she stated fiercely.

'Well, in that case,' Ben said, walking up to her and trying to pretend that his stomach didn't still hurt from the punch, 'let's go and get your books back.'

Aarya led Ben to the outskirts of the village. It was different here. Quieter. Less bustling. Ben supposed that most people were sheltering from the midday heat.

'My mother will be expecting me at home,' Aarya said.

'We won't be long,' Ben told her. 'Come on, Aarya. If you don't stand up to these people, they'll only keep on doing it.' Aarya looked down, and with a flash of insight Ben sensed that this had been going on for a long time.

They turned a corner and found themselves at one

end of a long street. There were a handful of beaten-up old vans parked on either side, and a thin dog sat in the middle of the road, its tongue lolling from the side of its mouth. Along each side of the road were wooden shacks, all of them closed up with rolling metal shutters and big locks. At the end of the street was a high, sand-coloured wall with an iron gate; and beyond that Ben could just make out the top of a house.

Aarya pointed down the road. 'Raheem lives there,' she said.

'Raheem?' Ben asked. 'Is he the one that took your bag? The one with the big nose?'

She giggled, despite herself. 'Yes,' she said. 'The one with the big nose.'

Ben looked at the building. It was imposing, some-how. 'You think he's at home now?'

'It is midday. Most people are.' And then, looking around nervously: '*We* should be.'

He chewed on his lower lip. 'All right, then,' he said. 'Let's just go and knock on the door. He won't want his parents to find out what he did, will he?'

Aarya snorted. 'His parents are worse than him.'

'What do you mean?'

The girl scowled. 'There are rumours, that is all.'

'What kind of rumours?'

'People visit them. People who are not from here. Just passing through.' She seemed reluctant to speak.

'They're allowed to have visitors, aren't they?'

But Aarya avoided his question. 'I think we should go home,' she muttered. 'I do not want anything to do with this family.'

'No,' Ben insisted. 'Come on – it'll be all right. What's the worst they can do?' He winked at her. 'Anyway, I'm supposed to be seeing the sights, aren't I?'

He strode forward. Aarya followed a few paces behind.

As they approached, the dog that had been sitting in the middle of the road scampered away, as though the approach of humans was something to fear. It seemed to Ben that it took a long time to walk the length of the road. His shirt stuck to his back from the sweat and the sun pounded on his head.

They were perhaps twenty metres from the gate when they stopped. A vehicle had suddenly appeared, pulling up outside Raheem's house after having turned into the road from the opposite end. Ben didn't know what it was that made him want to hide. Perhaps Aarya's nervousness had put him on edge; perhaps it was the vehicle itself. It was ordinary enough in its way – just a beige-coloured Land Rover – but it stuck out in this town where most of the vehicles were rusty and dented. It also stood out because there was a man hanging from the side, wearing black robes and with a rifle strapped across his back.

More by instinct than anything else, Ben pulled Aarya by the wrist and dragged her towards the cover of one of the vans by the side of the road. Once they were out of sight, they peered round the vehicle and watched.

'What is it?' Aarya whispered.

'I don't know,' Ben said. 'Let's just say I've just got a bit of a thing about men with guns. A few bad experiences in the past.'

Aarya nodded emphatically and they went back to watching.

The Land Rover stopped to one side of Raheem's gate and the man jumped down. Immediately two others spilled out. They were identically dressed and both carried weapons. One of them barked an instruction and the other two began looking around. The robed man Ben had seen first started walking down the road towards them, looking left and right as if checking that there was no one foolish enough to be out in the midday sun.

As if checking that there was no one out on the streets to see them.

Ben and Aarya ducked back out of sight. Ben sensed that his new friend was trembling. He wanted to whisper to her that it was going to be all right, but he didn't want to make a sound so they crouched in silence behind the beaten-up truck.

Ten seconds passed.

Twenty seconds.

And then, quite clearly, Ben heard footsteps. The armed man was still walking their way. He was now very close.

Ben's muscles tensed. The footsteps grew louder. From their hiding place behind the van, he saw a shadow approach down the middle of the road.

And then the sound of footsteps stopped.

He was holding his breath. They both were. Sweat dribbled down the side of Ben's face. If the armed man took another couple of steps forward, he would see them. Ben didn't quite know why, but something told him that *really* wouldn't be a good thing.

Time stood still. Across the road, Ben saw the dog that he had noticed earlier. It was sniffing against one of the stalls and he prayed it wouldn't notice them and give their location away. He realized that every muscle in his body was preparing to run, if it should come to that.

It didn't. To Ben's relief the shadow disappeared and he heard the footsteps disappearing back towards the Land Rover. Both he and Aarya breathed a deep sigh of relief. Ben wiped the sweat from his forehead and then, gingerly, peered round the corner of the van again. 'Don't!' Aarya whispered. But Ben ignored her, and soon she too was looking down the road.

The man was standing back by the Land Rover, but the other two had disappeared. The back doors of the vehicle had been opened and so had the gate to Raheem's house, leading Ben to suppose that the other two armed men had gone inside.

They watched and waited.

Movement at the gate. The black-robed men had reappeared, and with them was another man. 'Raheem's father,' Aarya whispered. 'But what is that they are carrying?'

Ben didn't know. Whatever it was, though, they were handling it with great care. It took two of them to carry what looked, from this distance, like a dark, cylinder-shaped case. They seemed to carry it with ease, but Ben thought he could make out a look of extreme concentration on the face of Raheem's father and the armed man who helped him lift it.

The object was placed in the back of the Land Rover, then the doors were firmly shut. Raheem's father was speaking to the three armed men, but they didn't seem remotely interested in what he had to say. A few banknotes changed hands before the armed men turned and made their way back to the doors of the Land Rover.

'They're going,' Ben whispered.

And it was just as he spoke that he felt someone tapping on his shoulder.

He spun round and, with a sickening feeling in the pit of his stomach, saw a face with thick eyebrows, dark eyes and a large, hooked nose.

'Raheem,' Ben whispered.

Raheem didn't reply. At least, not to Ben. Instead he shouted at the top of his voice in the direction of his father and the armed men. Ben didn't understand what he said, and he certainly didn't want to find out. He turned to Aarya and once more grabbed her by the wrist.

'*Run!*' he shouted.

Aarya didn't need telling twice.

'He shouted out that we were spying!' she exclaimed as the two of them sidestepped Raheem and started hurtling back up that deserted street. But as they ran, Ben felt Aarya lagging behind. She wasn't as fast as him and couldn't keep up. He looked back over his shoulder and saw not only that Raheem was chasing them, but also that he was closing on Aarya. Even worse than that, one of the armed men was running in their direction.

He heard Aarya shout. Raheem had caught her, and now she was struggling with all her strength to get out of his grasp. Ben stopped, turned and ran back towards her. Raheem gave him a nasty sneer and spat some words at him that Ben couldn't understand. Ben launched himself towards him; Raheem let go of Aarya and suddenly the two boys were grappling with each other. Raheem's grip was strong and Ben had to use all his strength against him. The two of them fell to the ground and continued wrestling in the dusty road.

On the edge of his vision Ben was aware of Aarya. He heard her voice. 'They're coming, Ben. *They're coming!*' He tried to break free of Raheem, but the boy was too strong and he found himself pinned down.

And then, standing over them both, they saw a dark, black-robed figure. His rifle was no longer strapped across his back; it was in his fist and pointing in their direction. The man shouted an instruction and Raheem immediately let go. Ben wanted to run, but he knew he couldn't. He had the business end of a gun pointing straight at him.

From somewhere he heard the dog bark twice; closer to hand, he heard Aarya sobbing with fear.

The man approached, an angry glare on his face. He was right above Ben now, and the gun was only inches away.

It happened in a single movement. The man twirled the rifle in his hands so that the butt was now facing Ben, and with a short, sharp jerk he cracked it hard over Ben's head.

A fierce pain burned through him; then a wave of nausea; then a weird kind of numbness. Ben tried to push himself to his feet, but he only got halfway up before blackness engulfed him and he passed out, falling heavily back down onto the road as he did so.

Chapter Five

The plane had been in the air for seven hours and now it was dark outside.

The SAS unit – Ricki, Toby, Matt and Jack – sat together. Ricki and Matt listened to music on their iPods; Toby and Jack were sleeping. The military transport was full of soldiers being ferried out to Afghanistan. Ricki noticed that many of them avoided looking at the stretcher beds that lined one side of the cabin. Each one had heavy straps and a drip stand, and he wondered idly how many of them would be filled with wounded men when the plane made its return journey.

Ricki pulled his earphones out of his ears. He wasn't really listening to the music, and anyway he could feel the aircraft losing height. They would be landing in Afghanistan very soon. He nudged Toby, who was sitting next to him. 'The bird's losing height,' he said.

As he spoke, a voice came over the loudspeaker. It was the captain. 'Ladies and gentlemen,' he announced, 'we are about to begin our descent into Kandahar. In accordance with current regulations, we will be switching off all the lights in the cabin and outside the plane. Please take this opportunity to put on your helmets and body armour. We will be landing in approximately fifteen minutes.'

Ricki pulled his helmet and body armour – or plate hangers, as the guys normally called them – from under his seat. He never knew quite what good they would do if the plane was hit by a ground-to-air missile, or even if they came under attack from small arms fire, but he put them on anyway and the rest of his unit did the same. Five minutes later, the lights were switched off. They were in total blackness, with only the high-pitched hum of the plane's engines for company. Nobody in the cabin spoke.

They must have continued their descent for another ten minutes, although time had very little meaning in that thick darkness. It was a relief when the plane juddered as the wheels touched down.

The lights flickered on. Toby turned to Ricki. 'Good to be back?' he asked.

'Yeah,' Ricki said with a grimace. 'Great.'

Twenty minutes later they had disembarked.

Kandahar Airbase was enormous, and home to more than 2,000 members of the International Security Assistance Force, or ISAF. Most of them were American, although there were soldiers from many other countries there. The unit headed straight towards the PX – a kind of American shopping mall – to get some food and a cup of coffee. Once they were transported from here to Helmand Province, luxuries of that kind would be in short supply. In fact, luxuries of any kind would be in short supply.

In a large coffee shop, they sat at a table by themselves, well away from the regular army boys. They talked quietly so that they wouldn't be overheard. At the table next to them, Ricki noticed, there was a woman sitting alone. Unlike almost everyone else they had seen since they landed, she was wearing civvies. She traced her forefinger around the rim of her cup and looked like she was deep in thought. She didn't look particularly happy.

'Cheer up, love,' Ricki said. 'It might never happen.'

She looked up and blinked at him. 'I'm sorry?'

'I said, cheer up, it might . . . Oh, never mind.'

The woman smiled politely, then went back to staring at her cup of coffee.

'This your first time out here?' Ricki asked.

The woman looked up again. 'How can you tell?'

'It's obvious, isn't it?' And to Ricki's mind it was. You

could always tell a rookie. For him and his mates, who were used to spending time in all the most dangerous parts of the world, it was easy to forget how scary somewhere like this was to a first-timer. 'You want my advice?' he said.

The woman didn't nod, but he gave it anyway.

'Keep your mind on the job in hand. Don't think about home. You'll be back there soon enough.'

The woman smiled. 'I'll be fine,' she said. 'I was just thinking about my son, that's all.'

Ricki nodded. 'I've got a kid and all. But he'll be all right. Probably forgotten all about me already. What's your boy's name?'

'Ben,' the woman said. 'His name's Ben. And you're right. He'll be fine.' She swigged a final mouthful of her coffee, then stood up. 'I'd better be off,' she said with a smile. 'Nice to meet you.'

Ricki inclined his head. 'Nice to meet you too,' he said, before turning his attention back to his three SAS mates and the cup of coffee that was sitting on the table in front of him.

Carl looked at Aarya's father, Saleem, in horror.

'What do you mean, they've disappeared?' he said.

They stood in the main room of the small house that doubled as both the charity's office in Kampur and Carl's own living quarters.

Saleem's hands were clasped together. He looked terribly worried. 'They have not come home,' he said anxiously. 'They left for school this morning. When they did not return at lunchtime my wife thought that Aarya would be showing Ben the sights. But look.' He stepped back, opened the front door and pointed outside. 'It is dark. Aarya has *never* failed to return before dark. It is unlike her. She would be back in time to pray. I am telling you – they have disappeared.'

Panic rose in Carl's chest. This had never happened to him before. His volunteers had always been perfectly safe. It crossed his mind that this would be terrible for the charity's reputation; but then he felt guilty that his initial thoughts were not with the young people. 'What can we do?' he asked. Back in England, of course, their first move would be to call the police. But there were no police in this village in the south-western corner of Pakistan.

'I have told my friends,' Saleem replied. 'They will tell their friends. Soon the whole village will know that Ben and Aarya are missing. By morning, God willing, they will be found.'

Carl nodded. 'I will tell everybody I know,' he said. 'The English teachers must be informed immediately. We will search all night, if necessary. Saleem, my friend, we will find them. I promise you we will.'

But he couldn't help an unspoken thought rising

in his mind. *What if we don't find them? What then?*

Aarya sat on a chair, her hands bound behind her back. Three men stood in front of her and her cheek stung where one of them had hit her. The same men that she and Ben had seen outside Raheem's house? Aarya couldn't tell – her vision was blurred because of the tears that filled her eyes – but she thought they might be.

A man spoke. His eyes were dark and one of them was half closed on account of a vicious scar running across it. 'Why,' he demanded in the Afghan language of Pashtun, 'were you spying on us?'

It was an effort for Aarya to speak through her sobs. 'We were not spying.'

The man raised his hand as though about to hit her again.

'*We were not spying! We only came to get back my books.*'

The man looked unconvinced. 'What did you see?'

'Nothing,' Aarya breathed. 'You put something in the truck. That is all.'

Now it was the turn of another of the three men to speak. 'They have seen too much. Our mission cannot be compromised. We must silence them.'

But the first man held up one hand. 'Who is the boy?' he demanded.

'His name is Ben. He is from England. He was only coming to help me—'

The man's attention had wandered. 'British,' he said thoughtfully. His dark eyes had narrowed. 'Perhaps these two can be of use to us.'

A thick silence filled the room, broken only by Aarya's sobbing.

And then, a decision: 'They come with us. I have a plan for them. We leave under cover of dark.'

With that instruction, the three men filed out, ignoring Aarya's desperate request to please – *please* – let her and Ben go back home.

It was dark. So dark that, at first, Ben wasn't sure if he had actually opened his eyes.

His head was so painful he thought it might be splitting open, and he felt sick. He touched his ribs down one side of his body, then winced. They were tender and sore. For a moment he couldn't work out where he was. In his bedroom in Macclesfield? He shook his head. He couldn't be there because the floor was cold and hard, and as he stretched out his arms around him he couldn't find a wall, or a light switch, or anything familiar.

Where was he?

Where was he?

And then, with a sudden, sickening flash, he

remembered. Aarya. Raheem. The black-robed man with his weapons, standing over him. The cracking pain as he was hit over the head.

Ben pushed himself up into a sitting position. He sat there for a few seconds, blinking and waiting for his eyes to get used to the darkness. But they didn't. It meant that it really was pitch black in here. Wherever here was.

He stood up and walked blindly with his arms outstretched. Three paces. Four paces. His fingertips touched a wall. It was rough and cold. He walked round the room, following the wall with his hands until finally he came upon what felt like a door. He searched for a handle, but there was none. Taking a couple of steps back, he ran at it, barging with his shoulder; but the door was solid and he simply gave himself another bruise.

Then a thought struck him. 'Aarya?' he called, trying to stop the panic from sounding in his voice. 'Aarya, are you there?'

Nothing. Not a sound. In an idle corner of his brain he wondered if this was a dream. But it was no dream. This was horribly real.

He found the door again. Clenching his fists, he pounded it. 'Let me out!' he shouted. '*Let me out!*' His voice sounded thin and weak. There was no reply.

He pounded again.

And again.

Nothing.

Ben started to panic. His mouth went dry and his blood ran hot in his veins. '*Let me out! Let me out!*' But no one came.

Time passed. He didn't know how long he'd been in there. Minutes? Hours? He couldn't tell if it was day or night. He fell silent and sat with his back to the wall. From one corner of the room he heard a scurrying sound. He didn't even want to *think* what that was. Hugging his knees with his arms, he did the only thing he could do: wait.

Ben had started to shiver when he heard voices. They were distant and muffled. He strained his ears to listen to them. Three voices? Perhaps four? He couldn't quite tell, but he *could* tell that they were men and that they were arguing.

The voices came closer. It sounded like they were in the adjoining room, and suddenly a small crack of light surrounded the door frame. Ben jumped up and for a moment had to steady himself because the bump on his head was making him dizzy. He realized he was holding his breath, half out of nervousness and half to block out the sound of his own breathing.

There were definitely three of them, he decided. They were speaking a language he didn't understand. It sounded different to the Urdu he had heard people speaking at school earlier that day.

He listened. And then, unable to listen any longer, he threw himself at the door once again and thumped his fists against the wood. *'LET ME OUT!'*

The men fell silent. There was a sound of footsteps approaching. Suddenly terrified, Ben backed away. His skin tingled as he heard a key clanking in the lock and the door was pushed slowly open.

Light flooded in, making Ben squint as it pierced his aching head. It was a few seconds before he could look directly at the open doorway. A figure stood there. He was dressed in black, with a black turban and a long black beard – one of the men he had seen outside Raheem's house, he thought. The skin on his face was dark and weather-beaten and his lips were curled into a sneer. One of his eyes was half closed, thanks to a scar that ran across it. He carried a rifle and looked like he was prepared to use it.

Ben mustered the courage to speak. 'Where's Aarya?' he demanded.

The man's expression didn't change and Ben realized he hadn't understood.

'Where's Aarya?' he repeated, slower this time. But as he spoke, the man stepped backwards into the adjoining room. For a moment Ben took that as an invitation to leave his dark prison. As he stepped forward, though,

his captor raised his gun sharply. Ben halted and, with a sickening twist in his stomach, watched as the other two men came into view. They weren't arguing now, he thought to himself. It was as if the one thing they could agree on was that Ben should stay right there.

'Let me out,' he whispered yet again. He knew, though, that they wouldn't. It was no surprise when the door was shut again and the sound of the lock reached his ears. With a sense of hopelessness, Ben crouched back down on the ground with only his sore body and the scurrying of the rodents in the corner for company.

It was the waiting that was the worst. Ben had been in some nasty situations before and it was always the unknown that was scariest of all.

Control your fear, he told himself. *Accept it. Master it. Think clearly.* It was difficult in that dark, locked room. He took deep breaths. He tried to think of a plan to get out of there. He thought of Ed, sneering at him while he fought the boys outside the school. He had seen it all happen. When everyone realized that Ben and Aarya had disappeared, he would explain what he'd seen. That would lead the adults to Raheem's house. And then . . . But there was nothing he could do while the door was locked, that much was clear. So he'd have to wait for them to come back.

Ben thought it was about an hour later when they

returned, but it could have been less. He heard them outside and once more moved away from the door. This time, however, he didn't step back into the room. He stood to one side of the entrance and prepared to pounce.

The door opened. Light spilled in, casting an unnaturally long shadow on the floor of the room. A moment of silence. Then a figure stepped through the doorway.

Ben launched himself at him. His sore ribs hurt as he smashed against the body of his unknown captor. They scuffled in the dark, but it was no good. Instantly he found himself pinned down on the cold floor by two men, with a third standing over him and pointing a gun directly at his head. The gunman gave a harsh-sounding instruction and Ben was yanked roughly to his feet. He didn't know whether to be relieved or even more scared when they pushed him into the adjoining room.

Before he knew it, his hands had been tied and one of the men was wrapping a dirty strip of cloth round his head and between his lips; the gag dug sharply into the corners of his mouth. He was then pulled – one man to each arm – through another door and up a flight of stone stairs, at the top of which was a room that looked very similar to the one in Aarya's house where they had eaten. Ben didn't get the chance to examine it very closely, however, because they kept him moving: through a dark hallway and out into the front courtyard of what he now realized was Raheem's house.

The sky was dark. *Everything* was dark. There were other figures in the courtyard, but their faces were in shadow. He tried to shout out, but because he was gagged the only sound he made was a weak groan.

The front gates ahead were open. Beyond them, Ben could see a vehicle with its lights on. He was dragged towards it. One of his captors – the man with the scarred eye – opened the back door and pushed him inside before jumping up into the back of the vehicle itself.

There wasn't much room. The floor was taken up by the object they had seen being loaded up earlier. Ben didn't pay it much attention: he was too busy looking at the girl who sat alongside it. Her face was bruised and her eyes filled with terror. Although she was not gagged, her hands had been tied behind her back like his. She was shaking with fear.

'Aarya!' Ben tried to say her name, but it was just a noise because of the gag. He heard the door shut; seconds later the Land Rover started to move.

'Ben!' she hissed back. 'We must escape. They are . . .' She became breathless. 'They are *terrorists*, Ben. We *must* escape.'

Ben couldn't speak. But had he been able to, he knew

what he would have said: *We can't escape. We can't escape because there is a man aiming a rifle at us. We can't escape because the truck is moving too quickly now. We're being taken away at gunpoint and we don't even know why . . .*

Chapter Six

The truck drove through the darkness. As time passed, the temperature dropped. Ben, who was wearing just a T-shirt and a pair of jeans, started to shiver from the cold.

They had been going for an hour, maybe more. Of the three people in the back, nobody had spoken. Ben and Aarya sat side by side. Opposite them was their guard. He looked to Ben like he was holding his weapon expertly, not pointing straight at them, but down and to one side, ready to swing it into action if need be. Now and then he caught Ben's eye, but Ben read nothing in his face except flat, flinty determination.

The road was bad and the truck shook as it went. It made Ben's sore body hurt even more. As they drove, he tried to work out what was going on. All they'd been trying to do was get Aarya's books back. She had seemed nervous about doing even that, but surely this was nothing to do with a schoolyard fight, no matter who it was with. No; something else was going on here. Something more sinister.

He thought back to the moments before they were captured. They'd seen the armed men and had hidden, then watched from their hiding place as the package now at their feet was loaded into the truck. There was something secretive about it. They hadn't wanted it to be seen. Maybe that was it – maybe Ben and Aarya were being abducted because they *had* seen it. He glanced down. The object at his feet didn't *look* like much. Just a cylindrical suitcase, a bit scuffed and beaten up. Surely not enough to risk kidnapping two people for . . .

The truck came to a halt. The two men in the front climbed out; Ben and Aarya's guard did the same and the three men spoke briefly at the back of the truck before each drinking from a bottle of water. Ben's mouth was impossibly dry. He shuffled to the back of the truck and got their attention by pointing at the water bottle.

The three men looked uncertainly at each other, but then one of them nodded. He approached Ben and removed the gag from around his mouth and handed him the bottle. Ben drank deeply and felt his body absorbing the water as it slipped down his parched throat. After he had taken several gulps he turned in order to pass it to Aarya; as he did so, however, it was snatched back from him.

'She's thirsty too!' he said, his voice croaky. But the men obviously weren't interested. Before he knew it they were off again, trundling into the darkness.

'We need to keep them talking,' Ben said in a low voice, not at all sure whether their captors spoke English. 'Can you translate?'

Aarya nodded, her eyes wide. Just then, however, their guard raised his gun and jabbed Ben in the ribs. He winced with pain as the man spoke.

'He says, be quiet,' Aarya said. 'He says, if we talk he will shoot us.' Her lower lip started to tremble.

Ben jutted his jaw out in the man's direction, but he kept quiet just as he'd been told to. There was, he knew, no point annoying a guy with a gun.

They continued in tense, nervous silence.

Another hour passed. Two hours. Gradually Ben became aware of the night fading away and a steely grey light illuminating the countryside around them. Ben always felt weird when he hadn't slept all night; time didn't seem to have much meaning and it surprised him when he worked out it could only be Tuesday morning, barely forty-eight hours since he had landed in Islamabad. The terrain on either side of the poor road was rocky and unwelcoming; and in the distance he saw mountains, majestic and craggy. The one thing he didn't see, he thought glumly, were any other vehicles. The whole area looked deserted, and all the more threatening for that. Suddenly, as he looked through the window, he found himself having to clamp his eyes shut. The sun had peeked up over the mountain range and was now shining fiercely into his face. A new day had come to Pakistan.

Still they drove, in silence and discomfort. Every now and then, Ben tried to say something; but he was always cut short by a vicious glare from the guard, or another poke in the ribs from the rifle if he was unlucky. The road started to slope upwards. They were travelling, Ben realized, into the hills.

His stomach burned with hunger and it crossed his mind that they hadn't eaten for twenty-four hours. At least *he'd* had some water. Aarya hadn't, and she looked the worse for it. Her eyelids were drooping, and even though she was clearly trying to stay awake, exhaustion was painted on her face. He gave her what he hoped was a reassuring smile; Aarya smiled half-heartedly back.

The cloth that bound Ben's wrists rubbed his skin. His every thought was about how they could escape; but held at gunpoint with their hands tied, he knew there was very little he could do . . .

*   *   *

Two hundred miles away, a Hercules C-130 had landed at Camp Bastion, the British military base in Helmand Province. It had touched down in darkness. The pilots had worn night-vision goggles, but the passengers had had to make do with the pitch black. By the time Bel disembarked, however, daylight was arriving and already the early-morning sun was warm.

Camp Bastion bustled with activity. Helicopters arrived and left; trucks carried supplies all over this massive base – food, water, ammunition. All the essentials of war. A man was waiting for her. He wore military uniform and had a friendly face with bright blue eyes and blond hair. His skin was tanned from the Afghan sun and he held out his hand as Bel approached. 'Dr Kelland?' he shouted over the noise of the airfield. 'Welcome to Bastion. I'm Major James Strickland. I'll be your liaison officer while you're here.'

Bel smiled. 'Pleased to meet you.'

'I'll show you to your quarters,' Major Strickland said. 'And then I'll explain to you how things get done in this neck of the woods.'

Bel's quarters were in a low concrete dormitory which she was to share with seven female intelligence officers when she wasn't out on the ground with the locals. It was basic – a low bed with a locker to one side for her things – but clean. Once she had stowed her things away, she followed Major Strickland to a briefing room. It was still very early, but she felt pleased that the room was air-conditioned: it was already very hot outside.

The room was simple. A whiteboard at one end and a load of chairs facing it. A bit like a school room, Bel thought. In front of the whiteboard was a map of the area on a stand. 'Helmand Province,' Major Strickland said. 'Camp Bastion is here.' He pointed to a position roughly in the centre of the province. 'We've arranged for your first visit to be to a small settlement here, between Sangin and Kajaki.' His finger moved to an area north-east of Bastion.

'How will I get there?' Bel asked. 'By car?'

Strickland smiled, as if it was a silly question. 'No, Dr Kelland. Not by car. Any journeys in this region by ground need to be undertaken in heavily armoured vehicles. Helmand Province is littered with landmines. The enemy have also covered the areas with IEDs – improvised explosive devices. Ground travel in Afghanistan is incredibly dangerous. You'll be transported by Chinook helicopter to a British Army forward operating base in the area. It's called FOB Jackson. You'll stay there for two nights. It's hardly luxurious, I'm afraid.'

'I didn't come here for luxury,' Bel said.

'Good. The villagers will come to you for *shuras*.

That's their word for a meeting. We have four *shuras* arranged for you over the next two days. If everything goes according to plan, we can arrange others for you in different parts of the province.'

Bel nodded. 'OK,' she said. 'When do we go?'

'In about an hour,' the soldier told her. 'A Chinook will be ready for you, assuming it's not needed for an emergency.'

'Like what?'

'Medical evacuation,' Strickland said briskly. 'We have soldiers engaging the Taliban all over the province. Those Chinooks are an important asset out here, Dr Kelland. I'm afraid you're not the only person who wants to make use of them. Now, if you'll excuse me, I have a few things to attend to.'

'Of course,' Bel murmured. She followed the major out of the room and into the heat of the Afghanistan day, a small part of her mind wondering what on earth she was about to do.

If they wanted us dead, Ben thought to himself as the Land Rover plodded on, *they'd have killed us already. There's got to be another reason why we're here*. It wasn't much of a thought to hang onto, but it was something. It made Ben feel a little bit bolder. He turned to Aarya. 'We're going to be OK,' he said with all the confidence he could muster. When he received another poke in the ribs from the rifle, he stopped himself from wincing and gave the man a stubborn look. For some reason, that made him feel a bit better.

The journey continued. It didn't take long for the heat to become immense. Sweat poured from Ben's body and he longed for another mouthful of water. Nobody offered him one. He tried to forget about his sandpaper-dry throat and concentrate on what he could do to get them out of this. But he didn't know where they were; they had no food or water; and their captors were armed. Flight seemed impossible.

It was mid-morning when they stopped. From the window of the truck Ben had watched as they climbed steadily higher into the mountains before taking a small road that started heading downhill. Now they had stopped by what looked like a very ancient low wall. A boundary. It stretched off into the distance and on either side the terrain remained rocky and unwelcoming.

'Why are we stopping?' Ben demanded. He didn't expect a response and he didn't get one. The back doors were opened and he was ordered off the truck with a flick of the guard's rifle. It was hotter outside the truck than in, and he felt faint with hunger and dehydration. From a bag, one of his captors pulled a large, flat piece of bread. He tore it into several parts while one of the others undid Ben's hands. He was given a piece of bread but, as before, Aarya was ignored. An obstinate look crossed Ben's face. Turning, he tore off a small piece of bread and held it to her mouth.

Immediately he felt an arm pulling him back.

'No!' he shouted. 'She's got to eat something. She needs water too.' Ben drew himself to his full height and squared up to the man who had pulled him – the man with the scarred eye.

The stared at each other. A tense moment. The guard's good eye narrowed. He hesitated, but then drew a bottle of water out from under his robes and gave it to Ben, who snatched it and immediately carried it to Aarya. He held it up to her lips, and she drank gratefully before taking a mouthful of bread.

Ben drank too, then they moved into the shade of the truck. The men were standing at a distance from them, talking quietly.

'Can you hear what they're saying?' he asked Aarya.

She shook her head. 'Not very well,' she replied. 'I think they are waiting for something.'

'What?'

'I don't know.'

Ben scowled. 'I don't understand this,' he muttered. 'Why are we here? Why are they doing this?'

Aarya gave him a stern look. 'I do not know why some people do anything,' she said darkly, and Ben remembered the story she had told him about her aunt.

He was filled with a new fear.

Just then they heard a sound in the distance. Their captors clearly heard it too, because they hurried to the other side of the truck to look down the road.

For the first time, they were on their own. 'Quick!' Ben whispered. He struggled to untie the cords that bound Aarya's wrists, then gently pulled her to her feet. He looked around. The landscape was barren and there was almost nowhere to hide. They could either run back along the road, or follow the low wall. The approaching noise became louder as Ben hesitated, looking this way and that.

Maybe if he hadn't, they'd have got away. At that moment, however, one of the men reappeared behind them. He saw that Aarya's hands were untied and shouted loudly. Almost immediately the others were there, guns pointing. Ben cursed under his breath as the man with the scarred eye issued an instruction.

'He said, "Move",' Aarya translated. 'To the other side of the truck.'

There was nothing they could do but obey. More dejected than ever, Ben led the way. It was then that he saw what was making the approaching noise.

There were three of them. Three trucks, large and ungainly. They were a sandy colour and almost the height of two grown men. The wheels themselves were a metre high and each vehicle had two spares, one on either side. There was an opening on the top of each truck, for some kind of top-gunner, Ben assumed, although there was no one making use of them. The vehicles were encased in armoured steel and trundled slowly towards them, coming to a halt perhaps ten metres from where Ben was standing.

The engines were switched off and an ominous silence filled the air. The three guards stared in awe at the vehicles. They had fallen quiet too.

One by one, the doors of the armoured trucks opened and more men appeared. Ben counted them as they climbed out: one, two, three, four, five, six. All of them in traditional robes – though not all black, this time; and all of them with rifles strapped across their backs. They were bearded, with dark skin, and their faces were serious. Ben could sense Aarya looking at them in undisguised fear as they approached.

The next few minutes passed in a haze. There was suddenly much talking, none of which Ben could understand. He wanted to ask Aarya what everyone was saying, but the question stuck in his throat. The man with the scarred eye took one of the newcomers to one side. They spoke quietly, looking towards Ben and Aarya all the time. They seemed to agree on something, then returned to the others.

Two of the new men went to the back of the Land Rover. When they reappeared, they were carrying the suitcase-like package that had been in the back. Ben had the impression that it was light enough for one person to carry, but they were just making sure. The package was loaded into the middle of the three trucks.

And then the new arrivals turned their attention to Ben and Aarya.

There were no words. Not at first. Just a flick of a gun. Ben could tell what it meant. *Get in the armoured truck.* One of the newcomers looked stranger and more sinister than the others. His eyes were different colours – one brown, one a kind of milky, albino white – and one side of his neck was scaly, red and damaged. He led them to the rear truck and as they walked, the men started talking again.

Aarya stopped. Her tired eyes went wide and she started shaking her head.

'What is it?' Ben asked. But she wasn't allowed to answer. A barked instruction from the young man and they were hustled up into the armoured vehicle.

It was hot inside. Like an oven. There were thin, hard seats along two sides and ugly armoured steel all around. This was not exactly travelling in comfort. Ben and Aarya sat next to each other, their strange new guard opposite them, his gun pointed firmly in their direction. There was more shouting outside; the doors of the trucks were slammed closed and the interior was plunged into gloom as there were no windows, just a few small ventilation holes covered with wire mesh.

Ben, though, wasn't paying any attention to the guard, or to the shouts, or to the surroundings. He was listening to Aarya, who had started to sob uncontrollably.

'What is it?' Ben asked. 'What were they saying, Aarya?'

She looked at him with panic in her tear-stained eyes.

'The border,' she replied. 'They're taking us across the border. We're going into Afghanistan . . .'

Chapter Seven

In Kampur, the mood was one of alarm.

Miss Messenger had her hands clutched together, like a woman praying. The redness around her eyes suggested she had been crying. Mr Sawyer and Mr Knight prowled at the front of the classroom where they had all congregated, their faces as dark as storm clouds. Carl kept running his hand nervously through his slicked-back hair, looking like he hadn't slept. The students just sat in silence.

'We need to know,' Mr Knight said, 'who the last person to see Ben was. Did anyone have any conversations with him after school yesterday? Anything at all?'

Ed kept his mouth shut and looked at the floor. He had seen Ben, of course, just before he went off to do his knight-in-shining-armour bit, showing off in front of the girl after the local lads had knocked him down.

But he wasn't going to tell anybody else that. He didn't like Ben Tracey and he didn't trust him. Chances were that he was just off hiding somewhere, making life difficult for everyone else. And anyway, if Ed *did* admit to having seen him, everyone would probably start blaming him. They always did. No, he thought. Much better to keep quiet like everyone else.

'All right, everybody,' Mr Knight continued when there was no answer to his question. 'I don't want anyone to panic. We've informed the British Embassy and they're sending someone out as soon as possible. In the meantime, we're all going to stay together.'

Rebecca put her hand up. 'Will we have to go home, sir?'

'Possibly,' said Mr Knight. 'We don't know yet. Anyway, I'm sure everything will be OK. Ben will turn up any moment. I've no doubt there's an explanation for this. He's a very sensible young man. I'm sure he's fine. Absolutely fine.'

Ed examined his teacher's face. He couldn't help thinking that Mr Knight didn't look too convinced. Nor did anyone else. But Ed kept quiet all the same, lowering his head and continuing to stare innocently at the floor.

Across the border, the vehicle's engine juddered into motion. Ben's senses were screaming at him to try and get out, but he knew he couldn't. He felt like he was in a moving prison.

Their guard did not take his eyes off them and Ben couldn't help staring at his strange face. The one albino eye seemed to see further than the other; and the scaly skin on the side of his neck made him look like a reptile. He wore a cream-coloured robe, embroidered round the neck. It was stained and dirty. The sandals on his feet were sturdy but well used. Everything about him made Ben's blood run cold.

The road was bumpy, which did nothing for Ben's sore body. Eyeing the rifle nervously, he saw that White-eye's finger was on the trigger and he hoped the bumps would not cause him to fire by accident. Next to him, Aarya was still sobbing. He stretched out a hand to comfort her, but immediately saw the man jerk his gun. Ben quickly held up his hands then lowered them onto his knees.

They continued in silence.

In the back of Ben's mind something told him he should be talking. Getting this guy's trust. Distracting him, even. 'Aarya,' he said in a low voice. 'Translate for me, OK?'

Aarya nodded. There were still tears in her eyes.

'Ask him what his name is.'

The girl spoke. It was clear she was addressing their

guard, but he refused to acknowledge her. Or even to look at her.

'Ask him again,' Ben urged when they received no reply.

Aarya opened her mouth to speak, but she was interrupted.

'You do not have to ask the girl.' Their captor spoke in slow, heavily accented English. 'I understand your language. To know a man's language is to know how he thinks, and I wish to know whatever I can about my enemy.' His eyes burned with hatred.

Ben nodded slowly. 'My name's Ben,' he said, doing his best to keep his voice level. 'What's yours?'

'Amir,' he replied with a curling lip. 'But it is not important to you.'

Ben shrugged. 'Just like to know who my travelling companions are,' he murmured.

'What did you say?'

'Nothing. Where are we going?'

Amir smiled. It wasn't a pleasant sight. He shook his head as though Ben had asked a stupid question.

'I only want to know where we're going.'

No reply.

'What do you want with us? Why have we been kidnapped?'

No reply.

Ben and Aarya exchanged a glance and the vehicle continued to trundle along.

It was another ten minutes before Ben spoke again. 'We could use some water,' he said.

Amir's white eye bulged slightly. 'You will get water when we give it to you,' he said. '*If* we give it to you . . .'

'I don't think so,' Ben replied boldly. 'We're here for a reason. I don't think you want us dying of thirst.'

Amir narrowed his eyes. He leaned forward slightly and whispered. 'I would very gladly kill you now,' he said. 'Do not think you are so important to us.' He sat back and gazed at them, seemingly pleased with what he had just said.

Ben's dry mouth turned drier. Now that he'd got Amir talking, however, he knew he had to keep it up; and he knew what his next question needed to be.

'What's in the package?' he asked. 'What are we carrying?'

Amir licked his lips and his eyes burned a little brighter. He looked from left to right, as if afraid that there was someone nearby who could hear him speak. At the last minute, though, he squinted suspiciously at Ben, drew a deep breath and clamped his lips shut.

Ben didn't give up. 'Something precious, I bet,' he said.

'Be quiet,' Amir said. To emphasize his point he nudged his gun forward.

'You all seemed to be carrying it very carefully,' Ben persisted.

'*Silence!*'

And from Aarya, a nervous warning. '*Ben . . .*'

Ben kept his eyes on Amir. 'What does it matter if we know? It's not like we can do anything about it.'

Amir was clearly struggling with himself. He wanted to tell – to gloat. Maybe, Ben thought, he should pretend not to be interested. Perhaps that would drive him wild. He shrugged. 'Fine,' he said. 'I bet it's nothing important anyway.'

The white eye burned. 'You do not know what you are talking about.'

Ben continued to look uninterested.

'What we are carrying,' Amir spat, 'will change the future of our war.' His face shone at the idea.

'I don't think so, mate,' Ben said nonchalantly. 'Looks more like a suitcase of old clothes to me.'

That smile again. 'A suitcase.' Amir nodded. 'Yes, a suitcase. But not full of clothes. No, not full of clothes.'

Amir was excited now. Ben could sense it, and he knew Aarya could too. She was holding her breath, listening to their captor's every word, even though the man opposite them refused even to look at her.

'A suitcase *bomb*,' Amir whispered. And then, as if he was playing his trump card: 'Nuclear!' His smile looked like it was going to take over his whole face. 'When I was just a child it was taken from the hated Soviets who occupied our land. They think it is lost. The whole world thinks it is lost. But the whole world is wrong! It has been hidden in many places since then. *Many* places. Always we have known the time will come when we will have need of it. That time is now upon us.'

He wasn't whispering any more. Far from it: he was almost shouting. And as he came to the end of his little speech, he appeared to realize that he had said too much. The triumph dissolved from his face and he reverted to a scowl. 'Now,' he said, 'you will be quiet. Unless you want this day to be your last.'

They had been driving for about three hot, un-comfortable hours when the vehicle came to a sudden halt. 'Do not move,' Amir instructed. 'Or it will end badly for you.'

They watched him open the door and get out. Sunlight streamed in. It made Ben squint, and by the time he had regained his vision, he felt himself being pulled roughly out of the truck by someone he didn't recognize. He was thrown onto the dry, stony ground while Aarya was also dragged out. 'Ow!' he shouted, but nobody paid any attention. They just manhandled Aarya down too.

Ben looked around. They had arrived at a small settlement – little more than two mud-walled compounds on either side of a wide dirt track. In the distance, Ben saw they were almost surrounded by high, craggy mountains. Outside one of the compounds there was a tree with green leaves – they appeared almost fluorescent against the deep blue sky and the beige, sandy earth. Ben wondered for a moment how a tree could survive in such inhospitable surroundings. Each compound had a rickety wooden gate and the one nearest to Ben was open. Men in traditional dress were standing outside. Ben searched for Amir, but couldn't find him.

They were hauled to their feet by armed men, then dragged through the gate and into the compound. Ben tried to work out the geography of the place. There was a main central courtyard with a stone well in the middle. Around the courtyard was a series of rooms, each with a wooden door. He couldn't tell what was beyond the doors, but he assumed that this was where people lived, because around him he saw the signs of habitation: clothes drying in the sun, the remnants of a fire, even a little patch of land where vegetables were being grown. Some elderly men sat in the shade of a wall. Their beards were grey and their faces as brown and grooved as a walnut. They watched Ben and Aarya with curiosity, though they did nothing to stop the rough way they were being treated.

Before Ben could take anything else in, he and Aarya

were led to one of these wooden doors. They were flung inside the room and the door was closed behind them. A scratching sound told Ben that it was being locked.

'We have to do something,' he hissed.

Aarya's tears had stopped, but now she had a shell-shocked stare and looked like she was a million miles away. She didn't reply.

'Aarya, come on – we *have* to do something.'

'Do something? What can we do?'

'I don't know,' Ben replied. 'Escape, I guess. Warn someone what's going on. I don't know what they're going to do with that suitcase bomb, but let's face it, I don't think they're saving it up for Bonfire Night.'

'For what?'

'Never mind.'

Ben turned his attention to the room. It looked lived in. Against the far wall there was a low bed with an old mosquito net hanging over it. An oil lamp lay on the sandy, dusty floor and there were clothes in piles around the bed. The only light came from a gap in the wall far too small for anyone to climb through. Ben peered through it. All he saw was an expanse of featureless desert, bleak and unwelcoming, with a wobbly haze of heat rising from the ground. He felt panic surfacing once more, and did what he could to suppress it. There was no time for that. They had to do what they could to get out of here.

'Aarya,' he whispered. 'We need to search this place. Find anything we can to help us.'

Aarya looked at him as if he was mad. 'We *can't* get out of here,' she said waspishly.

Ben barely heard her. He was already rummaging through the piles of clothes looking for something – anything – that they could use. He found a battery-operated torch, but it didn't work, and opening it up he saw that the batteries had long since started leaking a foul brown liquid. Under the bed there was a small cardboard box containing a few books, an old black and white photograph and a cigarette lighter.

Ben took the lighter, then turned his attention to the oil lamp. It was a chance . . .

He hurried over to the lamp. 'What are you doing?' Aarya asked, but Ben was concentrating too hard to answer. The lamp was ornate, with a brass bottom and a long glass bulb. Ben fiddled gently with it until he managed to take it apart. To his satisfaction he saw a healthy reservoir of oil in the bottom. Taking care not to spill any, he put it carefully on the ground, then returned to the pile of clothes. He found an old set of robes and tore off a strip of material before going back to the lamp and soaking the cloth with the fuel until it was all absorbed. He put the oil-soaked rag in one pocket and the lighter in another.

'What will you do with that?' Aarya asked.

Ben narrowed his eyes and crouched down to the floor, where he scooped up a large handful of dust. That too went in his pocket with the lighter. Only then did he turn to Aarya and answer her question.

'Listen carefully,' he said. 'I've got an idea . . .'

Chapter Eight

Bel Kelland stood near the landing zone at Camp Bastion, one hand cupped over her eyes to protect them from the billowing cloud of dust kicked up by the two rotary blades of a Chinook. It was unbearably hot – more so because of the body armour and helmet that she had been given to wear; but for a moment she forgot how uncomfortable she was and watched the chopper land.

She had expected it to arrive five hours ago, but each time the helicopter had set off back towards base, it had been called out on some emergency to a different part of the province. It had only finally appeared in the sky minutes ago, like some huge black insect against the intense blue.

The Chinook touched down in a swirl of sand and noise. Its tailgate opened like the mouth of a great iron beast; almost immediately several soldiers ran off, carrying with them a stretcher bed. Lying in the bed was a wounded man. Was he dead? Bel wondered. Probably not. He was being moved quickly: she guessed that meant he had a chance.

All the soldiers being spewed out of the Chinook looked exhausted and dirty, weighed down by their packs and their weapons. As soon as they were all off, Bel heard a voice. 'OK!' it shouted above the noise. 'Let's load up. Dr Kelland, are you ready?'

Bel looked over her shoulder. Privates Mears and Aitken – the two young soldiers who had been assigned to accompany her – also carried heavy bergens and standard issue SA80 rifles. They were thin and young, but looked a lot less battle-weary than the new arrivals.

Bel nodded at them. 'Ready as I'll ever be,' she shouted, before following them up into the belly of the chopper.

It took another ten minutes for the beast to be fully loaded. Ten minutes for Bel to think how nervous she was. Camp Bastion might have been strange and for-bidding, but now that she was about to leave, she realized how safe it really was. As soon as the Chinook rose up into the sky, she would be at the mercy of any enemy insurgents who felt like taking pot shots at them.

Private Mears seemed to know what she was

thinking. 'We'll be flying high,' he shouted at her. 'Out of range of most of the enemy's weapons.'

Bel nodded curtly. At the tailgate she saw a soldier taking his position with what looked like a machine gun. The engines of the Chinook suddenly changed pitch and Bel felt her stomach lurch as it lifted up from the ground, swooped away from Bastion and – very sharply, very quickly – gained height. She found herself gripping the edge of her seat.

Suddenly, from the rear of the chopper, she saw what looked like a firework explode in the air. 'Oh my God!' she shouted. 'What was that?' She looked around, unable to understand why nobody else seemed concerned.

'It's OK, Dr Kelland,' Mears yelled over the noise of the engines. 'They're just countermeasure flares.'

'What?'

'*Countermeasure flares*,' he bellowed back. 'We fire them from the back of the Chinook as we go. They confuse any heat-seeking missiles that are fired in our direction.'

Bel blinked. 'Right,' she said, feeling herself going a bit green. 'And does that happen a lot?'

Mears smiled at her. 'Not when we fire countermeasure flares it doesn't,' he said.

They hadn't been cruising for more than fifteen minutes when the Chinook started to lose height, again sharply and quickly – too quickly, Bel couldn't help thinking. The soldiers didn't look worried, though she noticed that the gunner at the back was still crouched in the firing position, ready to shoot at anyone who dared attack them from the ground.

And then, as suddenly as they had taken off, they landed, surrounded once more by dust and sand. The soldiers ran down the tailgate into the fierce, burning heat. Bel followed. Once she was a few metres away from the chopper, she stopped to take in her surroundings. They were just outside a high mud wall with rolls of wicked-looking barbed wire perched on top. In the distance she could see high, craggy peaks and over to her right there was an entrance gate made from huge, solid sheets of corrugated iron. The men from the Chinook were already disappearing through the gate and as Bel watched, she felt someone pull on her arm. It was Mears.

'Come on!' he shouted at her. 'We can't stay here. The landing zone could come under attack. Let's get you into the safety of the base!'

That sounded to Bel like the most sensible thing anyone had said all day. She nodded at the soldier, then followed him at a fast run through the iron gates. They closed behind her just as the Chinook rose once more into the azure sky above.

* * *

Back at Camp Bastion, Major James Strickland had gone distinctly white. He held the satellite phone to his ear with one hand; with the other he wiped a trickle of sweat from his brow.

'Disappeared?' he said. 'What do you mean he's disappeared?'

'Just that,' replied the voice at the other end – an official from the Ministry of Defence in London. 'The village is being scoured as we speak, but there's no sign of him.'

Strickland closed his eyes. This was all they needed.

'You need to inform the boy's mother,' the official continued. 'Rotten job, I'm afraid, but as you're the liaison officer—'

Strickland interrupted him. 'For crying out loud,' he said briskly, 'I don't mind telling her. But I can't. Not now. She's not at Bastion.'

'Where is she?'

'FOB Jackson, north of Sangin on the other side of the riverbank. She's there for forty-eight hours. Maybe longer. I can try and get her back sooner, but frankly the choppers are flat out.'

A silence. When the official spoke again, his voice was grim. 'Can you get word to her?'

'Negative,' Strickland replied. 'It's too dangerous.'

'Why?'

'If she thinks something's happened to her son, she'll

go ballistic. We need our people to be thinking clearly and acting rationally. I can't guarantee that she'll do that, and I can't risk her being a liability to our troops on the ground. I'll give her the information about her son when she's back in Bastion, not before.'

Another silence. And then, 'Roger that.'

Strickland sniffed. He didn't like it when non-military people used military language and there was something about this official, safely behind a desk in London, that brushed him up the wrong way. 'What you need to do,' he said, as if he was addressing a very junior soldier, 'is make sure you find that kid.'

'Don't you worry about that, Major Strickland,' the MOD official said rather primly. 'You deal with things on your side of the fence, we'll deal with things on our side. Is that clear?'

Strickland took a deep breath to hide his irritation. 'Roger that,' he said, with a little more meaning in his voice than he perhaps intended . . .

Night fell.

As Ben and Aarya's prison grew dark, the girl quietly took a blanket from the bed. 'What are you doing?' Ben asked.

'What I should have done this morning.' A calmness had descended over her. She laid the blanket on the ground, then lowered herself to her knees and bent her head to the floor. Ben watched quietly as she started muttering to herself in prayer. A strange sense of peace filled the room; and even though Ben could not understand the words that came from Aarya's mouth, he could tell they were said with quiet honesty.

When she had finished, she silently stood up again, folded the blanket and turned to Ben. 'I am supposed to do that five times a day, unless there is good reason not to.' She looked towards the door. 'I think *they* are good reason.'

'Yeah,' Ben said. 'I think you can say that again.'

Looking through the hole in the wall, Ben could see the moon rising and the sky brilliant with stars.

'What do you think they are doing?' Aarya said.

Ben shrugged in the darkness. 'I don't know,' he said. 'But look . . . that bomb . . . it's got to be something big. Some kind of terrorist thing. We've *got* to warn someone.'

They fell silent again. Somehow, locked in that room, their chances of escaping seemed pretty remote – plan or no plan.

They heard voices outside. Ben pressed his ear to the wall, desperately trying to get some sense of what they were saying. But to him, the language was gobbledegook. He couldn't even make out the individual sounds, apart from one word that they kept repeating, and that made no sense to him: '*Kahaki.*'

' "*Kahaki*".' He repeated the word to himself a couple of times. 'What does that mean, Aarya?'

Aarya shook her head. 'I do not know,' she replied. 'I do not recognize it. Perhaps it is a name, or perhaps a place . . .'

Ben wanted to bang his hand against the wall with frustration. 'Here,' he said. 'You listen. Can you hear what they're saying?'

She put her ear to the wall. 'Not well,' she replied. 'I think maybe they are preparing to leave.'

Ben felt his stomach twisting. It was bad enough in this strange, dark room; but the alternative was worse. And it came soon enough. There was a scratching sound as someone unlocked the door and then pushed it open. A figure stood in the doorway, one of their abductors, silhouetted against a crackling fire in the middle of the compound. He gave a harsh instruction, which Aarya translated. 'He says we should follow him.' Her voice trembled.

The figure turned and walked into the centre of the compound. Ben took Aarya's hand and led her outside. The only light was from the fire, and he was aware of a number of dark figures milling around the outskirts of the compound, watching them. From behind, someone approached. 'Get back into the truck,' a voice said, and Ben recognized it as Amir's. Somehow, he just knew that the terrorist would have a gun pointing in his direction.

They stumbled out of the compound to where the trucks were waiting for them, huge and sinister in the darkness. The engines were running, but Ben noticed that the headlamps were not switched on. They were about to make a journey in the dark without being seen. The door of the rear truck was wide open, and Amir pushed them towards it. Ben entered first, purposefully making sure that Aarya could sit nearest the door. Amir took his seat opposite them, resuming his guard-like vigilance with his gun pointed in their direction.

'Where are we going?' Ben demanded.

'Silence,' Amir replied. The door was shut, and moments later the vehicle started to move.

It was very dark in the truck, but it didn't take long for Ben's vision to adjust. He could see Amir's white eye, wide awake, flicking from Ben to Aarya, then back to Ben again. The stony earth crunched underneath them. Ben pictured the view he had seen from their prison. Featureless. Nothingness. Stuck out in the desert by themselves they'd be in just as much danger as they were now. If they were going to escape, they had to do so while they were near the compounds. The inhabitants might not be friendly, but at least they could try and break in, maybe steal food and water. At least they'd have options. Pretty slim options, but options all the same.

He glanced over at Aarya. She was clearly waiting for that glance. Waiting for the sign they had arranged; the sign that signalled their attempt to get out of here.

Ben coughed.

He sensed her holding her breath.

He coughed for a second time.

His hand was in his pocket. He grabbed a fistful of the dust he had collected from the compound floor.

And then he coughed for a third and final time.

Aarya didn't hesitate. She grabbed the barrel of Amir's gun and pushed it upwards. The terrorist shouted, and Ben half expected to hear the sound of a bullet ricocheting off the inside of the vehicle. The sound didn't come, though. He pulled his hand from his pocket and hurled the dust straight into Amir's face. Their captor choked loudly; he dropped his weapon and put two hands up to his stinging eyes. Aarya moved quickly to the door of the truck and opened it while Ben pulled the fuel-soaked rag from his pocket and lit it with the cigarette lighter. A flame rose slowly up the rag and he threw it onto Amir's lap. It wouldn't be hot enough to hurt him, but when he got his vision back it would make him panic and buy them a few precious extra seconds.

By now, Aarya had the door open. Ben threw himself towards it, grabbed her hand and they both jumped from the moving vehicle.

'*Now!*' he hissed. '*Run!*'

The two of them sprinted together away from the convoy and into the blackness of the desert night.

Ben didn't stop to take in the scenery. He just wanted to put as much distance between them and the trucks as possible. Aarya was slower than him, but he kept to her pace, vaguely aware of shouting behind them. Ahead of them, in the distance, he could see a faint glow: the compound, he assumed. They kept running towards it, even though it seemed like a very long way off.

Bang!

He heard the gunshot almost at the same time that he felt it: a ringing sound that filled the air, and then a sickening whoosh as the round zoomed past his head. Two more cracks of gunfire followed it in quick succession, nauseatingly loud and uncomfortably close. One of them went over his head; the other kicked up a cloud of dust as it hit the road to his side. 'They are shooting at us!' Aarya wept. '*They are shooting at us!*'

'Yeah,' Ben hissed, still running at full pelt. 'I kind of noticed.' And with that, they both hit the dirt and started scrambling to the side of the road like demented crabs. Ben looked around desperately for some kind of cover – a rock, a ditch, anything. But all he could see in the light of the moon was a vast expanse of nothingness; all he could hear was the sound of angry voices, and of footsteps sprinting towards them.

The voices were louder now. 'They are coming!' Aarya gasped. *'Ben! They are coming!'*

Hands. Big, rough, calloused hands all over them, pulling them to their feet. Ben felt a blow to his stomach, so painful that it even masked the distress he felt that their escape attempt had failed. He doubled over, just as he heard Aarya being slapped hard across the face. A fist grabbed his hair and, still gasping from the punch, he was dragged towards the trucks and bruisingly thrown back into the hard metal shell of that moving prison. A distraught Aarya joined him, and then Amir. His ugly face was curled into an expression of absolute loathing, and as he retook his seat he poked the butt of his gun into Ben's belly.

'You are lucky,' he hissed. 'If you had been shot we would leave you bleeding by the roadside. If I see you move again, that is what I will do.'

One look at his captor's eye told Ben that Amir meant it.

The trucks rolled on, and so did the night. Amir was like a warrior owl, never closing his eyes, never moving his gun. At Ben's side, Aarya nodded from exhaustion, but Ben was determined to stay awake. Or maybe he was just too scared to fall asleep.

Towards morning, the temperature fell and he found

himself shivering. His limbs became numb and weak. If Amir was cold, he didn't show it, nor did he give Ben any sign of sympathy – not that Ben was expecting it. He was hungry and his mouth was dry with thirst: he really didn't think he could cope with being in this vehicle much longer.

'Are we going to stop soon?' he asked. His voice surprised him – it was thin and rasping.

Amir sniffed and looked like he was deciding whether or not to reply. He shrugged. 'Before sunrise,' he said. 'We have people expecting us in a nearby village. They will give us shelter while we wait once more for the cover of night.' He sneered – an expression that suited his face. 'These people are our friends. We have friends all over the country. They help us in our struggle against the hated Americans and British. You should not try any foolishness – they will not be forgiving if you try to escape.'

Ben tried to moisten his lips with his tongue. 'Are you going to leave us there?'

Amir spat to one side. 'Of course we will not leave you there. We have taken you for a purpose.' He grinned – a singularly nasty expression. 'You should be glad that you are useful. If not, you would be dead.'

'What's so useful about us?' Ben demanded. 'What can we do that you can't?'

'Nothing!' Amir announced. 'It is not what you can do, but who you are that is important.'

'But you just kidnapped us at random. I don't understand.'

'Of course you do not understand. You are just a stupid child.' Amir's lips curled again. 'You are both stupid children. Stupid, because you think you can escape from us. And stupid because you know nothing of how our war is fought. *Nothing.*'

'Then why not enlighten me?'

For a moment Amir was quiet. Ben shrugged, as though it made no difference to him whether his captor carried on talking or not. Amir, though, could clearly not resist. 'Where we are going,' he said, 'there are many foreign troops. But they are not true fighters. Not true fighters at all. If they think there are' – Amir searched for an unfamiliar word – 'if they think there are *civilians* with us, then they will not attack us with their aeroplanes and their bombs. And if they think one of the civilians is British . . .'

Amir's smile grew broader than Ben had yet seen it. Triumphant, as though he had just made the winning move in a game of chess. Ben looked at him in horror, then over at Aarya. Her head was still nodding, and there was nothing to suggest that she had heard anything Amir had said. One small part of Ben wished the same could be said of him too. He felt sick as the full implication of what Amir had just said sank in. He didn't know where they were going or what they were about to do, but what he did know was this: he and Aarya were travelling in a convoy with a group of terrorists in charge of a nuclear suitcase bomb, and they were being used as human shields. And as long as they were being held at gunpoint by the fanatical terrorist in front of them, there was absolutely nothing they could do about it.

Chapter Nine

Tuesday became Wednesday. Ben didn't know whether to be relieved or frightened when the convoy came to a halt again. His body was bruised from the juddering journey; he was weak with hunger and dry with thirst. Aarya looked even worse.

Amir ordered them off the truck and they stepped weakly down, finding themselves once more on the outside of a compound. Ben could tell that day was not far off, but the grey light of morning had yet to break through the darkness as the silent, shadowy, dark-robed figures dragged them roughly into the compound itself.

If they hadn't been driving all night, Ben would have wondered if they'd moved at all since their last stopover. As far as he could tell, the place was almost identical. The only exception was the fire in the middle of the courtyard, which was now just a pile of glowing, smoking embers.

'Stop!'

It was Amir talking. Ben and Aarya waited while the men around them discussed something.

'What are they saying?' Ben whispered.

Aarya's voice was weak. 'They are talking about where to keep us,' she said, then listened again carefully. 'Somewhere empty, where there is nothing we can—'

Ben never got to hear the rest of the sentence, because Aarya never finished it. Instead she flinched, holding her hands to her ears. A booming sound exploded. It was far away, but not *that* far away, and it seemed to shake through Ben's body. And then, suddenly, the sky in the distance became illuminated with a bright light that lingered for perhaps twenty seconds before fading away.

And then, louder this time, another boom.

It was too much for Aarya. She started screaming. *'What is it? What is that noise?'* And then she reverted to her own language, crying with stress and panic.

Their captors had no time for it. One of them strode over to where Aarya was standing, before raising one of his hands ready to beat her on the head. A sudden anger filled Ben. He stepped forward and grabbed the man's wrist, just as he was trying to hit Aarya.

'No!' he shouted. 'Leave her alone.'

The man turned. His eyes were wide and angry. It didn't take much for him to escape Ben's grip and he looked for all the world like he was about to launch himself at both of them. Ben stood in front of Aarya, who was now sobbing hysterically, and stuck out his chin.

'Amir!' he demanded. 'Where's Amir?'

Amir's face emerged from the gloom.

'If they touch her,' Ben shouted, 'if they hurt her in any way, I'll spend every second trying to escape. Have you got that? The only way you'll be able to stop me is by shooting me. And what will happen to your precious human shield then?' He was full of anger, and he stood there in front of Aarya as a line of faces stared flatly at him.

There was a tense pause. Then Amir gave an instruction and another man suddenly forced them roughly into a room at the other side of a compound. The familiar noise of a key in the door hit Ben's ears and before they knew it, they were alone again.

'Ben!' Aarya sounded angry. 'What are you doing? These are dangerous people. They will kill you . . .'

Ben shook his head in the darkness. 'No,' he said stubbornly. 'They won't kill us. At least, not yet. We're here for a reason, Aarya. If we come under attack, they'll stick us up on the roof of their trucks – make it clear they've got civilian hostages. They seem to think that'll stop the army from blowing them up.'

Aarya paused. 'But . . .' she stammered. 'But that is monstrous.'

'Yeah,' Ben muttered. And then, cryptically, 'Welcome to my world.'

'What do you mean?'

Ben looked away. 'Let's just say Amir and his buddies aren't the first people to try and play dirty when I'm around.'

Aarya looked confused. 'I do not understand, Ben. Are you saying these people know who you are?'

'Course not. I'm not exactly in the Afghanistan phone book—'

'*Ben!* Stop speaking to me in riddles.' There was a sudden fire in Aarya's voice as she stepped purposefully towards him.

He shook his head, cross with himself. 'I'm sorry,' he said. 'I just seem to have this habit of walking into trouble. This is all my fault – I wish you didn't have to be involved.'

Silence. And then, a hand on his shoulder. 'This is not your fault, Ben. It is theirs, the men outside. You were very brave to stand up to them.'

Ben didn't reply. At that very moment the door opened. He couldn't see who it was, but he could hear the thump as something was thrown in before the door was shut once again. Scrabbling around on the ground, he found a bottle of water. He quickly opened it and handed it to Aarya, who drank deeply before giving it back to Ben. As he gulped down the water, he felt his whole body soaking it up and, like a wilted plant that had just been fed, he was revived.

'What was that noise?' Aarya asked. 'The booming noise and the light in the sky?'

For a moment Ben didn't answer. He had been asking himself the same question and he didn't much like the conclusion he'd come to. 'I reckon,' he said finally, 'that the light was some kind of flare. You know, for the army to light things up a bit. Spot people moving around in the dark.'

'And the sound?'

'Weapons,' Ben said. 'Artillery. Something like that.'

'At night? When people are sleeping?'

Ben thinned his lips. 'Yeah,' he said, 'or *not* sleeping. I get the impression we're going to be hearing a bit more of that. Think about it, Aarya. They've got a nuclear suitcase bomb. If they're going to use it, they're going to use it where they can cause maximum damage. And if they need you and me as a human shield, it means they're taking us somewhere they expect to come under fire. Some kind of battleground. If those flares are anything to go by, I'd say we're pretty close.'

As if to highlight his point, in the distance they

heard another muffled thump. Ben sensed Aarya shaking on the ground where she sat.

'I want to go home,' she said in a small voice.

'Me too,' Ben replied. 'Me too.' And then, because he thought he didn't sound positive enough, he added, 'We will.'

He knew Aarya didn't really believe him.

They sat in silence for several minutes.

'Ben?' Aarya asked finally, her voice calmer than he had heard it for ages.

'Yeah?'

'If the British Army attack us, they would be less willing to risk a British citizen than a Pakistani girl, wouldn't they?'

Ben felt himself tense up. 'I don't know.'

'I think they would. I think it means that you are more use to these terrorists than I am. I think it means they would kill me if they had to.'

Ben took a deep breath.

'That's not going to happen, Aarya,' he said firmly. 'I promise you that's not going to happen.'

But he only said it because he could think of nothing else to say. He watched quietly as his friend, her body trembling, settled down for her morning prayers. He almost felt like praying himself.

Bel's first night at FOB Jackson was uncomfortable

and noisy. Her quarters were little more than a thin bed covered with a mosquito-net tent, all propped up against a low wall. She had eaten ration packs with the soldiers – a sludgy mess of sausages and beans – then turned in early so that she could be ready for the *shura* that would happen early the next morning. All night, however, she was kept awake by the light of the flares being sent up into the sky, and by the booming sound of weaponry far and wide. Around midnight she had climbed out of bed and walked around the base. She had met Private Mears, who had explained to her what the noise was. 'Enemy activity to the north,' he had said. 'We're sending in mortar fire to suppress their movement.'

'Enemy movement?' Bel asked, alarmed. 'That, er . . . that doesn't sound very good.'

Private Mears winked at her. 'Welcome to Helmand,' he said. 'Don't worry about it. Tonight's no different from any other. The base is well defended – they'd have to be suicidal to attack us here.'

Bel took some comfort from Private Mears's words as she padded back to bed. Some, but not much. As she lay there, she thought about Ben, and smiled. He'd been so keen to accompany her, but this was no place for a person his age. Come to think of it, it was no place for a person of any age. Bel absolutely could not wait to leave here and get back home.

Dawn arrived. Everyone in the camp who wasn't on lookout duty rose with the sun. Bel washed her face using water drawn from a well in the middle of the camp, then went to find Mears. The young private was drinking a cup of tea with a few mates.

'Morning, Dr Kelland,' he said. 'You look like you could use a brew.'

Bel *could* use a brew, but she didn't get the chance to say so, because just as she opened her mouth there was a loud noise and something screamed over the top of them.

'*Get down!*' Mears yelled. '*RPG!*' He threw his tea to one side, then wrestled Bel heavily to the ground like a rugby player. All the wind was knocked out of her lungs as the rest of the soldiers hit the dirt as well, their arms covering their heads while, only a few metres away from them, Bel heard something explode in the air, followed by the sound of shrapnel raining onto the ground.

'That was close!' someone shouted.

'What's an RPG?' Bel gasped, her face still pressed into the ground.

'Rocket-propelled grenade,' Mears stated flatly. 'Bit of a Taliban favourite.'

Bel looked up. The soldiers were pushing themselves to their feet, and there was urgent movement all around. 'Get up!' Mears instructed, and she felt him pulling her from the ground just as another rocket whistled over them. 'We need to get you to cover. *Now*.'

'I thought you said the enemy would have to be suicidal to attack us here,' Bel shouted.

Mears gave her a grim look. 'Yeah,' he yelled back. 'Trouble is, some of them are.' He pulled her by the arm and they ran across the open ground of the base to where a high wall of sandbags had been constructed at right angles to the main compound wall. They threw themselves to the ground and pressed their backs against the sandbags while yet more rockets flew overhead.

'Come on,' Mears muttered to himself. 'Come on. *Come on!*'

'Come on, what?' Bel demanded.

'The enemy must be close if they can lob RPGs into the compound like that. We need to return fire, quickly.' He peered over the top of the sandbags, then quickly sat back down again. 'GPMG gunner climbing up to the compound roof now,' he reported.

'What's a GPMG?'

'General Purpose Machine Gun. You might want to cover your ears.'

Bel did what she was told, but the sudden grinding, thundering noise from the rooftop weapon seemed to go through her all the same, like a hundred tiny explosions in a line. Private Mears barely flinched – Bel supposed that he was just used to the noise.

The GPMG fire continued in short, sharp bursts,

ringing out over the top of the compound. There was shouting all around, and every time Bel thought the firing had stopped, it would start up again.

'Sounds like we've suppressed the enemy fire,' Mears said. He had sweat pouring from his face.

'What?'

'The enemy. They've stopped firing. Guess they haven't got quite the taste for a fight they thought they had.' Mears was grinning and Bel realized that he was excited by the contact. She wished she could say the same.

'Does that happen a lot?' she asked, her voice trembling.

Mears shrugged. 'Attacks on the base, no. Morning contacts, yes. When it gets hotter, the enemy all go inside to get out of the midday heat. Then things start to kick off again later in the afternoon. But I can tell you one thing.'

'What?' Bel was out of breath just from the sheer terror of it all.

'After that little display, they won't be letting the locals into the base this morning. I reckon your *shura*'s going to have to wait for another day.' He smiled at her. 'You might as well make yourself at home, Dr Kelland. Looks like you're going to be here for a bit longer than you thought. Now if you'll excuse me, I'm going to clean my rifle. If the enemy are going to be bolshie, I'd feel a lot better knowing everything's in good working order. Know what I mean?'

The man from the British Embassy who arrived in Kampur was stiff-backed and stern-faced. Even the teachers looked a bit scared of him. He was accompanied by two others – a man and a woman, who had the bearing of police officers, even if they didn't have the uniforms. The Embassy man spent a good deal of time with the teachers, explaining the arrangements he had put in place to get them all back home as quickly as possible, as well as consoling Aarya's distraught parents. It was up to the other two to interview the pupils.

Ed didn't like the look of them. They were steely-eyed, no-nonsense types. He could instantly tell that pulling the wool over their eyes wouldn't be like deceiving his friends, or his teachers. As they all lingered outside a classroom in the village school, waiting to be interviewed one by one, Ed felt the pressure mounting. His mouth was dry; he was sweating badly. Telling them the truth about Ben's schoolyard antics was out of the question, of course. The lie was too deeply ingrained now. He was just going to have to see it through.

The door opened. Rebecca, the first to be interviewed, walked timidly out with a slightly wild look in her eyes. The woman appeared, clipboard in hand. 'Ed Hughes,' she announced. 'Ed?'

All the others looked at him. Ed drew himself up to his full height and walked confidently past them, though his fingernails were dug deeply into the palm of his hand. The woman stepped aside to let him into the classroom, then closed the door and took her place behind the teacher's desk, alongside the man.

'Sit down, Ed,' she said, indicating a seat opposite them.

Ed did what he was told.

A silence as the two adults looked at him.

The woman peered over her half-moon glasses at him. 'We just want to make sure, Ed, that there isn't anything about Ben Tracey and his exchange partner Aarya that you've forgotten to mention.'

'There isn't,' Ed replied quickly. Too quickly.

The adults looked at each other. 'You seem very sure about that, Ed,' the man suggested. 'Been thinking about it a lot, have you?'

'Not really.' Ed did what he could to withstand the man's stare. It took some doing.

'Sure about that?'

'Of course I'm sure.' Ed's body temperature was rising and he knew he appeared flustered. It didn't seem to worry either of them, though: they both looked at him calmly.

'I suppose we don't need to tell you how serious this is, Ed,' the woman pressed. 'If we don't find Ben and Aarya, you'll be having interviews with people a lot fiercer than us. Sure you don't want to tell us anything?'

'*I haven't seen them, all right?*' Ed was half shouting now, and his face had gone very red. Both adults raised a single eyebrow, and suddenly Ed heard himself gabbling. 'Tracey's an idiot, OK? He's probably just hiding somewhere. You shouldn't waste your time on him.'

Another silence. 'Do you really think we're wasting our time, Ed?' the woman said. 'Or is there something personal between you and Ben?'

Ed looked at the floor. This wasn't going well and he knew it. 'No,' he muttered. 'Nothing.' He heard the scratching sound of pen and paper as the two grown-ups each wrote something down. 'What are you writing?' he demanded. 'Look, I don't know anything, OK? I haven't seen anything.'

'No, Ed,' the man replied. 'It seems to me that you may have mentioned that once or twice before.' Again, the two of them glanced at each other.

Ed felt a drop of sweat run down the back of his neck.

'You'll be leaving Pakistan tonight,' the woman told him.

'All of us?'

'All of you.'

Relief crashed over Ed. He didn't like it here. Back in England he could pretend none of this had ever happened.

'We might want to speak to you again, though. Back home. That would be all right, wouldn't it, Ed?' They were looking directly at him now. Piercing.

Ed shrugged. 'Whatever,' he said.

'Good. Well then, I don't think we need to keep you any longer.' The man's words were friendly, but his voice wasn't. Ed stood up and walked to the door.

'Ed,' the woman's voice called softly before he had a chance to open it. He stopped and turned round.

'What?'

'We'll know if you're lying. You do realize that, don't you?'

Ed frowned. He gave them a hard look, then dug his fingernails a little more firmly into the palm of his hand. Then he shrugged again, opened the door and walked out.

They were just trying to put the frighteners on him, he told himself.

They didn't suspect anything.

Even if they did, they had nothing on him. Nothing at all. He just had to keep up the pretence. Do everything he could not to crack. And he knew he could do it. After all, there was no way he was going to let Ben Tracey, of all people, get any help from him . . .

Chapter Ten

The day passed slowly and uncomfortably. As light trickled into their new prison, Ben saw that they had indeed been put into a room that contained nothing they could use to their advantage: just a low bed with a thin mattress and very little else. He let Aarya take the bed while he lay on the hard, dusty floor. Sometimes he would fall asleep, only to be woken with a start by the booming of weaponry in the distance, or the occasional muttering of Aarya's regular prayers. Whenever that happened he would look around, confused and not knowing where he was. But then he'd see Aarya's terrified face and the locked door and it would all come back to him in a sickening flash.

Evening arrived and the door opened. It was Amir, his ever-present gun slung by his side. He placed another bottle of water on the floor along with a wooden bowl of food. 'Eat this,' he said with a glare at Ben, 'then prepare to leave. We depart at nightfall.' Ben noticed that he refused to address Aarya.

The water was welcome, as was the food – a strange, bland porridge which Ben might have turned up his nose at if he hadn't been so hungry. As it was, both he and Aarya gobbled it down. And when they had finished, the waiting continued.

'You think they will take us towards where the guns are firing?' Aarya asked.

'Yeah,' Ben said. 'I do.'

It was fully dark when the door was opened again. Nobody needed to tell them what to do. Ben and Aarya walked out, covered as always by men with guns, and were marched from the compound under the watchful eyes of the owners.

'I don't know why they don't help us,' Ben muttered under his breath.

'Maybe they don't want to help us,' Aarya breathed. 'Or maybe they know things will go badly for them if they do.'

One of their captors barked a command. It was not in English, but Ben understood its tone. *Silence!*

Amir was waiting for them, with some of the others, outside the compound; but instead of the three heavy armoured trucks they had used before, there were two much smaller Land Rovers. As Ben and Aarya stood under armed guard, they watched the suitcase bomb being lowered into one of them. Only then did Amir approach them. He pointed at Aarya. 'You,' he said. 'Get into the front truck.'

Aarya meekly did as she was told. Ben made to follow her, but immediately felt a hand on his shoulder. 'Not you,' Amir snarled at him. 'You get into the other vehicle.' As Ben opened his mouth to protest, Amir interrupted him. 'Forget about being a hero,' he hissed. 'The girl is no use to us. If you do not do what you are told, we will kill her first.'

Ben stared at him furiously, but the terrorist's words had frozen his muscles. Glancing over his shoulder, he saw a terrified Aarya being placed in the front truck; he was left with no option but to follow Amir into the rear vehicle.

The suitcase bomb was on the floor in the back of the truck; there were seats on either side. Ben sat down carefully, unwilling even to let his leg brush against it. Amir sat opposite him, along with another of the dark-eyed, bearded terrorists. A third man took the wheel and waited for the vehicle ahead to move away before following it.

It wasn't long before another flare lit up the sky and Ben wasn't surprised to see that they were heading in the general direction from which it came. 'We're moving into the battle zone, aren't we?' he quietly asked

Amir. His captor made no response; he just continued to stare at him, the milky eye glowing eerily in the dark. So Ben persisted, wanting to keep the conversation going – not so much for tactical reasons, but rather to keep his mind occupied.

'Why two trucks?' he asked.

Amir narrowed his eyes, as though he didn't understand the question.

'You're travelling at night,' Ben said, 'without any lights. You obviously don't want to be seen. Surely one truck would be safer than two.'

Amir sneered. 'No,' he rasped. 'One truck is not safer. In fact, one truck is a great deal more dangerous.' He turned to his colleague and said something in his own language which made them both laugh.

'Why?' Ben demanded.

There was a glint in Amir's eyes now, a kind of wild excitement. He leaned forward as he spoke, slowly and with a snake-like hiss to his voice. 'There may be landmines on the road ahead,' he whispered. 'We drive in the tracks of the vehicle in front. So we know *we* will not hit one.'

A cold, prickling sensation went down Ben's back. Landmines – he'd seen the damage they could do in the Congo. 'But – but the truck in front. What if that hits a mine?'

Amir's eyes widened. 'In that case—' He jerked his

121

hands up, palms downwards, and made a low noise in the back of his throat. The sound of an explosion. Then he tapped the suitcase bomb at their feet. 'That way,' he sneered, 'our weapon will be safe.'

Ben leaned over and looked through the front window of the Land Rover. The other vehicle was a good twenty metres ahead, travelling slowly.

'But the people in there,' he whispered, 'don't they . . . ?'

'They are honoured to take the risk,' Amir said, his eyes still glinting. 'They know that if they die, it will be in a good cause.' The fire in his expression grew stronger. 'And your friend? She is just a girl, after all . . .'

Ben didn't know how to reply to such a statement. He thought of Aarya, exhausted and scared, sitting in the back of that truck. Did she have any idea of the danger she was in? Did she have any idea why she was in front or what might happen?

Ben hoped not. Sometimes, he decided, it was better not to know.

It was midnight, Ben estimated, when they hit a main road. By most standards it was a shoddy track, but it was a lot better than the ones he had begun to get used to. They didn't stay on it long, however. The driver made his way north, back into the desert, carefully staying in the tracks of the vehicle ahead. Every second, one half of Ben's mind expected to hear the brutal sound of the front truck exploding, while the other half argued: It *won't* happen. It *can't* happen. Aarya's going to be OK.

He wasn't sure that he was doing a great job of persuading himself.

There were moments of silence, moments when the distant boom of weapons disappeared and the night sky remained unlit by flares. They never lasted long. Whenever they started up again, they were always louder than the time before, and brighter. Ben knew that meant only one thing: they were getting closer to the hotspots.

'What if the army sees us?' he asked. 'Won't they attack?'

Amir sneered. 'They will only attack if they see us carrying weapons. That is their weakness. And they are too scared to patrol when it is dark. That is why we travel at night. Now, you will stop asking me questions.'

Even if Ben had wanted to, there was little chance left. It was well after midnight, he estimated, when the truck came to a stop. 'What is it?' he demanded, before looking out of the window. He blinked. Peering into the darkness, he realized that the surrounding desert was no longer the featureless plain he had grown used to. Suddenly, only metres away from the Land Rover, there were trees. Lots of them, and a field of something growing.

'From here,' Amir announced, 'we go by foot. The green zone is not fit for vehicles. Get out.'

Ben did as he was told. Outside, he saw Aarya being thrown to the ground. He ran over and helped her up. She gave him a tired smile.

'What's the green zone?' he whispered. 'Amir said that's where we are.'

Aarya looked around. 'I think it is what they call the area surrounding the edge of the river bank. In the summer, the river is very low, but the area around it is fertile. Crops grow there, and it is where many people live.' She gave him a solemn look. 'I have heard people say that, in Afghanistan, it is also where there is lots of fighting.'

A whole host of questions flooded Ben's mind, but at that moment they were surrounded by their captors. 'Walk,' Amir told them. He was still holding his gun, but now he had something else strapped to his body: the suitcase bomb, which he carried on his back. It looked cumbersome and rather heavy – the veins on Amir's neck stood out from the strain of carrying it – but portable nevertheless. The very sight of it made Ben shudder.

They walked in single file – two of the terrorists in

front of Ben and Aarya, the rest of them bringing up the rear. 'Keep close to me,' Ben whispered as they walked. 'Maybe we can—'

'*Silence!*'

The ground was treacherous. Both Ben and Aarya stumbled as their feet became trapped in unseen holes; the soil underfoot became marshy and wet, then hard and dry as they walked alongside a high field of some crop Ben didn't recognize. All around it was silent – just the footsteps of their little party disturbing the night and once, chillingly, the howl of a dog echoing through the air. They'd been walking for a good fifteen minutes when they came to an area thick with compound walls, much like the ones where they had stayed on the previous two nights. There was one big difference, however: these walls bore the scars of battle. Holes of all different sizes had been blasted into them: small ones where, Ben assumed, rifle fire had sprayed against them; and larger ones, where heavier artillery had battered the compounds.

Amazingly, though, the walls were still standing and it was towards one of them that Ben and Aarya were led. There was a low wooden door in the middle of it; their captors opened it, then pushed them through. A dog howled again, closer this time – and Ben realized that it was in this very compound. Suddenly it came scampering up to them – a thin, poor-looking thing that sniffed around their feet as though they were the first human contact it had had for months. It soon scuttled away though, tail between its legs and whimpering, as a huge explosion rocked the sky, shaking the ground beneath them.

Amir removed the suitcase bomb from his back, propping it against the inside wall like it was just a hitchhiker's rucksack. Then he turned and looked around the compound. A group of men – nine or ten of them – were waiting for him. They were all dressed in Afghan robes and they approached the new arrivals with smiles. There was much embracing and a good deal of chattering that Ben couldn't understand, but that didn't matter. His attention was firmly fixed on something else.

It was difficult to make it out in the darkness, and he had to squint. There was no mistaking what it was, however: a vast array of weaponry, much of it propped up against the far wall of the compound in the same way that Amir had propped up the suitcase bomb. It was an impressive arsenal: rocket launchers, rifles, a big hunk of metal that looked to Ben's untutored eye like a machine gun. And then there were boxes, piled high, which he supposed were full of ammo.

Ben and Aarya exchanged a glance. 'I don't reckon they use that sort of gear to shoot birds,' he breathed.

Aarya shook her head, then they looked back over at

the others. Their captors' chatter had become more animated and they stood around the bomb, pointing at it like it was some precious artefact. Ben then heard Amir's voice above the others, and the men all turned to look across at them. It was clear that he and Aarya were now the subject of conversation.

Ben stepped nervously back, but that only took him deeper into the compound. Suddenly Amir barked a short order, and the two of them were immediately surrounded. Ben's instinct told him to run, but he knew there was no getting away and it was only moments before he felt strong hands on him as they were yet again manhandled into a dark room on the edge of the compound, where the door was locked.

Once more they were left alone.

Very alone.

And very, very scared.

Chapter Eleven

The British base at Sangin. One hour before dawn.

Platoon commander Andy Bishop groped in the dark. By his bed – if you could call it that – lay his helmet, to which he had strapped a head torch. He switched on the torch. The area around his bed became flooded in a dusty red light. No white light allowed here – too easy to see from a distance.

Immediately there was the sound of the men around him stirring and groaning. 'Morning, campers,' Andy said in a voice made gravelly by the Afghan dust. 'Rise and shine. Time for a stroll on this lovely Thursday morning.'

His gear was neatly squared away beside him and he started to put it on. Desert fatigues, body armour, SA80 rifle which he had meticulously cleaned only hours before. All around him the members of his platoon arose; in that red light they looked like zombies, but Andy knew that in two minutes they'd be transformed from sleepy men to highly alert fighting machines. And that was what they needed to be if they were going to patrol deep into the green zone of Sangin.

Minutes later Andy was boiling water on a small stove and making a much-needed cup of tea. As the water bubbled he heard the sound, on the opposite side of the base, of some vehicles starting up. That would be the fire support unit. It was their job to take position in the high ground nearby and keep watch over the green zone with their high-powered viewing devices and heavy, accurate weaponry. If Andy's platoon got into trouble, the fire support guys would be able to use their guns to hit the enemy. Not a bad insurance policy to have, Andy always thought.

They had been briefed the previous evening at 1730 hours. From the base they would head north, directly into the green zone. This area was an enemy stronghold and there had been a lot of activity there over the past forty-eight hours. The purpose of their operation was to quell that activity. To make the enemy know that their presence would not be tolerated.

In other words, they were out looking for a fight.

It was still dark when they prepared to leave: twenty men, heavily tooled-up with weapons, communications systems, ammunition and litres of water. There was a low buzz of conversation. Not nervous, exactly. Just prepared for any contact that came their way.

'Ready, Andy?'

It was Major Graves, the commanding officer.

'Ready, sir.'

'All right, then. Let's take it to them.'

The wide metal gates of the base slid open, and the men stepped outside into the town of Sangin, all their senses hyper-alert.

The darkness could go only halfway to blanketing the destruction all around them. Buildings had been flattened; there were great craters in the streets where artillery shells had landed. Once, Andy knew, this part of town had been lively and bustling. Not any more. It would be impossible to live here – impossible because of the constant fighting, and because all the houses had been destroyed. No wonder so many of the townsfolk had fled.

They walked steadily north, their boots crunching on the stony earth, taking care not to wander too close to each other. Bunch up and they would present an easy target for any brave sniper that might be hidden behind a mound of rubble. Andy kept his gun ready. You seldom got any warning that a contact with the enemy was about to start, so you had to be constantly vigilant.

Somewhere, a dog howled. The sound disappeared

eerily into the night sky. The men continued to march.

Dawn. Just a glimmer of light in the sky at first. To Andy's right, the shell of a building that was once a school. The only thing you would learn there now would be about the destruction of war, and that was something the people of Afghanistan knew enough about already.

It always surprised Andy how quickly the green zone arrived. It was as if someone had drawn a line: on one side of the line was the bombed-out remains of the town; on the other side were thick green fields, trees and trickling streams. It made Andy think of mermaids – beautiful creatures who entranced sailors and tempted them to their deaths. The green zone was beautiful too, in its way. But set foot inside it and you'd be taking your life in your hands.

In the grey light of morning, Andy saw a small group of Afghans in a field perhaps fifty metres away. They stared at them as they entered the green zone. They might be peaceful, ordinary villagers; or they could be enemy spies. Their gnarled, weather-beaten faces gave no suggestion that they either welcomed or disliked the soldiers. Either way, there was no sign that they were carrying weapons, so the soldiers could do nothing but walk past them and continue into enemy territory.

They walked in single file along a line of trees. Between

the soldiers and the trees was a ditch; to their right was a field of low dry stalks. Andy recognized it as a poppy field – he'd seen enough of them during his time in Helmand, after all. He felt vulnerable. Beyond the poppy field were two compounds; between the compounds and the soldiers there was nothing but open ground.

And open ground, as they well knew, meant they could easily come under fire.

Still, Andy thought to himself, they'd come out here to pick a fight. Some kind of sixth sense told him that a fight was exactly what they were going to get . . .

Ben awoke from a half-sleep to the sound of voices outside. He pushed himself up from the ground. Aarya was already by the door, her ear against the lock.

'What's going on?' Ben whispered.

'Shhh!' she hissed, waving a hand at him in irritation and keeping her ear pressed to the door. 'I'm trying to listen.'

Ben joined her by the door and pressed his own ear against it. There was definitely activity in the compound. 'What are they saying?' he breathed.

'I do not know,' Aarya replied. 'I heard them say the word "soldiers", but I cannot hear anything else.'

More activity outside. Muffled voices. 'I think we can safely say they're not getting ready to leave,' Ben muttered. 'Not during daylight.'

Aarya shook her head. 'No,' she said. 'They are arguing. Some of them want to fire their weapons. Amir is telling them not to.' A pause. Aarya looked like she was going to say something, but as she opened her mouth there was a very different kind of noise from outside. The unmistakable sound of a gun being fired.

'The weapons!' Ben hissed. 'The ones they had against the wall. They're using them to attack someone. Aarya, we've got to do something.'

'What *can* we do?' Aarya demanded. 'We're locked in.'

Ben banged his fist angrily against the wooden door. 'Let us out!' he shouted. '*Let us out!*' His words, however, were drowned by a sudden burst of fire. 'You said they were talking about soldiers!' Ben yelled. 'They must be firing on them!' He took several steps back, then ran at the wooden door, barging it with his shoulders. The door rattled, but it remained locked.

It was just as he was preparing to bash his bruised shoulder against the door for a second time that Aarya grabbed him. 'Don't be foolish, Ben!' she scolded. 'We are safer in here than out there.'

'But we've got to stop them.'

'*They* are men with guns, Ben. We have nothing. We need to take shelter.'

With that, she tugged at him. Ben, reluctantly realizing she was right, didn't resist. The two of them ran to the far side of the room. Ben upturned the thin mattress from the only bed and propped it up in front of them. It was hardly robust, but it made them feel a bit better as they listened in horrified silence to the sound of their captors' guns, and wondered what kind of devastation was going on outside . . .

There was a stillness in the air. The sun had only spent fifteen minutes in the sky, but already Andy could feel its heat. He wanted to drink some water, but that would mean stopping. And there was no way he was going to st—

'*GET DOWN!*'

Andy heard the barked instruction from one of his men just as a bullet whizzed over his head. Just inches away? He couldn't tell, but it had been very, very close. Andy threw himself to the ground, then rolled heavily into the ditch. He felt his clothes becoming soaked with water, but just now that was the least of his worries. The enemy had opened fire, and all of a sudden the air was alive with rounds. Keeping himself pressed down against the oozing mud at the bottom of the trench, he loosened his rifle and prepared to return fire.

All his muckers had performed the same manoeuvre. As a single body of men, they had taken cover in the ditch. 'Is anyone hit?' Andy shouted as he propped the end of his rifle against the edge of the ditch. '*I said, is anybody hit?*'

'*Negative!*' came the reply. And then: '*They'll have to do a bit better than that!*'

A wave of relief crashed over Andy. He was responsible for the men in his platoon. If any of them died, he'd live with the guilt for the rest of his life.

The British soldiers returned fire, and for a moment the air sounded like Bonfire Night. Andy's ears went numb from the sound of his own weapon and everybody else's.

A minute of sustained fire from both, and then the guns fell silent.

Andy was out of breath; sweat poured from him. The shooting might have stopped, but they were still in the enemy's sights. Moving out of that ditch was a no-no – they were pinned down, easy pickings for any snipers in the enemy compound. Keeping his head low, he crawled on all fours, past six of his men to where the commanding officer was stationed.

As he crawled, however, there was a screaming sound in the air.

'*RPG!*' someone shouted, and Andy pressed himself face down in the ditch once more. The grenade exploded somewhere behind him – too close for comfort. Andy stayed put as he counted five more grenades being fired, one after the other in quick succession. By some miracle, none of them found their target.

Andy pushed forward another twenty metres. Major Graves had his back against the wall of the ditch, a map of the area opened out in front of him. To his side, a radio operator was speaking coordinates into his communications system.

'I'm calling in an artillery strike on the compound,' Graves told Andy.

'Roger that,' Andy replied. He turned to the radio operator. 'Time till impact?' he asked.

The radio guy held up one finger as he listened to his earpiece. 'Forty-five seconds,' he said.

They waited. In one corner of his mind Andy found himself praying that the artillery shells hit their target accurately. The enemy compound was only a hundred metres away. It didn't leave much room for error.

A boom in the distance. Then another.

Andy held his breath and covered his ears.

Impact.

The whole ground shook as though a sudden earthquake had hit them, and from the direction of the compound there were two terrible explosions.

'*Three more coming in!*' the radio operator yelled. Andy tensed up and waited for them to hit. The shells slammed into the compound with three brutal booms just as the acrid smell of cordite drifted towards them.

Then, silence.

Major Graves spoke. 'Andy, we're going to advance

on the compound and clear it. Your platoon to flank round to the south; we'll take the north.'

Andy nodded. He pushed himself to his feet and then, keeping his head low, ran back down along the line, gathering his men and preparing to advance on the enemy – or at least what remained of them.

When the artillery shells had hit, Amir was a long way back from the front wall. He had been in enough battle situations to know how it would go. They would exchange fire for a while, then the hated British soldiers would call on their more powerful assets to bring the contact to an end, like cowards. It did not make his brothers any less eager to fight, but Amir feared for their weapon. If some kind of ordnance hit it, the explosion would be bigger than anyone expected. Amir did not care about losing his life – that was in the hands of forces greater than himself anyway; but the green zone of Sangin was not where anyone wanted the bomb to go off.

They had different plans for that weapon. Very different plans.

So it was that he had strapped the suitcase bomb to his back and was preparing to leave the compound when the stunning blast of the first artillery shell threw him to the ground, knocking the wind out of him and causing a shower of rubble and shrapnel to fall painfully onto his body. He gasped as a big hunk of metal, twisted and contorted into a lethal weapon, landed inches from his head.

A second shell thumped into the ground. From somewhere in the compound he heard the sound of screaming. Amir pushed himself up with difficulty – the suitcase bomb was weighing him down – and looked towards the other side of the compound.

He counted three dead men, and one more who looked like he wouldn't last more than a minute or two. The man's arm had been blown off and was lying on the ground, metres away, while blood gushed from the open wound. The screams – bloodcurdling and fierce – came from his strangled throat. They were growing weaker, though.

Amir had only been on his feet for seconds when the remainder of the shells hit, throwing him back to the ground once more. Suddenly the compound was full of smoke – Amir coughed and choked, unable to see his hands in front of him. For a moment, he hugged the ground. In the back of his mind he was aware that the screaming had stopped, and he knew what *that* meant.

He pushed himself to his feet again. The smoke was settling, but Amir still coughed and spluttered. The whole compound was littered with dismembered bodies now. He didn't stop to identify them and he'd have had trouble doing so anyway: the faces of the dead were burned away and mashed up by shrapnel. There were, however, three other men standing. Their faces were bleeding; one of them had a wound to his arm. But their eyes were bright and they looked to Amir for instructions.

'The soldiers will be coming!' he barked. 'We must get the weapon away from them. We must leave this area.'

The three men nodded. They immediately headed for the compound gate.

'Wait!' Amir shouted.

The others stopped and turned. Amir looked meaningfully at a locked door towards the back of the compound. 'The children,' he said.

There was a brief pause before one of the men – bigger than the others, with a fresh wound across the side of his face and a bandolier of ammo across his back – stepped forward. His name was Anuar, and Amir always suspected he fought not for the cause, but because he liked it.

'If the soldiers come,' he said, 'they will find them. And if they find them, they will learn about the weapon.' He sniffed, then looked Amir straight in the eye. 'Leave it to me,' he continued. 'This is my task to fulfil. I will kill them now.'

Chapter Twelve

'No!'

Amir's voice was firm. It made Anuar stop in his tracks. 'What is wrong?' the man with the wounded face demanded. 'Do not tell me you have suddenly gone weak, Amir.'

'Don't be stupid,' Amir spat. 'They are no use to us dead. We need to take them with us.'

'But they will slow us down,' Anuar said. 'We cannot risk it.'

Amir narrowed his eyes, then stepped forward and grabbed Anuar by the throat. 'You will take your orders from me. Is that understood?'

Anuar's lip curled, but he nodded. 'Yes,' he hissed. 'It is understood.'

'Good. I am leaving now. I can move more quickly by myself. You take the children. Meet me in the caves behind Sangin. We will be able to hide there while things quieten down. Then we will continue our journey.'

Anuar nodded, a surly look on his face. He turned and headed towards the place where the children were imprisoned while Amir, the suitcase bomb still strapped to his back, moved swiftly across the compound. He needed to get out of here, quickly, before the British soldiers arrived.

Ben and Aarya didn't know what had been causing the explosions, but they knew it was something big. Each time the shells hit, the ground shook and they were showered with dust from the cracks that were appearing on the ceiling. Aarya had screamed, but the sound was minute compared to the noise of the explosions. Ben's ears hurt so much he had to touch them to check they weren't bleeding. His whole body was trembling from the shock of the impact.

And then the silence. In some ways it was worse than the noise.

'What was that?' Aarya breathed.

'I don't know,' Ben replied. 'Whatever it was, I'm glad we weren't right underneath it.'

It struck him that the force of the blasts might have weakened the door. He ran over to it and gave it a sturdy kick. Nothing. He was about to try again when, suddenly, it opened.

Three men entered. One of them had a bleeding wound on the side of his face and a bandolier of ammo; all of them had stern, unfriendly expressions. No one spoke. Two of them grabbed Ben, while the man with the bleeding face took Aarya. A rough piece of cloth that stank badly was wrapped around Ben's mouth and tightly tied at the back and his hands were tied again. Aarya received the same treatment before they were hustled from the room and out into the central courtyard of the compound.

Ben couldn't believe the destruction. Or the death. Bodies lay all around on the ground, disjointed and disfigured. Blood was everywhere, and for a moment Ben thought he was going to be sick. To his horror, he saw the dog that had approached him when they arrived sniffing at the dead bodies, and even licking the blood from one of the faces. Ben shuddered.

Their captors, however, didn't give them any more chance to take in the sights. They were clearly in a great hurry, and before they knew it Ben and Aarya were dragged out of the compound.

They found themselves on a rough pathway, high compound walls on either side. There was no sight of anyone else. *That figures*, Ben thought to himself. *I reckon I'd have got the hell out of here too*. The three men didn't hang around. With their guns pointing, they forced Ben and Aarya to the left, then continued through a maze of compound walls. They went quickly and were, Ben sensed, running from something. Or someone.

Maybe he should shout – alert people to their presence. If there were British troops in the area, surely the sound of an English voice would make them come running. But one look at the man with the bleeding face soon put him off that idea. The terrorist had something about him. An aura. Ben believed he would fire that rifle given half the chance – and he didn't look like the kind of guy to waste his ammo on a warning shot.

They ran along tree lines, through fields and in ditches – anywhere that gave them cover. The sun beat on Ben's head like a hammer and sweat trickled down the nape of his neck. There was no let-up. If either of them stumbled – and they often did – they were just pulled roughly back up again; if they slowed, a rifle was poked into their guts. Ben's chest burned with exhaustion; he could only imagine how Aarya felt.

Suddenly the greenery stopped. Ben found himself looking out over a bleak desert landscape. Ahead of them were hills, rising sharply into the near-distance. They were sandy, craggy and forbidding. Ben and Aarya were forced to run towards them.

They didn't climb the first hill they reached, but instead skimmed round the foot of it so that they were no longer in view of the green zone. Only then did the men allow them to reduce their furious pace, and not by much. They started to climb. Ben had to help Aarya, who was stumbling more than he was. From somewhere in the far distance he heard the booming sound of artillery, but none of it was directed towards them.

Not yet, at least.

They climbed and climbed. At the brow of one hill they dipped down, but only to then climb another. There were no paths or landmarks, but the men seemed to know where they were going. Nor did they seem to be affected by the heat in the same way as Ben and Aarya, who were weak with exhaustion.

When a plane flew high overhead, Ben stopped and waved manically to it.

Bad idea.

A brutal kick behind the knee knocked him to the ground; he was grabbed by the hair and pulled up again. The man with the wounded face didn't speak, but his look told Ben all he needed to know: *Do that again, and you're history.*

They ran for an hour, maybe more, before the scenery started to change again. Up ahead there was a craggy, cliff-like structure dominated by the wide open mouth of a cave. They were quite high up now, and behind them Ben could see the green zone from which they had just run, a mile or two in the distance, with a river snaking lazily through. He didn't get the chance to stare for long, however, because they were forced towards the cave at gunpoint.

They were still several metres from the mouth of the cave when the air grew colder. Ben didn't know whether to be relieved by the drop in temperature, or scared by the strangeness of it. They stepped into the cave's mouth, out of the burning brilliance of the sun, and he felt as though he had been blinded.

It took a moment for his eyes to get used to the gloom. The cave walls were high and craggy. A little way from where he was standing he saw a bed of ash where a fire had recently been lit – clearly this place was no stranger to humans and in one corner of his mind he wondered if animals lived here too.

'Get further into the cave!'

It was Amir's voice. Ben spun round to see the man standing just behind him. His face shone with sweat, his milky eye bulged and he had placed the suitcase bomb at his feet. He untied their hands before instructing, 'Both of you. Now! Further!'

Neither Ben nor Aarya could speak because of the rough, stinking gags round their mouths. They had no choice, though, but to do as they were told. Ben took Aarya's hand and, timidly, they crept towards the back of the cave.

'Wait!' Amir hissed.

They stopped.

Their captor walked up to them. 'These caves do not end,' he said. 'If you try to run away, you will be wandering around them for the rest of your lives. Which will be very short, without light, food or water.'

Ben narrowed his eyes as menacingly as he could. He pulled Aarya away and they continued walking into the caves while the men started talking in low voices. He could tell from the sound of their voices that they were discussing their next move.

He looked over his shoulder as they walked: ten metres, twenty metres. Amir was right: the cave seemed to go on for ever and the light from its mouth did not penetrate very far. Near-darkness soon engulfed them. When he was sure they were out of sight of the men, however, Ben stopped. He turned Aarya round and untied the gag from her mouth.

'Ben—' She started to say something, but he just pointed at his own gag. Moments later, that too fell to the floor.

'Quick,' Ben whispered. His voice was like sand-paper. 'They've just got us out of the way because they don't want you to overhear what they're saying. They'll come and get us any minute.' He peered into the dark-ness. There were openings off to either side – mini caves. It looked like Amir had been telling the truth. If they tried to escape, they'd get hopelessly lost.

'What can we do?' Aarya asked in a small voice.

Ben set his jaw. To flee into the unknown darkness of these caves would be madness, but there was no way he was going to give in to this without a fight. He drew a deep breath and tried to clear his mind. They couldn't fight these men with guns. No way. They'd have to be cleverer than that. More subtle.

The beginnings of an idea started to form in his brain. It was a long shot, but it was the only shot they had . . .

The pieces of cloth that had been used to bind their mouths were lying on the cave floor. Ben picked them both up. 'Wait there,' he told Aarya.

'What are you doing?'

'Just wait.' He headed further into the cave system, dropping one piece of cloth about fifteen metres away from where Aarya was standing, then continuing and dropping the other one even further in. He ran back to her and looked at his work. He could only just see the first piece of cloth; the second was obscured by the darkness of the cave.

'If you were one of them and saw that,' he whispered to Aarya, 'what would you think?'

Aarya's eyes widened as she understood what Ben was doing. 'That we had gone further into the caves.'

Ben nodded. 'Come on then,' he said. Together they ran quickly into one of the smaller caves to the side.

It was impossibly dark in there. Thick, velvet

blackness. 'We need to hold hands,' Aarya breathed. 'If we are separated, we'll never find each other again.' They grasped each other's hands; Ben used his free arm to feel his way in the darkness, touching the side wall of this new cave as they moved away from its entrance to make sure he knew where they were. In his head he counted paces. Five, ten, fifteen . . . They were twenty paces from the opening of the cave mouth before they stopped.

'We'll wait here,' he said, speaking so quietly he could barely hear his own voice. 'With a bit of luck they'll follow the bits of cloth and not look here.'

'With a bit of luck?' Aarya said. She didn't sound too convinced.

'Yeah,' Ben replied. 'I reckon we're due some, don't you?'

'And what then? They will not leave the bomb un-attended. Someone will stay at the entrance to the cave.'

'I know,' Ben said. 'But if we can get them to split up, that's got to be a good thing, hasn't it?'

'They have guns, Ben. All of them.'

'Well, if you've got a better idea, Aarya, I'm all ears.'

'Do not be cross with me, Ben,' Aarya scolded. For a moment she sounded for all the world like Ben's mum. 'I am trying to make sure we have thought of everything.'

Ben nodded. 'You're right,' he said. 'But come on – we won't have much time before they realize we've pulled a fast one. If you're going to think of something else, think fast.'

A silence. Aarya clearly *didn't* have a better idea. 'I hope you are right about this, Ben,' she said finally. 'I *really* hope you are right.'

'Me too,' Ben breathed. 'Me too.'

They waited.

In the darkness, a second seemed like an hour and Ben tried not to think about what else they might be sharing this cave with. He closed his eyes – it made no difference, after all – and took some deep breaths. He was exhausted, but he knew he couldn't give in to it now.

His clothes had become sweaty in the scramble up to the caves. Now, the moisture was pulling all the heat from his body. He started to shiver, and he felt Aarya doing the same.

Not long now, he told himself. *Not long now and we can make a run for it . . .*

'They're coming . . .' Aarya whispered.

Ben strained his ears. Sure enough, he heard noises. Voices. Muffled and distant. Ben could barely make them out, but they sounded angry. And they were getting louder.

He held his breath. *Find the cloth*, he said to himself. *Whatever you do, find the cloth . . .*

Lights.

Ben cursed under his breath. He hadn't counted on them having torches. At the mouth to the small cave, beams of light flashed in, then out again.

Don't come in, Ben thought. *Don't come in . . .*

A shout. The torchlight receded.

'What did they say?' Ben asked.

'I think they've found it,' Aarya whispered so quietly that she was almost inaudible.

A hubbub of voices. And then one, louder than the others. Ben recognized it of course. Amir. He was shouting angrily, giving instructions.

'What's he saying?' Ben hissed at Aarya. 'Tell me what he's saying.'

Aarya's breath shook as she spoke. 'He said, "Find them,"' she told him. 'They're splitting up, Ben. They're going deeper into the caves.' She squeezed his hand. 'Your plan's working.'

Ben took another deep breath. The *first* part of his plan might be working, he thought to himself. Now, though, they had to escape. And *that* was going to be the difficult bit . . .

Chapter Thirteen

On the opposite side of Sangin, the fire support unit looked out over the town and the desert hills beyond.

Major James Black looked through a high-powered, handheld military telescope. Behind him were five armoured vehicles, each laden with heavy weaponry manned by the fifteen men that made up his unit. In the distance he could clearly see the opening to a network of caves. He looked at the young soldier standing next to him. 'Are you sure?' he asked.

'Positive, sir. He ran into the cave and hasn't come out since.'

'And he was carrying a weapon.'

'Roger that, sir. Looked like an AK-forty-seven.' He grinned. 'Bit difficult to see from this distance though.'

'Cut the funnies, soldier,' Major Black instructed. 'If I order a strike on those caves and we find out there are civilians in there, all hell's going to break loose. I'll ask you one more time. Are you sure you can give a positive ID on an enemy combatant entering that cave system?'

Chastened, the soldier nodded. 'Yes, sir,' he said quietly. 'Positive ID, sir.'

Black lifted the telescope to his eye again. The mouth of the cave seemed to wobble with the heat haze. As he looked, his mind ticked over. He was trained to make life or death decisions like this, but that didn't mean it got any easier. If there were enemy hiding up in that cave system, it was his duty to call in an airstrike. But what if his soldier was wrong? What if the person he had seen was not an insurgent or a terrorist, but an ordinary, law-abiding citizen? What if his AK-47 wasn't an AK-47, but a pitchfork?

A voice behind him. 'Awaiting your order, sir.'

Black sniffed. It was decision time. In the distance, the cave continued to shimmer in the heat.

And then, suddenly, movement.

He kept perfectly still. A figure had appeared at the mouth of the cave. Major Black adjusted the focus on his telescope, zooming in digitally onto the figure. And as he did so, a flicker of a smile played on his lips. The man in his sights was armed, all right. The soldier had been correct – he bore a rifle and it was being held ready to use. There was also something on his back – a bergen of some description, only slightly bigger and more cylindrical in shape. Major Black didn't know what it was, but that didn't matter. He'd seen all he needed to see.

He turned to the radio operator standing behind him. 'You have the coordinates for the cave?'

'Yes, sir. American bomber turning and burning, awaiting your order.'

'Good. One five-hundred-pound bomb, two milli-second delay. Let's deal with these guys before they have a chance to kill any British soldiers, shall we?'

'Yes, sir,' came the crisp, efficient reply.

Major Black handed the telescope back to the soldier, then returned to the cover of the armoured vehicles.

'Two minutes to impact,' the radio controller announced in a loud voice. 'Two minutes to impact!'

Ben and Aarya started to retrace their steps, hand in hand. Ben used his free hand to follow the cave wall back to the opening, counting his paces as he went. The exit was exactly where he expected it to be. He carefully peered out.

'Can you see them?' Aarya asked.

Ben looked to his left. Further into the cave system he thought he saw the flash of a torch. But then nothing. Darkness. He looked to his right. The main entrance was in the distance, glowing like a solitary eye.

'Come on,' he whispered. Together they pushed forward towards the light.

Ben's skin tingled with tension. He walked carefully, silently. Make a noise and it could all be over. All sorts of doubts pinged around his mind. What if they had seen through his plan? What if the terrorists hadn't carried further on into the cave at all? What if they were watching them from the sides at that very moment? Up ahead, silhouetted against the mouth of the cave, he saw a figure. It was impossible to see his face, but Ben recognized the cylindrical shape on his back well enough. Amir was also carrying his rifle and was pacing up and down. Ben thought he seemed nervous.

They were close now. Fifteen metres, maximum. Ben tapped Aarya on the shoulder and pointed towards the side of the cave, where they huddled down against the wall.

'We need to move quickly,' Ben whispered. 'The others could come back any minute.'

'What are we going to do?'

Ben frowned. 'We have to use the element of surprise,' he said. 'That's all we've got. We need to get as close as possible, then jump him from both sides. If we do it quietly, and get our timing right, we might get him onto the ground before he has a chance to—'

'To what, Ben?'

'To use his gun.' They fell silent for a moment. 'You

154

wait here,' Ben continued. 'I'll go to the other side of the cave. On my signal we'll move forward. When we get close, wait for me to give you the nod, then we'll just charge him as quickly as we can. He can't move fast with that thing on his back, so we should manage it.'

'And what then?'

'We take his gun.'

Aarya's eyes widened. 'But, Ben, surely you would not . . .'

'Of course not, Aarya. But I'd rather the gun was in my possession than his, wouldn't you? At least we'll be able to make a run for it and warn someone what's going on.'

Aarya nodded mutely.

'All right, then,' Ben said. 'Remember. Watch for my sign.'

Crouching low, he left Aarya and tiptoed over to the other side of the cave. Then he looked back, held up his arm and emphatically pointed towards the exit.

The two of them crept forward. Every tiny crunch underfoot was magnified in Ben's hearing a thousand-fold. He could feel his blood pumping in his veins.

Amir grew closer. If he turned now, and looked in the right direction, he would be able to see one of them. But he had his back to the cave mouth and was looking out over the desert. The sun, shining overhead, cast a short shadow. Ben looked down at it: his eyes were drawn to the cylindrical outline of the suitcase bomb, and the long, wicked shape of the man's rifle. He closed his eyes, took a deep breath and prepared to give Aarya the signal.

He raised his arm.

And then, slowly, he lowered it. There was a noise. It was distant at first, just a low hum like a lazy bee on a sunny day. It clearly alarmed Amir, however. Their captor looked up into the sky, then quickly shook his head left and right. With a sick feeling, Ben realized he was looking for somewhere to run.

The buzzing sound grew louder.

And louder.

Instinctively, Ben knew what it was.

'A plane,' he whispered. Heading in their direction. It had frightened Amir, and he wasn't the kind of man to be scared by shadows. 'We have to get out of here,' he muttered. And then, louder, more urgently: '*We have to get out of here! Aarya! RUN!*'

There was no place for caution. Not any more. Ben pushed himself up to his full height and started sprinting towards the cave mouth. The sound wasn't a buzz any more. It was a roar, filling their ears like an angry lion. He sprinted as fast as he could, aware of Aarya running across just metres behind him. Bursting through into the sunlight, the thunder of the approaching aircraft jolted through him. He bore left, down the hill and away from the cave mouth. As he ran he looked over his shoulder, checking that Aarya was still with him.

She wasn't.

She had stumbled and fallen. She was pushing herself up even now in a desperate attempt to leave the cave.

'AARYA!' he shouted, stumbling at the same time and falling heavily to the stony earth.

The plane was directly above them now. His ears were numb from the noise. Instinctively he curled up into a little ball, cradling his head in his hands.

'AARYA!' he yelled. 'AARYA! GET OUT OF THERE! GET OUT—'

On the high ground above the town, the fire support group waited for the bomber to arrive. In the distance they could already hear its thunder.

'Thirty seconds!' shouted the radio operator.

Major Black watched the cave through the viewfinder of his telescope. The enemy combatant was still there, that strange, cylindrical bergen still strapped to his back. Suddenly the man looked up into the sky, aware of the approaching plane.

He looked left and right.

And then he ran.

Black cursed. The approaching plane was deafening

his ears now, and he was about to lower the telescope. Just then, however, he saw something else. Two more figures, running out of the cave. He frowned. They didn't look like locals. More to the point, they didn't look like combatants. They wore western clothes – a rarity in this part of Helmand Province – and there was no sign of weaponry.

He threw the telescope to the ground, spun round and held his hands up to his mouth. '*Abort mission!*' he yelled. '*ABORT! ABORT!*'

But above the roar of the jet engines, nobody could hear him.

He ran towards the radio operator, who looked at him in utter astonishment. '*ABORT!*' Black screamed again.

The radio operator's eyes widened as he realized what his superior was saying. He repeated Black's instruction into his receiver: 'Abort! Abort!' Even as he spoke, however, he looked out towards the cave.

The aircraft had curled upwards, climbing vertically into the sky. It was what was happening on the ground, though, that mattered. A small dot was falling through the air, directly above the cave mouth. To the eyes of Major Black and the radio operator it looked like it was falling in slow motion, but they both knew that was a trick of the mind. They both knew it took almost no time for a 500-pound bomb to hit the earth from that height.

158

Black saw the explosion: a flash of red. A fraction of a second later he heard it: a great thump echoing across the desert. A huge cloud of dust mushroomed up into the sky, obscuring everything. Black lurched forward and grabbed the telescope. It took a couple of seconds to focus it, but even when the view was sharp, he was none the wiser. The cave mouth was hidden. The whole area was a scene of blasted dirt and devastation.

He scanned left and right. He scanned down the hill. He continued to alter the focus, desperately trying to take in the whole scene. Desperately trying to see some sign of movement.

Desperately trying to make out the figures he had seen running from the cave.

He saw nothing. Just the rubble, settling on the ground.

No sign of movement.

No sign of life.

He let the telescope fall from his eye and turned to look, with a haunted expression, at the radio operator.

Neither man spoke.

A million unwanted thoughts rebounded in Major Black's mind.

What had happened?

What had they just done?

Who had they just killed?

Chapter Fourteen

'AARYA!' Ben yelled. 'AARYA! GET OUT OF THERE! GET OUT—'

And then he hugged the earth.

He had never known a noise like it – almost as though he himself was part of the explosion. There was heat too: the air around him became furnace-like. It burned, singeing his skin and his hair. The earth shook. Not a slight tremor, but a sickening shudder as though someone had picked up the ground and thrown it about.

Ben stayed crouched on the earth, head in hands. The air around him was solid with dust. He tried to breathe in. Bad move: his lungs rejected the filthy air, forcing him to cough, splutter and spit. The noise of the blast ebbed, echoing away across the desert, but his ears were still full of sound: tiny stones, a hailstorm of

160

them, raining down on him. They pelted his back, hard and fast. Nearby, Ben was conscious of a much bigger piece of rubble thumping down onto the ground. A few inches closer and he'd have been pulverized. He tucked his head down further and steeled his body against the showering debris.

For thirty seconds it continued. Thirty seconds of intense, painful battering. By the time the rubble had all fallen back to the ground, Ben felt as if he had taken a hundred brutal kicks to the back. He tried to straighten himself up, wincing with the pain. And then he opened his eyes.

For a moment he thought he had gone blind. He was surrounded by a sandy mist so thick he couldn't see his hand in front of him. Then his eyes smarted and started to sting and water, so he shut them again. Realizing he was still holding his breath, he pulled his T-shirt up over his nose, then gingerly breathed in. The air stank of dust and cordite, but he managed to get some oxygen into his lungs before trying to look into the cloud of dust again.

It was a little less thick now, but Ben's visibility was still no more than a metre. He staggered, totally disorientated, not knowing which way was which. '*Aarya!*' He shouted her name, then dissolved into a fit of hacking coughs that bent him double.

Stay where you are, he told himself once the coughing

had subsided. *Wait till you can see where you're going. Wait till . . .*

He blinked, then rubbed the gritty moisture away from his eyes. The cloud was thinning faster now and he could see something emerging in the distance. It looked ghostly, like a dream, bathed in the sandy tones of the dust cloud. The entrance to the cave. At least, what *used* to be the entrance to the cave. Now it was just a thick, tumbledown wall of boulders. Half the mountain looked like it had been blown away.

Ben stared at the destruction in disbelief. And as he stared, two thoughts went through his head. Firstly, nobody who was still in the cave at the time the bomb hit was ever going to get out, even if they were still alive. And secondly, he had not seen Aarya leave the cave mouth.

A twisting sensation in his stomach. Ben felt like retching. He ran to the wall of rubble that blocked off the cave and started climbing over it, looking for a way in or out. Nothing. It was absolute devastation. He started shouting Aarya's name, his voice hoarse and ragged. Mustering all his strength, he tried to pull heavy rocks out of the way, noticing as he did so that the backs of his hands were cut and bleeding from the rain of rubble. He couldn't budge a single stone.

'*Aarya! Aarya, are you there?*'

No response. Just the distant hum of the aircraft and

the sudden boom of another battle raging many miles away.

'*Aarya! Aarya!*'

But the more Ben shouted, the more he realized that it was useless. If Aarya was still here, she couldn't hear him. And that meant only one thing.

Ben found himself gasping as a weird mixture of grief and panic raced through him. He jumped down from the boulders and started searching the area, looking for some sign of his friend, or indeed his enemy. Amir had been well ahead of them, the suitcase bomb strapped to his back. The very fact that Ben had not been blown to smithereens meant the bomb had to be intact. Unable to see Amir anywhere, he deduced that the terrorist had escaped with his treasured weapon.

Ben stopped. He felt himself being ripped apart with indecision. He wanted to stay and look for Aarya, but he didn't know where to look. He wanted to chase Amir, but he didn't know where he had gone or what he could do even if he found him. Clutching his head in his hands, he tried to clear his brain. To decide on the right thing to do.

More than anything, he realized, he needed help. But how could he find help, stuck here on a blasted hillside in the middle of the Afghan desert, unable to speak the language and with the sun beating down like a brutal weapon?

Another boom in the distance. The whole area was a battleground, riddled with enemies being hunted by the British Army.

The army.

Suddenly Ben saw things more clearly in his mind's eye. That's what he needed to do. Find some soldiers. Tell them what was happening. Amir. The bomb. Everything. They would be able to find him. And what if he had Aarya with him? Then they'd find her too. She had to be still alive. Ben refused to believe anything different, despite the bleak evidence to the contrary.

Now that he had decided what to do, he didn't hesitate. He just started to run, ignoring the agonizing pains down his back as he hurried down the hill, retracing his steps into the green zone.

'AARYA! GET OUT OF THERE! GET OUT—'

Aarya heard Ben's voice, but only just above the roar of the jet engines overhead. She didn't need any urging to get out of that cave, though. Having stumbled, she pushed herself to her feet and ran faster than she had ever run before.

When the bomb hit, she assumed she was going to die. A silent prayer flashed though her head as her ears were deafened by that unbelievable noise. The impact threw her off her feet, forward into the air. She thought about her mother and father as she hit the ground, a crumpled mess of limbs. She imagined them weeping. As she opened her eyes and saw nothing but a sandy-coloured fog all around her, she wondered for a split second if this was what paradise looked like.

But then she realized how much she was hurting. There was no pain in paradise. She knew that was true. Aarya pushed herself up to her feet and continued to run, just as the rubble started to rain down on her. She put her hands over her head and staggered blindly into the mist.

Out of nowhere, a face. One dark eye, one the colour of milk. A body. Very close. Within grasping distance.

Aarya's heart jumped into her mouth. He looked like a spirit, and an evil one at that. 'Amir!' she whispered.

Amir didn't reply. He just grabbed her and started to pull her away from the caves, moving quickly despite the package on his back. She opened her mouth to scream, but immediately it was filled with thick, unpleasant dust and all she could do was spit and retch.

Still Amir pulled her. He seemed impervious to the rubble that was raining down on them. Impervious, almost, to pain. A small stone struck Aarya's face. She felt blood. It dripped into her eyes and blinded her. Amir continued to pull, refusing to stop when she stumbled and just dragging her through the dirt until her feet could catch up again.

The rubble storm stopped. The fog cleared. Looking

over her shoulder, Aarya searched for Ben; but they had moved round the hillside now, and she could see nothing. Just the edges of the devastation.

'The men in the cave!' she whispered. 'We need to help them.'

But Amir just gave her a dead-eyed look. 'They cannot be helped,' he stated. He narrowed his eyes, as though he was judging Aarya in some way, like a doctor. Then he pulled a bottle of water from inside his robes and handed it to her. Aarya put the bottle to her lips and drank the warm water gratefully. She felt like she could have drunk for ever, but after a few seconds Amir pulled the bottle from her lips, allowed himself a little water, then put it away.

'They cannot be helped.' He repeated his earlier statement. 'You are lucky not to have joined them. If you are not silent, you will. I will keep you alive only so long as you are useful to me.' To emphasize his point, he grabbed Aarya by the throat and squeezed hard, so hard that she made a weak, croaking sound.

With that, he tugged her even more firmly and dragged her further away from the bombsite. Where to, she did not know.

Ben stumbled as he ran. He was so parched he felt like his body was made of sand, so weak he knew he could collapse at any moment. He needed water, but he saw nothing except dryness all around, shimmering in the heat.

He fell, knocking his shins against a rock, but there was no energy left in him to cry out. In his muddled brain something nagged at him. What was it Amir had said, an age ago when they were driving through the night? *There may be landmines in the road ahead* . . . An image filled his mind. He was in the Congo. A mine had exploded. There were body parts everywhere.

It could happen to him, he knew, as he pushed on through the heat. But what could he do? To stay here now, in the sweltering afternoon sun when he was so dehydrated, would be to sign his own death certificate.

'I need to find the British Army,' he whispered faintly to himself. 'I need to find them . . .'

His head was pounding now. Ben raised his hands above it – a vain attempt to shelter himself from the sun's rays. Stopping to catch his breath, he looked ahead. The green zone was there, but with the heat haze he couldn't tell how close it was. All he could do was continue towards it, and hope he reached some sort of civilization before the heat defeated him.

A tree. With the sun so high in the sky, it barely cast a shadow. Ben staggered past it, then squinted. A field in the distance. He scanned the greenery, looking for people. But he saw nobody. Why would he? Who would be working in this intense, intolerable heat?

A ditch. A thin trickle of muddy water oozed along the bottom of it. It was smelly and unappetizing, but to Ben it looked as tempting as a fountain full of the clearest, freshest water. He stopped and stared. For a moment, he considered drinking it. He even found himself bending down, his hands cupped, ready to take a draught. But then, at the last minute, sense kicked in. The water wasn't fresh. It was foul. He had to look elsewhere.

Ben drew himself up to his full height. But the very process of doing that made him giddy and nauseous. He took a step. The giddiness increased.

And then, although he tried to stop it, Ben felt himself tumbling into the ditch. He was vaguely aware of the muddy water soaking his clothes before he lost consciousness.

Chapter Fifteen

Bel had spent two days at FOB Jackson now. Two hot, sticky, traumatizing days and she wished she could be anywhere but there. After yesterday's rocket attack, she felt like she was afraid of her own shadow. And while the soldiers around her had taken the hostilities in their stride, she could sense that some of them had still been rattled by that short, sharp contact.

She had spent most of her time trying to keep cool and drinking as much water as she could. This was drawn from the well in the centre of the compound, then sterilized using little white tablets. The water itself was warm with a rather unpleasant aftertaste on account of those tablets, but she gulped it down never-theless. She realized that she had forgotten to remind Ben to drink plenty of water back in Pakistan and she chided herself for the oversight. But it was OK, she consoled herself. Ben was a sensible boy. He knew how to look after himself.

Private Mears would check on her every couple of hours, a smile constantly on his young, earnest face. 'All A-OK, Dr Kelland? Feel free to sunbathe if you like . . . What do you mean, you didn't bring your bikini?' Under other circumstances she would have found his chirpy comments annoying; out here she was grateful for them. They helped take her mind off gloomier thoughts.

'Any news on the *shura*?' she asked, just after noon on the Thursday.

Mears smiled apologetically and shook his head. 'Looks like you'll be staying here another night,' he said. 'We're going to have to start charging you board and lodging soon. I know the room service isn't up to much, but—'

It was a noise that interrupted him. A huge, booming noise. It was distant, but still very loud – louder, certainly, than the occasional explosions Bel had become well used to over the past forty-eight hours.

'What was that?' she asked sharply.

Mears's jokey expression had fallen from his face. 'Sounds like an airstrike. Wait there – I'll find out what's going on.'

He sprinted across the courtyard of the compound, past the well in the centre and up to where one of the radio operators was crouching with his equipment. Bel watched as they spoke. The radio operator pointed in a northerly direction and Mears nodded as he listened to what the guy had to say. Then he came jogging back.

'I was right,' he said. 'Airstrike on a cave system to the north. Enemy combatants seen entering. Sounds like we gave them a bloody nose.'

'Sounds like you gave them more than that,' Bel murmured. 'Sounds like you gave them a *lot* more than that . . .'

Ben didn't know what it was that made him regain consciousness: his aching body or the sound of strange chattering voices all around him. Whatever it was, he didn't feel inclined to open his eyes, so he just lay there, trying to make some sense of the confused fog in his mind.

Where was he? he wondered. It was warm. Very warm. Was he on holiday? Or maybe he was lying in his garden at home and the chattering voices were those of his mum and dad. But if that was the case, why couldn't he understand them? He gave an impatient sigh, then forced himself to open his heavy eyelids.

When he did, he got the shock of his life.

A face was looking down at him, close enough for Ben to feel breath on his cheek. It had dark, leathery skin so deeply lined that for a moment he wondered if it was actually human. He told himself not to be stupid. Of course it was a human face. It was a man. He had a long white beard and intense blue eyes that looked like they were seeing right through him. On his head was a kind of embroidered cap. The man was leaning over him, his face only an arm's length from Ben's, and he barely moved.

Ben grew frightened, and then all the events of the past couple of days crashed back into his head. He looked from left to right, trying to get his bearings; but still the man staring at him did not move.

'Who are you?' he tried to say. But his throat was so dry that he simply couldn't speak. He wondered how long he had been out. Was it still the same day?

Like a stationary lizard suddenly moving, the man stood up. He said a single word, and as he opened his mouth, Ben saw that what teeth remained were yellow and crooked. Pushing himself up to a sitting position, he realized that he had been lying on a thin mattress in the shade of a tree. The tree itself grew in the middle of a compound and surrounding him, in a ring, were ten – maybe fifteen – people. The chattering sound came from the children, who became even more excited when he turned to them. The adults, however, looked on with a solemn lack of expression.

Suddenly he became aware of someone else standing next to him. He saw a girl – Aarya's age, perhaps a bit younger – holding an earthenware cup. She handed it to Ben, then nodded encouragingly. Ben took the cup and looked inside.

Water.

He put it to his lips, closed his eyes and drank. The water tasted warm and stale, but that didn't matter. It was still the best drink of his life.

When he had finished he handed the cup back to the girl. 'Thank you,' he said. The girl looked at him a little shyly, then disappeared.

Ben's head was still throbbing. He looked down at himself and saw that his clothes were scorched and full of holes – a souvenir from the bomb blast, he supposed. The skin on his hands and arms was cut and sore; his muscles shrieked at him. The water had barely gone halfway to reviving him, but he suddenly felt alert again. Alert and full of purpose. 'I need to speak to the British Army,' he addressed the strange-looking man. 'It's urgent.'

The man's expression didn't change. He certainly gave no sign that he had understood what Ben was saying. Ben looked around at all the other people staring at him. 'English,' he said. 'Do any of you speak English?'

The silence with which they replied spoke volumes.

Ben hauled himself up to his feet. A moment of dizziness: he steadied himself against the tree trunk and looked around again – blank expressions, all except the children, who seemed to have lost interest in the strange newcomer and were now tearing around the compound. Looking for the exit, he saw a rickety wooden door set into the wall. It looked as though it could easily have been a hundred years old. Ben staggered towards it, but immediately there was someone in his way – a younger man with a short, brown beard. He shook his head emphatically and then mimed the action of someone shooting a gun, before wagging his forefinger in Ben's face.

'I *have* to find someone,' Ben said, his voice hoarse. He spoke slowly, as if that would help the Afghan man in front of him understand.

The man shook his head again, before pointing to himself, then to the door and making a walking motion with his two forefingers. He smiled again and nodded.

Ben gave him an uncertain look. The man appeared to be suggesting that he would go and find a soldier. But what was Ben going to do? Stay here? He didn't much like the thought of that. His experience of compounds such as this hadn't been all that great, after all. But then he looked back at the inhabitants. They had clearly picked up his unconscious body from the ditch, brought him here and laid him in the shade. They had given him water. These Afghan locals had shown him more kindness in the two minutes he had been awake than his terrifying captors had since they had been abducted. If he could trust anyone, he thought to himself, he could trust these people.

And besides, if he walked out of this compound now, where would he go? The locals looked strange to him: imagine how he must look to them. Imagine the attention he would draw, wandering aimlessly through the green zone in his ripped jeans and T-shirt, desperately seeking a British soldier but not knowing where to look. In a dangerous place like this, he'd be a magnet for trouble.

He turned back to the young man. 'Thank you,' he said. 'Please hurry.'

The Afghan man grinned, nodded and sprinted out of the compound.

Ben returned to his mattress, glad of the shade that the tree offered. When the girl reappeared with more water, he accepted gratefully, and as he drank it he looked over the brim of the cup. He was still being stared at and he tried to ignore those alien glares by closing his eyes and trying to get his head in order.

Amir still had the bomb. That much was clear. Did he have Aarya too? Ben decided that he must have, even though a nagging voice told him he was only thinking that because he couldn't bear to imagine the alternative. And everything that had happened since their abduction suggested to Ben that he had plans to use the weapon, and soon. When their convoy through the desert had stopped for the daylight hours, the owners of the compounds where they stayed had been expecting them. Amir and his men had a plan. They knew where they were going and what they were doing. It was an operation of some kind. Ben shuddered to think what the consequences might be.

Time passed. In the corner of the compound a woman lit a fire. Ben watched as she took flour and water, then kneaded it expertly into big sheets of dough and cooked it over the fire. When it was ready, she tore some off and gave it to Ben. He thanked her profusely and wolfed it down, suddenly aware that he was hungrier than he could ever remember being. Two children, a boy and a girl no more than five years old, shyly approached him. The boy had a small toy car – metal, very old and dented. The paint had long since peeled away, but he presented it proudly to Ben as though it was the finest treasure in the land. Ben smiled at him, then handed the toy back. The two of them sat in the dirt beside him and played happily, etching roads in the dust and making engine sounds. They could have been any kids anywhere.

At one point, everything went quiet and there was suddenly hardly anyone around. Ben felt a moment of panic, until he realized what was happening: the villagers were praying, and he remembered Aarya explaining that it should be done five times a day. Everyone soon re-emerged and continued to go about their business.

Gradually, Ben realized, he was becoming less of a curiosity. The inhabitants of the compound had stopped looking at him like he'd just walked off a spaceship and had started getting on with their lives: washing clothes, cooking food or just sitting and talking in low voices.

Ben became drowsy, but despite the welcome he had been given he didn't feel at all comfortable falling asleep here, so he stood up and walked round the tree. He felt much better now that he had food and water inside him . . .

Suddenly there was a shout.

It came from the direction of the compound entrance. Ben spun round just in time to see the door being kicked open and two men in desert combats, big sunglasses and military helmets burst in, their rifles directed straight into the compound. One of them shouted a word Ben didn't understand before a whole line of soldiers ran in. Some of them took up positions around the compound; others sprinted into the living quarters that ran along the walls, re-emerging only when they appeared confident they contained nobody who posed a threat. The children playing near Ben scurried to a far corner of the compound, clearly terrified; the grown-ups just looked on with that emotionless stare Ben had come to recognize – all of them except the young man who had gone to fetch help. He was out of breath, but his eyes shone. Ben gave him a curt nod of thanks.

And then a voice. Relief flooded over Ben as he realized it was speaking English.

'Compound secure!'

One of the soldiers stepped towards Ben, removing his sunglasses and propping them up on his helmet.

Ben stepped forward to meet him. 'Are you a sight for sore eyes!' he said.

The soldier looked at him warily. 'Major Simon Graves,' he introduced himself.

'Ben Tracey.'

'I see.' Major Graves sounded curiously like a schoolmaster. 'Well, perhaps you'd care to tell me, Ben Tracey, what the hell you're doing in the middle of Helmand Province . . .'

Chapter Sixteen

'To be honest,' Ben said, 'it's kind of complicated . . .'

'Why am I not surprised?' Major Graves muttered. 'All right, son, hold your tongue for now. We'd better get you back to the base.'

'But I've got information,' Ben objected. 'Important information. A terrorist strike, or something. I need to tell you now—'

'Look, son,' Graves interrupted him sharply. 'You're surrounded by British soldiers in the middle of the green zone. That's a bit like being covered in jam in the middle of a wasps' nest. We haven't got time to sit around here chatting – you can tell me what you need to tell me back at base. Until then, you stick with me and you do what you're told. Got it?'

'But these people here are friendly. They helped me – and there isn't *time*. It could happen any—'

'*Got it?*'

Ben scowled. 'Yeah,' he replied. 'Got it. Just tell me, is it still Thursday?'

Graves widened his eyes. 'Yes, son, it's still Thursday.' He turned to his men. 'All right,' he announced. 'Fast extraction. Let's not give the enemy any time to find out where we are. This village might be friendly, but it doesn't mean we're safe here.'

The soldiers didn't hesitate. Two of them left the compound and covered the exit.

'Ben, listen carefully. We're going to perform a leapfrogging manoeuvre. Half of us advance, then we stop and wait for the other half to overtake us while we give them cover. Then they stop and let us advance. Do you understand?'

Ben nodded.

'Stay close to me, but not too close. There's an enemy sniper somewhere in the vicinity, and if we bunch up we're more of a target for him. About five metres should do it, OK?'

'OK.'

'If we come under fire, hit the ground and do exactly what I say.'

'Right,' Ben said. 'Er, how likely is that, do you think?'

Major Graves avoided the question. 'Just do what you're told, son, and you'll be fine.'

Ben nodded, then followed him out of the compound.

They ran along the compound wall. After fifty metres they stopped. All the soldiers crouched down and Graves gestured at Ben to do the same. His companions raised their rifles and covered both ends of the narrow path while the remainder of the soldiers ran past them.

They continued this manoeuvre past compounds, through ditches, along fields and past the occasional local, who stared at them in that way Ben was getting accustomed to. The going was slow. Every time they were in the open, Ben had to suppress his natural urge to run. Any moment he expected the sound of footsteps and heavy breathing to be replaced by the noise of a sniper shot ringing through the air, but he tried to put that thought from his mind. He was well protected by heavily armed soldiers. Nothing was going to happen . . .

The green zone stopped suddenly and Ben found himself walking into the rubbled remains of a town. Great hunks of masonry were piled up where buildings used to be; shrapnel littered the ground. Ben had the sense of a once-bustling town completely destroyed, a place from which the inhabitants had long since fled.

And up ahead, at the end of a long road of devastation, he saw a high wall with barbed wire curled up over the top of it. As they approached, a huge pair of metal gates swung open to reveal a bustling military base: men in camouflage gear, heavy armoured vehicles, crates full of ammunition boxes. Under other circumstances it would be a most unwelcoming place, but Ben couldn't wait to get through those gates.

'*Shooter!*' A voice from behind them. '*Shooter! Get down!*'

Ben didn't even stop to think. He hurled himself to the earth and covered his head with his hands. Just in time. He felt the bullet pass inches above him. It hit a large piece of rubble several metres past where he was lying, then ricocheted back down onto the ground.

'*Enemy fire!*' It was Major Graves's voice. '*Cover us!*'

From the top of the walls of the base up ahead there was a sudden thundering of weaponry. Ben felt himself being pulled up to his feet. '*Run!*' Graves told him. '*Get through the gates! Now!*'

Ben didn't have to be told twice. He sprinted towards the base as the guns continued to blast out of the shelled remains of the town. Did the sniper still have him in his sights? There was no way Ben could tell. He just had to trust that as a moving target he was too difficult to hit.

The soldiers behind him were firing back now, their rifles sounding tinny against the huge guns from the base. Ben just continued to sprint, sore, out of breath and sweating. He made it through the gates, unspeakably relieved to get some solid walls around him.

The rest of the soldiers came bundling in. They all had sweat dripping from their faces and stern, serious expressions. Major Graves stood by the gates, counting them all back in again, then shouted the order for them to be closed. The metal doors slid shut and only then did the heavy firing from the top of the walls cease.

Graves approached Ben, pulled off his hat and, for the first time since they had met, smiled at him. 'Well done, son,' he said. 'You did well.' He raised one arm and gestured all around him. 'Home sweet home,' he announced. 'Sangin DC. Not much, but it keeps the rain out. At least it would if there was any rain. How you doing?'

Ben raised one eyebrow. 'I'd be having a much better day if people stopped trying to kill me.'

'Wouldn't we all, son. Wouldn't we all. Now then, we're going to get you patched up. And then I think you've got a bit of explaining to do, don't you?'

They gave him water – litres of the stuff – which Ben guzzled like there was no tomorrow. An army medic sat him down on an empty ammo case and cleaned him up, binding some of the larger cuts with Steri-Strip. 'You'll live,' he told him.

'I was planning to,' Ben replied, trying not to think about how close he had just come to being shot.

As the medic worked, Ben talked. Major Graves

stood silently nearby as he explained everything: the abduction, the suitcase bomb, Amir, Aarya and the caves. The airstrike. Graves listened carefully. When Ben had finished, he was momentarily silent. 'Stay there,' he said. 'I'm going to radio back to Bastion.'

Ben waited. The base around him was bustling with activity – men cleaning their weapons, vehicles being checked over. Ben himself was largely ignored and he couldn't help feeling a bit grateful for that. Now that he had warned the army, his thoughts had moved to Aarya. Where was she now? Struggling under the rubble of the airstrike? Or being dragged by Amir through the desert yet again? Their captor's sinister face rose once more in Ben's mind: the scarred, scaly skin; the albino eye. What was he going to do with that bomb? What was his plan? Ben felt his fear being replaced by a sudden anger. This was all his fault. If he hadn't insisted on going after that idiot Raheem . . .

He shook his head. There was no point thinking like that. Aarya was still missing, still in the hands of that frightening terrorist. Ben's job was to do whatever was asked of him to make sure she was rescued.

He looked up to see Major Graves standing over him, his face serious. 'I've spoken to Bastion. They seem pretty interested in what you've got to say. We've had rumours for a couple of weeks now about some top-secret enemy operation. No one knows where or when. Special Forces boys are all out on the ground trying to gather intel. Sounds to me like you might have stumbled across a pretty major lead.'

Ben was only half listening. His mind wasn't on intel, or special forces, or leads. That stuff was out of his hands now. It was on his friend and what he could do to help her. 'I think Amir's taken Aarya,' he said urgently. 'He's got something planned for the bomb and he's using her as a human shield.'

Graves narrowed his eyes. 'Did you see her after the airstrike on the caves, son?'

Ben took a deep breath and looked at the ground. 'No,' he said quietly.

A pause. When Graves spoke his voice was quieter. 'I've got to tell you, Ben – you were incredibly lucky to survive that.'

Ben gritted his teeth. 'Amir survived it, didn't he? He had the bomb on his back. If that had gone off, we'd know all about it . . .'

'Maybe,' Graves replied. 'Maybe not. I guess we'll have to send people up to check out the area.'

Ben stood up. 'I want to go with them. I owe it to Aarya.'

Graves fixed Ben with a calm look. 'You're a brave lad, Ben, but I've got to tell you there's no way that's going to happen. I'm waiting for my instructions, but

I'll put a month's wages on you being on a flight out of Afghanistan within twelve hours.'

'No way,' Ben said flatly. 'I'm not going anywhere till I know Aarya's OK.'

'This is the army, son,' Graves said brusquely. 'I'm afraid you do what you're told.'

Ben was about to reply when a young private respectfully walked up to them. 'Bastion on the radio, sir.'

Graves nodded. 'Stay there, Ben,' he said, before striding purposefully to the other side of the base. He returned less than a minute later with a frown on his face. 'Looks like you might be staying here for a bit longer than I thought,' he said, unable to keep the disapproval from his voice.

Ben narrowed his eyes. 'Why?'

'They're sending some people this way to talk to you.'

'People? What sort of people?'

Graves eyed him carefully. 'SAS,' he said. 'I guess they want to hear the details of your story straight from the horse's mouth.'

And with that, he turned abruptly and walked away, leaving Ben alone once more. Alone to wonder and worry about what was going on around him.

'*Keep walking!*'

Amir's voice was harsh. No nonsense. The voice of a

man who didn't deal in idle threats. Aarya wanted to obey him, but her legs wouldn't do what her brain instructed. Her knees collapsed and she fell to the desert ground.

Then she screamed. Amir had grabbed a clump of her dirty, matted hair and was now twisting it tightly while pulling her up at the same time. She tried to stand, but she just couldn't do it and so she was left hanging by her hair. 'Please,' she begged. 'Please let me rest, just for a minute.'

Amir let go of her hair and she fell to the ground once again with a thump that jolted through her whole body. For a fraction of a second, she felt relief. He was letting her rest. But then she heard footsteps. Looking up, she saw Amir stepping away from her, then turning and aiming his rifle in her direction. He used his brown eye to look through the viewfinder, leaving the albino one to gaze at her directly.

'*No!*' Aarya gasped. '*No . . . please . . .*' She pushed herself back along the ground.

'You are slowing me down,' Amir said, his voice suddenly very calm. 'If you slow me down, you are not useful. You are a hindrance. That is why I am going to kill you.'

Aarya didn't know where she found the strength. Fear? Adrenaline? Whatever it was, she managed to haul herself up to her feet once again. 'I won't slow you down,' she whispered, her voice racked with fear. 'I promise I won't slow you down.'

They stood there, man and girl, tiny in the vastness of the desert. And then, gradually, Amir lowered the rifle.

'Walk,' he said.

Aarya continued to stagger through the desert. She wanted to whisper her prayers, but she did not dare and she hoped she would be forgiven for that. To take her mind off the pain that seemed to flow through her whole body, she tried to think of other things. Her mind turned to Ben and a twisting sensation of anxiety corkscrewed into her stomach. Was he safe? Was he even alive? She had felt terrified when she was with him, but was even more terrified now he wasn't there.

She looked around as she walked. The scenery hadn't changed since they had left the cave: a seemingly never-ending expanse of stony, sandy earth and undulating hills. Aarya didn't understand how Amir could know where he was going, but he was directing her with purpose and confidence. He didn't have the aura of a man who was lost.

The day wore on; Aarya continued her superhuman effort. As the fierce afternoon heat died away and evening came, she started to wonder if even the threat of being shot was enough to keep her moving. And it was at just that point that she looked up and saw something in the distance.

It was a conurbation of some sort. A village? A town? Aarya couldn't tell. To the left of it, she saw the river. The evening sun sparkled on the water. Aarya, with her parched throat and exhausted limbs, felt teased by the sight. Amir too seemed affected. 'Angoor,' he said, almost to himself. 'My home town. We will be there in less than an hour.'

Amir's home town? By rights, Aarya knew, it should be a place to fear; but in fact, the very sight of it gave her a renewed surge of energy. Even if it meant she was to be locked up once again in some awful prison, at least she would be able to rest.

'Keep walking!' Amir told her. 'I am still prepared to shoot you, even though we are close.'

Aarya stumbled onwards.

They attracted attention as they entered the outskirts of the town. Attention from the children playing in the dirt; attention from the adults going about their business, transporting goods in rickety wheelbarrows or sitting outside open-fronted stalls that lined certain streets. The evening air was thick with the smell of food cooking. On street corners, she saw members of the Afghan police force. They leaned on their weapons, smoking cigarettes and joking amongst themselves and with other locals. Certainly they did nothing about the local men with guns who paraded up and down with a brash swagger that made them look like they owned the place. One of these men – a swarthy guy with broad shoulders – shouted a greeting to Amir. Amir nodded at him, but didn't speak.

Through the mist of her exhaustion, Aarya could sense that this place was tense and lawless. It was weird, but she wanted to stay close to Amir. Many people stared at him as they passed, but these were stares of respect. As long as she was with him, Aarya sensed, nobody would approach her.

Amir, despite the load he was carrying on his back, walked with renewed urgency. He clearly knew these streets well, and before long he had guided them off the main road that ran through the centre of town and into a maze of side streets – wide and spacious, but ramshackle and full of houses that looked like they were near collapse. He stopped outside one of the few two-storey houses and kicked three times on the wooden door. Aarya looked up. On the first-floor balcony she saw an armed man looking down with an unfriendly stare. A shiver went down her back as she waited for the door to open.

Amir was expected, just as he always was. As they entered the house – it was dark and didn't smell at all good – five men greeted him like a brother, then stood back to admire the suitcase bomb, which he had unstrapped from his back. One of the men, who wore a plain black robe, spoke to him in Pashtun: 'Where are the others?'

'Fallen,' Amir spat. 'At the hands of the hated invaders.'

A shadow passed over them. A silence. It was only then that any of them even noticed Aarya. 'Who is she?' the man in the black robe demanded.

'It is not important *who* she is,' Amir replied. 'She comes with me as a hostage. See to it that she is put under lock and key – and I suppose she should be fed if she is not going to perish on me.' He didn't even look at her as he spoke.

Aarya felt strong hands on her arms. Struggling wasn't even an option as she was dragged into an adjoining room and locked in.

If Ben was here, she thought to herself, *he would try to do something clever . . .* But Ben wasn't here. She was completely alone and too exhausted even to move. She collapsed on the floor barely a metre from the door and just lay there, already almost asleep. Through the fog in her mind, however, she heard voices on the other side of the door. Half of her wanted to sleep; the other half told her she should listen, so with a massive effort she tuned her ear in and concentrated on what was being discussed.

Amir was speaking. 'It has been a difficult journey,'

he said. 'The hostages were a last-minute decision and they have caused us a great deal of trouble. But I will continue with the girl. The closer we get to the ISAF forces, the more useful she will become.'

'The ISAF forces,' his friend said lazily, 'will not approach this town. We control it.'

'Your other companions,' another voice said. Aarya thought it was the man in the dark robe. 'You think they are dead?'

'I do not see how they could have survived the airstrike,' Amir said. 'But we must not dwell on that until after the operation is complete. When we destroy the dam, all of Afghanistan will know of it. Then we may celebrate their lives, not mourn their deaths.'

The men grunted in agreement.

'In any case,' Amir continued, 'it may be that things will be easier now. Kajaki is heavily defended. It will perhaps be easier for the girl and me to approach un-noticed. The bomb must be planted as close to the dam as possible if we are to destroy it completely.'

'God willing, you will be successful in your mission.'

Then a new voice spoke. 'You said you had more than one hostage?' There was something accusatory in his voice.

'Yes,' Amir said quietly, and Aarya could just imagine his white eye burning as he spoke. 'A boy. I think it likely that he was killed in the airstrike.'

'And if he wasn't killed?' the third voice persisted. 'What, then? Will he not try to alert the invaders?'

Amir snorted. 'The boy is an idiot. I would not trust him to do anything successfully. And besides, he knows nothing of my mission. No, we do not need to worry about him. Of that I can assure you. Even if he does alert anybody, they will have no time to stop me. It happens tonight. I will take the bomb to Kajaki after dark.'

'I hope you are right, Amir. This operation has been a long time in the planning. It would be unacceptable for it to fail on account of one boy.'

'It will not fail,' Amir stated. 'That is all I have to say.'

The black-robed man spoke again. 'What will you do with the girl?'

A pause. Aarya held her breath.

'As I have told you, she will accompany me to the dam. If I need to sacrifice her to ensure the success of the operation, I will.' He laughed – a short ugly laugh tinged with cruelty. 'Of course,' he said, 'once the bomb is planted, she will be of no more use. I will kill her then. Whatever happens, tonight will be her last on this earth . . .'

Chapter Seventeen

A few miles to the south, a Black Hawk helicopter kicked up a huge cloud of dust as it came in to land. Ricki, Toby, Matt and Jack disembarked at the landing zone of the British base at Sangin, leaving the two pilots in the chopper.

The four-man SAS unit each wore ultra-modern digital camouflage made up of tiny squares, and carried M16 assault rifles with hologram sights that had been painted an olive-green colour. On their heads were dun-coloured helmets with night-vision goggles propped up on the tops. Each man wore an ops waist-coat. Ricki and Toby had their handguns attached to their waistcoats just in front of their chests; Matt and Jack had them strapped to the inside of their thighs. Personal preference. They all wore knee-pads on both legs, apart from Ricki, who wore one only on his right knee, to protect it when he was in the firing position. On each ops waistcoat, just below the neck, was a small Union Jack; and each man's name and blood group was marked on their clothes. Toby carried a rucksack with the few essentials they'd need in the field: radio, medical pack, a bit of food.

This SAS unit was travelling light.

They bent down to protect themselves from the air currents caused by the spinning rotary blades; and as they ran towards the main base, the SAS unit passed ordinary green army soldiers running the other way, well armed with their SA80 rifles so that they could protect the Black Hawk while it was stationary at the LZ.

Ricki was the first through the gates and immediately drew stares from the regular army guys at the base. Hardly a surprise, considering the way they were tooled up: they looked like men from a different planet. He was greeted by a soldier with the bearing of a commanding officer, who held out his hand. 'Major Graves,' he said. 'Always a pleasure to play host to the Regiment.'

Ricki held out his ID card, then nodded at him and shook his hand as the others congregated around and the gates to the base were swung shut. 'Where is he?' Ricki asked.

Graves pointed to a position about thirty metres

away. A lone figure was sitting on a large ammo case. He stood out, not only because he was much younger than everybody else here, but also because he was wearing civvies: jeans, T-shirt and trainers. They were ripped and dirty. This lad looked like he'd been through the wars.

'We need to speak to him now,' Ricki said.

'Roger that,' Major Graves replied crisply. 'His name's Ben Tracey.' And then, more quietly, 'Go easy on him, guys. He's had a rough day.'

Ricki didn't reply. Rough day or not, Ben Tracey needed to tell them everything he knew. *Everything*.

The unit ran over to where Ben was sitting. Close up, he looked even more ragged than at a distance. 'Ben?' Ricki said.

Ben nodded.

'I'm Ricki. This is Toby, Matt and Jack.'

'You look different from the other soldiers.'

'Yeah,' Ricki said. 'We are, a bit. SAS. Special forces. Sounds like you've got some information that could be useful.'

The unit listened as Ben spoke. Occasionally they exchanged glances. 'You're lucky to be here, Ben,' Ricki said when Ben had finished. 'Very lucky.'

'Yeah,' he replied. 'I'd kind of realized that. When are you going to go back to the caves, to . . . to try and find Aarya?'

Another glance among the unit, then Ricki came and sat next to Ben. 'It's getting dark, Ben,' he said. 'There's no point going up there now. And anyway, you need to prepare yourself for the worst. Not many people survive an airstrike like that.'

'I did,' Ben replied hotly. 'Amir did.'

Ricki inclined his head. 'Yeah,' he said. 'And Amir's got to be our number one priority. Those suitcase nukes aren't toys, Ben. We've been on the ground for four days and hearing intelligence chatter about a major terrorist strike in the area but haven't picked up on any details yet since we've been in country. Is there anything you haven't told us? Anything that might give us a clue where Amir is headed?'

Ricki watched as Ben closed his eyes and shook his head. 'No,' he said. 'No, I don't think so. They spent most of their time talking a different language. It was only Amir that spoke English. I mean, I overheard them speaking, but it was all just—'

And then he stopped.

'What is it, Ben?' Ricki urged.

Ben's eyes were still scrunched closed. 'There was one thing they said. It was when we were locked up – I was listening through the door. I couldn't make out anything they were saying, but there was one word they kept repeating. It sounded like *khaki* . . . no, wait . . . *kahaki*—'

Toby interrupted. 'Kajaki,' he said.

'Yeah,' Ben replied, snapping his fingers. 'Yeah, maybe that was it. Kajaki.'

Matt gave a low whistle and Ricki jumped to his feet. 'The dam,' he said, as the pieces of the jigsaw fitted into his head. 'They're going to make a hit on the dam.'

'What dam?' Ben demanded, but there was no time to talk about it now. Explanations would have to wait.

'Toby,' Ricki instructed. 'Get on the radio back to base. Tell them what we know. All lookout posts around the dam to keep an eye out for this guy, but they mustn't fire on him. If that thing goes off by accident . . .'

But Toby was already in action, stepping to one side and extracting his radio from his backpack. Ricki turned back to Ben and an idea crept into his head. It was a lot to ask of the kid, but if they didn't stop this thing from happening . . .

'Ben,' he said. 'This Amir. Would you recognize him if you saw him?'

Ben nodded. 'Yes,' he said emphatically. 'Anywhere—'

He was interrupted by Jack. 'Ricki, mate,' he said. 'You can't be thinking of—'

But Ricki held up one hand to silence him. 'If we're going to stop this guy, we need someone who can give us a positive ID. Without that, we'll just be groping in the dark. It'll mean coming with us.'

'Where to?' Ben said uncertainly.

'Wherever the trail leads. Look, Ben – I can't force you to do this, and I can't pretend it isn't going to be dangerous. It is, very. Probably the most dangerous thing you'll ever do in your life. Say no if you want. Nobody will think the worse of you. But we're well trained. We'll do everything in our power to look after you.'

Ben frowned. *He's going to say no*, Ricki thought to himself. *And then what?*

'If this bomb goes off,' Ben said, 'people are going to die, aren't they?'

Ricki gave him a serious look. 'If this Amir is doing what I think he is,' Ricki replied, 'we're talking major disaster. Code red. Trust me, Ben – it could change the course of the war, and not in our favour.'

A pause. The four SAS men looked down on him and waited expectantly for his answer.

And then Ben spoke.

'All right,' he said. 'I'm coming with you.'

War, Bel realized, could be many things. Terrifying. Tragic. Exciting. But also boring.

She was bored now. Stuck in FOB Jackson with nothing to do but keep out from under the feet of the soldiers who were supposed to be looking after her but who really had more important things on their minds.

Another day was drawing to a close – the sun was sinking and darkness wasn't far round the corner – and she didn't relish the thought of yet again trying to sleep while the brutal noise of warfare blazed all around her.

She couldn't face another mouthful of army rations, either – those bland, sludgy sachets of almost-food that had to be heated up in boiling water before they were opened. Still, it was that time of day and Private Mears was offering to cook her up some food. 'Don't get me wrong,' he said. 'I'm no Jamie Oliver, but it keeps the wolf from the d—'

A sudden shout from a lookout post up on the walls. '*Enemy approaching! Enemy! Get to your positions!*'

Mears stopped mid-sentence and looked around. The whole base was a sudden hive of activity. He turned back to Bel. 'You know where to go?' he said curtly.

Bel, whose stomach was suddenly knotted by the fear of another contact, nodded. She ran to the protection of the sandbags where she had taken shelter during the brief rocket attack on the nearby base the previous morning, wishing that the boredom of a few seconds ago could magically return. Fat chance of that happening, though. As she huddled down by the sandbags she put her hands over her ears. She knew what to expect this time. Noise. A lot of it.

The GPMG gunner on the compound wall

discharged his weapon. It thundered into the air: one burst, two bursts. There was shouting all around, chaos and confusion. And then, from outside the compound, another sustained burst of fire. Bel was no military expert. She didn't know what kind of gun it was, or what kind of ammunition. All she knew was that it sounded intense.

A sudden shriek from inside the compound walls. '*MAN DOWN!*' came the cry. '*MAN DOWN!*'

Bel looked over the wall of sandbags in alarm. Three soldiers were rushing up the stairs that led to the top of the compound wall. The GPMG gunner was on his back, one arm draped over the inside of the wall. He lay perfectly still, and Bel thought she could see something dripping from the end of his arm. Blood.

Another soldier took up position at the GPMG post and started firing out from the compound. Bel watched in horror as the wounded man was carried off the roof and laid on the ground just by the wall. Two medics surrounded him, ripping off his clothes to find the entry wound, shouting instructions as they went. 'We need morphine here, now! And get me a drip.'

Bel couldn't take her eyes off the scene, so much so that she became almost immune to the sound of the GPMG raging above her. The medics worked tirelessly, inserting a drip, binding wounds, pressing on his chest. Urgent. Relentless.

But then, almost as if someone had flicked a switch, they stopped and stood up.

'He's gone,' she heard one of them say. 'We've lost him.'

Bel blinked. Her skin tingled with shock. For a moment nobody in the compound moved. It was as if they had all been numbed. The faces on each and every one of them changed. They became grimmer. More determined.

And then they sprang into action once more.

Suddenly there were five or six of them on the roof, supporting the GPMG gunner with rifle fire. Their rounds cracked in the air just as Private Mears ran over to Bel.

'What's happening?' she demanded.

'Enemy on all sides,' Mears said, his voice tense. 'We don't know how they got so close, but there's loads of them.' All traces of his chirpy, jokey nature had left him.

'The . . . the dead man . . .' Bel stuttered.

Mears clenched his jaw. 'A friend of mine,' he said. 'And I'm not going to let them get away with it. You need to stay here, Dr Kelland. You're the only civilian here and you need to keep out of the way. This is going to be ugly. Whatever happens, stay by the protection of these sandbags, OK?'

Bel nodded, her eyes wide with fright.

Mears stood and started to sprint towards the area of the wall where the GPMG gunner was perched. He was only halfway across the compound, however, when a massive explosion seemed to rock the very foundations. Mears was thrown to the ground as a great cloud of smoke billowed up in front of him.

More shouting.

'The gates!' someone yelled. 'They've hit the gates!'

And as the cloud cleared, Bel saw that it was true. The entrance to the compound – those huge sheets of sturdy corrugated iron – had been blown inwards. Their edges were now splintered and jagged; more alarmingly, there was now a gaping hole looking out into the surrounding area. It was almost completely dark now, so Bel couldn't tell what – or who – lay beyond the gates. She didn't know whether to be relieved or worried about that.

Bel found herself hyperventilating. She tried to get a hold of herself as Mears scrambled to his feet and ran back towards her. His face was dirty and he had a great slash across his left cheek, a souvenir from the blast that had just blown the doors open.

'*Get down!*' he shouted. '*They've blown the entrance! They could be in here any second!*'

Bel hit the ground as Mears knelt in front of her, pointing his rifle in the direction of the gates. Immediately the air inside the compound was filled with rounds being fired in from outside. They hit the far wall, kicking up a cloud of dust and masonry.

'What was that?' Bel whimpered.

'Enemy fire. Stay down.'

Bel wanted to. She tried to. But no matter how much she feared the flying bullets, she had to know what was going on around. Pushing herself up to her knees, she peered over the sandbag wall to see four soldiers, two on either side of the doors, their weapons at the ready. One of them held up three fingers. Then two. Then one.

'Go!' he shouted. 'Go, go, go!'

The four men swung their weapons round and jumped in front of the entrance, where they started to fire, steadily and heavily. The GPMG joined in the attack and the four men walked forward.

But they never made it through the door.

The unseen enemy returned fire, not with rifles but with a more powerful weapon, a rocket of some kind. It hit one of the four men bang in the abdomen, throwing him back about five metres before it suddenly exploded in a starburst of shrapnel. Bel watched, sickened, as the remaining three men ran back, away from the shrapnel and the mashed body of the man the rocket had hit. A second soldier had just died in front of Bel's eyes. She wanted to be sick.

Mears was cursing. 'Air support,' he hissed. 'We need air support. Where is it?'

The only answer he got was another burst of fire from the GPMG as more soldiers came forward to cover the entrance. They didn't make the mistake of trying to step through it this time. Instead, six of them positioned themselves in two columns – three on either side of the gates – and fired at a diagonal trajectory out of the compound. Their rate of fire was slow – one round every ten seconds or so. Bel just prayed it was enough to stop the enemy advancing.

Mears turned. When he saw that Bel had put her head above the sandbags, he gave her an angry look and pulled her back down. They sat with their backs against the bags. 'It's a stand-off,' Mears said tersely. 'The enemy can't advance, we can't fight them back. We need support from the air.'

Bel put her head in her hands. 'What . . . like a bomb or something?'

'No,' Mears said. 'Not a bomb. The enemy are too close to us. We need an attack helicopter, something that can hover over them. But they won't like doing it in the dark . . .' He made a strange whistling sound through his teeth, and Bel realized that he too was try-ing to control his breathing. 'We need it now. We can't defend ourselves in this position.'

Bel gave him a worried look. 'If the enemy make it

inside the compound, what will they do? Take us hostage or something?'

The young private took his head. 'No,' he said. 'They won't be taking any hostages . . .'

He didn't need to finish the sentence.

His meaning was perfectly clear.

Chapter Eighteen

They found Ben some body armour and a helmet. The armour was a bit big for him, and very heavy; but it felt good to slip it over his head and strap it tightly around his sides. Ben shook Major Graves's hand. 'Good luck, son,' he said. The look on his face made it clear he thought this was all a very bad idea.

Ricki put one hand on his shoulder. 'Ready, Ben?' he asked.

Ben nodded. 'Ready as I'll ever be,' he said.

'When the gates open, Toby and Matt will go first. Then you. I'll follow with Jack. Keep your head down and stick with us to the landing zone. If you hear gunfire, hit the ground. Otherwise your objective is to get into the Black Hawk as quickly as you can.'

'All right,' Ben said, a bit nervously. The body armour really *was* quite heavy.

Ricki smiled. 'Don't worry, son. It's normally the guys with guns that attract fire.' He held up his weapon. 'Let's go.'

The gates slid open and Ben ran out, flanked by the four-man SAS unit. It was a fifty-metre sprint to the landing zone, where Ben saw the chopper, its blades already spinning. As he ran, he did his best to ignore the great hunks of rubble that surrounded the military base, each one of them a potential firing point. The chopper itself was surrounded by green army soldiers, all of them on one knee and pointing their guns outwards. It felt good to get within the defensive ring they formed around the aircraft; it felt even better to climb into the Black Hawk itself.

The inside of the chopper was drab and uncomfortable. The floor was covered with a thick, rubbery material and the sides were plastered with hooks.

Two pilots sat up front with a bewildering bank of controls at their fingertips. Propped up on their helmets they had a pair of night-vision goggles: darkness, after all, was just around the corner. It seemed impossible to Ben that only that morning he and Aarya had left the green zone and gone into the caves. A radio crackled noisily. Just behind the pilots were the positions for two side gunners. The guns themselves looked like something from the Second World War, with long links of ammunition trailing out beside them. The rest of the unit bundled in. Matt and Jack took the side-gunners' positions, while Ricki, instead of closing the side doors, just slung a piece of rope across the opening. He had barely taken his place before the chopper rose suddenly and swiftly into the air. Looking out of the window, Ben saw the military base grow smaller, before the Black Hawk tilted in mid-air and then swerved sharply. The next thing he knew, he was gazing down onto a huge river that stretched as far as he could see into the twilight distance.

'The Helmand River,' Ricki shouted above the noise of the chopper. 'It travels the length of Helmand Province. The Kajaki dam is at the northern end. That's where we think your man must be headed.'

Ben listened carefully. 'How big is this dam?' he shouted over the noise.

'Big,' Ricki replied. 'And important. It's the site of a hydroelectric turbine. When the turbine is fully operational, it can supply electricity to millions of people in Helmand Province. It's a major piece of infra-structure and heavily defended. The enemy are constantly trying to attack it.'

Ben shook his head. 'I don't understand. Why would the Taliban want to destroy it?'

'Not all of them do,' Ricki shouted back. 'Most of them just want to control the ground. But some of them don't *want* there to be electricity. Some of them want life to be like it was a hundred years ago.'

Ben blinked. He seemed to remember Aarya saying something similar back in her village.

Ricki carried on talking. 'It's not just the turbine that's the problem,' he said. 'If the dam gets blown up, it could flood the whole of the Sangin valley. There are settlements up and down the river that could just be washed away. We're talking thousands of deaths, Ben – not just now, but in the years to come from the radiation. That's why we *have* to stop this bomb.'

Ben paused for a moment while the reality of what they were doing sank in. Outside, it was almost dark; Ben thought he could see the lights of individual settlements dotted along each side of the river. He shuddered to think that, if Amir got his way, all those lights would suddenly – and permanently – go out.

'The bomb,' Ben asked Ricki. 'Is it really big enough to take out the whole dam?'

Ricki exchanged a meaningful look with the rest of his crew. 'If it's what I think it is,' he said, 'then yes. I've heard of these suitcase nukes. We all have. To be honest, I wasn't even sure if they existed – you know, just part of military folklore. The Russians made them back in the nineteen seventies, but they've all been lost.'

'Or hidden,' Toby interrupted.

'Or stolen,' added Jack.

Ricki nodded in agreement. 'Whatever happened to

them,' he said, 'rumour is they have an explosive capability of a couple of kilotons.'

'Is that a lot?' Ben asked.

Ricki nodded. 'Forget the Kajaki dam,' he said. 'That's enough to take out Niagara Falls.'

Ben couldn't help feeling slightly sick at the thought.

The pilot was wearing his NV goggles now. Suddenly his radio burst into life. *'Attention Alpha Three Tango'* – an urgent voice came over the loudspeaker – *'Attention Alpha Three Tango. Do you copy? Over.'*

The pilot replied with a calm, steady voice. 'This is Alpha Three Tango. We copy. Over.'

'We have an emergency situation, Alpha Three Tango. Forward Operating Base Jackson. Enemy advancing on the FOB. Several men down and one British civilian on the ground, a Dr Bel Kelland. All available helicrews diverted to assist. Over.'

Ben's eyes widened and his blood ran cold. 'That's my mum!' he screamed. 'Ricki, that's my mum. We've got to turn back!'

But Ricki said nothing. It was the pilot's call to answer. 'This is Alpha Three Tango. Currently on course for Kajaki. Priority one, repeat, priority one. Cannot divert. You must have other guys in the area.'

'Affirmative,' came the reply. *'Alpha Three Tango, you are cleared to continue your operation. Over.'*

'Roger that,' the pilot replied. 'Over and out.'

'NO!' Ben screamed. *'We can't just leave her there!'* He got to his feet.

Instantly, Ricki pushed him back down. 'No one's leaving anyone anywhere, Ben. If your mum's in trouble, they'll be sending air crews in to extract her right now.'

'But—'

'No buts, Ben. Listen to me. If she's at FOB Jackson, the most important thing you can do is stick with us. That base is right by the river. If the dam blows, she'll be underwater before you know it.'

Ben stared at him. Everything seemed to be crashing around about his ears. First Aarya, now his mum. Amir's face, with its one milky eye, hovered on the edge of his vision. The very thought of him made Ben's lip curl.

The SAS man stared back at him. A cool, level gaze. He could tell there was no way he'd be changing his mind.

'All right,' he said finally. 'Let's go and sort this out.' Ben looked out of the window, and watched the Afghan darkness slip by.

At FOB Jackson, a weird silence had descended. Weird and terrible. Darkness all around. The dead soldier lay in front of the gates, motionless. No one could get to his body because to do so would mean stepping into the enemy's line of fire. There was an occasional burst from the GPMG, but Bel sensed that these were just warning shots. As if to confirm this suspicion, Mears hissed: 'They haven't got a fix on the enemy. They don't know where they are.'

Bel closed her eyes and tried to get rid of the utter dread that was seeping through her body. She thought of Ben, and of Russell, her husband. Where were they now? Did they have any idea of what was happening? Would she ever see them again?

A noise in the distance, from somewhere overhead. Mears breathed out a heavy sigh of relief.

'What?' Bel asked.

'Apache,' he replied.

'A *what*?'

'An Apache attack helicopter.'

'How can you tell?'

Mears shrugged. 'You get used to the sound. It'll be here any second.'

He wasn't wrong. Before Bel knew what was happening, the noise became louder and she could discern the sound of rotary blades.

A flash of light from the sky, then the Apache flew overhead, incredibly low – only metres above the wall of the compound, like some huge spirit in the sky. The beams of light shooting from it lit up the compound, illuminating both the dead and the living. The noise of the blades pulsated through Bel's body as it slipped over the compound and hovered just outside the gates.

And then it fired.

The noise of the attack helicopter's weapons made the GPMG sound like a toy gun. It fired short bursts, and although Bel couldn't see what was happening, she could well imagine how destructive they were. She never thought a weapon of such destruction would bring her such relief.

She found herself holding her breath. Mears put his head over the top of the sandbags and Bel followed suit, just in time to see the Apache rise into view again above the compound walls. It hovered there for a few seconds.

And then it happened.

Bel didn't hear the sound of the ground fire above the noise of the chopper. But she definitely saw its effects. A flash of red as a blast hit the Apache, just below the rotary blades, and the huge metal machine suddenly started to spin dangerously out of control. The beams of light flashed then receded like some terrifying fairground attraction. There wouldn't be any candy floss tonight, though.

'What's happening?' Bel shrieked. *'What's happening?'* For once, Mears didn't have an answer. He too looked on in shocked astonishment as the Apache, twirling now like some sort of demented, shining spinning top, sank from view.

And then came the explosion.

It made the walls of the compound shake. A great ball of fire rose up into the air – even from where Bel was hiding she could feel the heat – and an enormous, dull red mushroom cloud billowed up into the sky.

'*Apache down! Apache down!*' Somebody was screaming the news at the top of their voice, even though there was really no need. There couldn't have been a single person in the vicinity of that explosion who didn't know what had just happened.

Suddenly Bel felt Mears pulling at her arm. 'We need to get to the back of the compound!' he shouted. 'Away from the chopper.'

'Why?'

'Those Apaches carry Hellfire missiles. If one of those goes off, they'll take out the front of the compound and who knows what else. Run, quickly!'

Bel did as she was told, and they weren't the only ones who had that idea. Six or seven soldiers ran with them, and as they hit the back wall of the compound, they formed a protective ring around Bel with their rifles pointing directly towards the entrance. Through the blown-apart gates Bel could see thick black smoke and orange flames. Her thoughts turned to the pilot of the Apache. There was no way he could have survived that.

The body count, Bel realized, was mounting. 'How many men on those things?' she screamed.

'Two,' a voice replied.

Her whole body was trembling now. It was like the worst nightmare she'd ever had, only there was going to be no waking up from this. Mears was next to her, his own breathing heavy and trembling. 'The enemy won't want to approach,' he said. 'Not with the Apache burning between us and them.' He sounded like he was trying to reassure himself more than Bel.

'But . . . but . . .' Bel was finding it difficult to speak. 'Will they send another helicopter? We need someone to get us out of here. You said we were surrounded!'

Mears kept his weapon pointed at the entrance and didn't look at her. 'They'll have to be careful,' he said tersely. 'Normally those Apaches scatter the enemy as soon as they appear – just make them run away. If that didn't happen, it means they're confident. I don't know what they used to shoot the thing down, but our commanders aren't going to want to send in another one until they know what they're dealing with.'

'But it's night-time,' Bel said. 'How are they going to find out?'

Mears breathed out deeply. 'I don't know, Dr Kelland. I just don't know.'

Fear and frustration almost overcame Bel. She felt

her knees going weak. '*Well, what are we going to do in the meantime?*' she hissed.

Graves turned to look at her. His young face was determined but serious. 'The only thing we *can* do,' he said. 'Wait for reinforcements. And until they come, defend ourselves to the last . . .'

Chapter Nineteen

Ben felt the Black Hawk losing height. They were coming in to land, but through the window of the chopper, he could see nothing but darkness.

'Where are we?' he asked.

Ricki waited until they were on firm ground before he answered. 'About half a mile from a small town called Angoor.'

'Shouldn't we go straight to the dam? I mean, if that's where Amir's headed . . .'

Ricki shook his head. 'The dam's being watched by British troops. They'll let us know if they see anyone approaching, but we want to find this guy before he gets close. Angoor's an enemy stronghold. That means no troops. It's the closest place to the dam that Amir could be sure of not bumping into ISAF forces. We're going to ask a few questions, see if anyone can put us on the right track.'

'Right,' Ben said. 'Doesn't that, er . . . doesn't that make it kind of dangerous for us?'

Ricki nodded. 'Yes,' he said. 'It does. We've landed at a distance, so we need to approach the town on foot. When we're there, we're going to ask a few people a few questions.'

'Who?'

The SAS man winked. 'Wait and see,' he said. His face became serious again. He held up his rifle. 'Listen carefully, Ben. You're not armed and you're not going to be. But if anything happens to the rest of us, you need to know how to use one of these.'

Ben looked apprehensively at the weapon.

'This is an M sixteen,' Ricki continued. As he spoke, he pointed out the different parts of the weapon. 'This is the trigger. You know what that does. This is the safety catch. It's on at the moment, but you can switch it to semi-automatic or fully automatic. On semi-automatic the gun will fire one shot every time the trigger is pulled. On automatic, the weapon will continue firing until the magazine is exhausted or you take your finger off the trigger. Have you got that?'

'Yes,' Ben replied. 'I think so.'

Ricki pointed to the other side of the weapon. 'This is the magazine release catch. This thing coming out of the bottom is the magazine. Holds thirty rounds. Once you've loaded a new magazine you pull back these two lugs.' He indicated a lever at the back of the weapon. 'When you've done that, your weapon's fully loaded, so the safety catch *has* to be on unless you're going to discharge it.'

'I'm sort of hoping I won't have to.'

'Me too,' said Ricki. At the back of the weapon there was an extendable telescopic arm. 'This digs into your shoulder to keep your gun steady,' he went on. 'Flick this switch here to move it in and out and get it into a comfortable firing position.' He held the weapon up and tapped on a cylindrical object at the top. 'This is a hologram sighting system. Look through it.'

Ben did as he was told.

'Do you see a red dot?'

'Yeah, I see it.'

'That's where the rounds will fall.' He lowered the gun. 'This tube at the end of the barrel is a suppressor. It silences the sound of the gunfire. We use these so that if we're in a contact situation, it's difficult for the enemy to locate our position.' He gave Ben an extremely serious look. 'Listen to me, Ben. This thing is *not* a toy. The sights aren't zeroed in to your eye and you've never fired one before. You *only* touch it if you're in the worst case scenario. Have you got that?'

Ben nodded.

'OK.'

At the back of the chopper there was a flight case. Ricki opened it and pulled out a number of stained Afghan robes. 'Dishdash,' he said curtly as he handed them round. He gave one to Ben. 'This should fit you,' he said. 'We're never going to look like Afghans, but if we put these over our clothes, we should merge into the background a bit better, and for longer.'

Ben pulled his robe over his head. It was heavy and made from a coarse, uncomfortable cloth. It also didn't smell that good. He noticed that the others kept their M16s hidden under their dishdashes: in seconds they'd gone from looking like awesome fighting machines to regular guys.

'Let's go,' Rick instructed.

The team dismounted from the protective metal casing of the Black Hawk onto the stony earth. Almost immediately the chopper rose into the sky.

'Where's it going now?' Ben shouted. 'To get my mum?'

'Don't count on it,' Ricki replied. 'It'll go wherever it's told. Those things are in short supply in Helmand. There's always a call for them somewhere.' He looked into the distance towards the town. 'We walk in single file. Ben, you stay at the back and try to follow in our footsteps.'

'Why?'

'Landmines,' Ricki said.

Ben frowned, then nodded.

As the chopper disappeared, silence surrounded them. Silence, and darkness. Ben felt horribly vulnerable as he followed the unit through the desert sands, trying not to think too hard about where he was putting his feet. Half of him didn't want to reach the town of Angoor; half of him couldn't wait to get out of the desert and away from the threat of landmines.

They walked in silence for at least half an hour before the boundary wall of the town approached. Even in the darkness, Ben could tell that it was made from the same material as the walls of the compounds he had been in: some sort of mud and straw mixture, baked hard by the sun. It looked very old. The unit skirted around the wall until they came to an opening – a rough arch, unguarded. They slipped inside.

The outskirts of the town were almost deserted. The SAS team wove their way between the walls of compounds that made up this part of town. Occasionally an Afghan national would appear at the end of one of these side streets; without exception, they would melt immediately into the darkness, looks of suspicion on their faces.

'Ever get the feeling,' Ricki muttered once this had happened for the third time, 'that you're not really wanted?'

'You can say that again,' Toby replied. Ben just stayed silent.

Angoor was not a big town, and so it wasn't long before the compounds in the outskirts were replaced with single-storey buildings that looked like they were made of concrete. The streets which they lined were wider, but still stony and rubble-strewn. There had clearly been fighting here in the not-too-distant past: many of the buildings were peppered with bullet holes and a few had even been destroyed. Some of the buildings had metal shutters closed down over them – shops, Ben assumed, but closed now it was dark. There were piles of rubber tyres dotted around, and big sheets of rusty corrugated iron propped up against buildings for no apparent reason. A smell of diesel permeated the air. This wasn't a nice place.

There were more people here too, mostly men who eyed them darkly as they passed. A few of them had mobile phones held to their ears. Ben was taken aback to see them, but there were enough phones around for him to realize they were commonplace. To his surprise, there were a number of vehicles lining the street: beaten-up trucks here and there, but more frequently motorcycles. 'It's how the enemy like to get around,' Ricki told him quietly. Ben just nodded.

Their weapons might have been hidden, but they

clearly weren't fooling everybody. The further they walked, the more attention they attracted. Groups of men congregated in the evening darkness and gazed at them with unfriendly stares as they passed. More than once, Ben saw rifles slung across their backs, though thankfully nothing as heavy-duty as the M16s the SAS team were carrying under their robes. Behind them, he heard the low hum of a motorbike. Somebody was following them, and they weren't making much attempt to be subtle about it. The unit just carried on, grim-faced and alert. They seemed to know what they were looking for, and they weren't going to be put off by the unfriendly, dangerous atmosphere.

A street corner. And standing there, smoking a cigarette and eyeing them uncertainly, was a man in uniform. The unit stopped.

'Stick close to us, Ben,' Ricki said.

'What's happening?' Ben breathed.

'You see the guy on the corner?'

Ben nodded.

'Afghan national police. Some of them are fine. Some of them I wouldn't trust as far as I could throw them. But if there's any buzz on the street about something going down, these guys will know.'

'If you don't trust him,' Ben objected, 'how do you know he's going to tell you the truth?'

Ricki just raised an eyebrow. 'Trick of the trade,' he

said mysteriously, then led the unit across the road to the Afghan policeman.

The policeman had the butt of his rifle on the ground and was leaning against it. He continued to smoke his cigarette as the unit approached, finally breathing out a lungful of smoke into Ricki's face as the SAS man stood in front of him. He went to take another drag, but Ricki grabbed the cigarette from between his fingers and threw it to the floor.

'Bad for your health, my friend,' he said. 'You should give up.'

The policeman's eyes widened. He straightened up a little.

'Another thing that's bad for your health,' Ricki continued, 'is not doing what we ask.' As he spoke, he raised his dishdash slightly to reveal the end of his M16. 'You speak English?'

The policeman didn't reply, but he nodded warily.

'We're looking for someone,' Ricki said. 'Ben here's going to tell you what he looks like, and you're going to tell me if he's been seen. Do you understand?'

The policeman shrugged. Ricki turned to Ben. 'All right, Ben,' he murmured. 'Let's hear it.'

'Tall and thin,' Ben said. 'One of his eyes is white and he has scars on one side of his face. He was wearing white robes. And' – he said this last bit defiantly – 'he's probably got a young girl with him.'

'Ringing any bells?' Ricki demanded.

The policeman narrowed his eyes. 'Perhaps, yes,' he said. They were the first words he had spoken. 'Perhaps, no.'

Ricki sniffed. He raised his dishdash once again and for a tense moment, Ben thought he was going to draw his weapon. The policeman obviously thought the same thing too. He took a nervous step backwards.

But Ricki didn't touch his M16. Instead, from a pouch in his ops waistcoat, he drew out a handful of crumpled notes. He peeled off three of them and waved them under the policeman's nose. Instantly the man's expression changed from one of suspicion to one of greed. He tried to grab the notes, but Ricki pulled his hand away. 'Information first,' he said. 'Money second.'

The policeman sniffed and his eyes flicked left and right, checking to see who was watching him. Ben looked over his shoulder. There were people in the street, but for the moment nobody seemed to be scoping them out, and the motorbike that had been trailing them was out of sight.

'I know the man,' the policeman said quietly. 'He arrived this evening. He had the girl with him.'

Ben felt a surge of excitement. *He had the girl with him.*

'Where are they now?'

The policeman gave another lazy shrug and eyed Ricki meaningfully. The SAS handed over a couple of notes. 'The house where they are staying, it is not far from here.'

'Show us.'

The man shook his head and a smile came across his face. He lifted one finger and shook it.

'Show us where it is, you'll get more money.'

But the policeman continued to shake his finger. 'It is too dangerous for me,' he said. 'But I will tell you where to go.'

The SAS team looked at each other. Something seemed to pass between them, some kind of unspoken agreement. Ricki turned back to the policeman.

'All right,' he said. 'Start talking. We're all ears.'

Aarya was paralysed with terror.

She didn't know what was worse: the waiting, or the prospect of what was to come. She found herself shivering as she curled up into an exhausted little ball in the corner of that dark room; when the door opened, she trembled even more.

Amir stood in the doorway. 'Get up,' he said.

Aarya had no option. She pushed herself to her feet and walked timidly towards him. Amir stepped away from the door frame and allowed her to walk into the adjoining room. The others were still there, eyeing her darkly and without speaking. Propped up against the wall was the suitcase bomb.

She watched as Amir slowly walked round the room, embracing each of the five men in turn. She didn't dare speak. Amir was just walking towards the bomb when there was a noise. A ringing sound.

A phone.

One of the men pulled a chunky mobile from inside his robes and put it to his ear. He listened carefully, without speaking, then grunted once and hung up. He looked at Amir. 'You must leave,' he said. 'Now.'

Amir's brow furrowed. 'Why?'

'That was a tip-off. Local police. There are foreigners in town. They have been asking about you. They know where you are.'

Amir's lip curled. '*How* do they know?' he demanded. 'Who told them?'

The man shrugged. 'Probably the policeman himself. You know what these dogs are like. They take with one hand and give with the other.'

But Aarya's captor didn't seem to be listening. 'Get out onto the streets,' he said. 'You must defend the house, with your lives if necessary.' If this instruction worried the five men, they didn't show it.

The man who had taken the call started giving orders. 'You get back up on the balcony,' he told one of his colleagues. 'You,' he told another, 'go outside. If you see anybody suspicious approach, shoot them. The rest of us will take positions inside the house, ready for them if they should be so foolish as to enter.' He turned to Amir. 'You will take the secret exit? You will carry on alone?'

Amir nodded. 'To the death. Get to your positions,' he said. 'Now.'

The men moved with a sudden sense of purpose; moments later, Aarya was alone with Amir. He strapped the suitcase bomb to his back, grabbed his rifle and pointed it in her direction. 'Out,' he said shortly.

Still trembling, Aarya walked out of the room with Amir following right behind. At the end of the corridor in which they found themselves, she saw the last of the five men disappearing and started to follow them; but then Amir tapped her shoulder with the gun. 'Not that way,' he said. 'Left. Through the door.'

There was indeed a door on the left-hand side. Aarya opened it. She was met by a staircase that led down-wards. The gloom was so deep that she couldn't see to the bottom of the steps.

'Down,' Amir instructed, and to emphasize his point he poked her in the back with his gun.

Aarya stumbled forward. Amir followed, closing the door behind him so that they were in total blackness. For some reason, she didn't know why, she counted the steps. Fifteen of them, and then they were at the bottom, where the smell was musty and foul. She heard Amir moving around in that pitch-black basement and somewhere at the back of her mind she considered running back up those steps and trying to flee; but she knew it would be hopeless. And so she waited.

A clicking sound. Amir had found a door and opened it. It led into another basement room which had a small candle burning on a wooden table and yet another door beyond it. A short instruction from Amir, and Aarya walked through this door and into a further room. Amir brought the candle with him, then opened a final door which led to the foot of a flight of steps. They climbed up them, and Aarya found herself in an entirely different house. Deserted, or so it seemed.

They crept through the house, guided only by the light from Amir's candle, until they reached the front door. Here they stopped. Amir put the candle on the floor, shuffled the suitcase bomb on his back to a more comfortable position, then pressed his ear to the door.

For a moment, silence. And then, from nowhere, voices. Shouting.

Amir's face grew steely. Aarya held her breath.

And it was then that the air started to ring with the sound of gunshots . . .

Chapter Twenty

The instructions that the Afghan policeman had given led them to the top of a wide side street. They peered out from round the corner, not wanting to be seen. There were houses on each side, but they were very poor places, some of them looking as if they were on the point of collapse. About fifty metres away there was a single building that was two storeys high, with a balcony on the top floor.

'That's it,' Ricki said. 'That's the building he said.'

The rest of the unit grunted their agreement. Matt pulled a small cylindrical device from his ops waistcoat and put it to his eye. 'One man on the balcony,' he reported. 'Armed. Another guy covering the front entrance, about ten metres from the door. Also armed.'

'Anything else?' Ricki demanded.

Matt replaced the scope. 'Negative,' he said. 'Just the

two of them, but there'll be more inside. I don't suppose they'll be offering us a nice cup of tea when we come knocking.'

Ricki turned to Ben. 'Listen carefully,' he said. 'You need to do exactly what I say.' Ben nodded. His stomach was twisted with nerves. 'We need to gain entrance into that house. There's going to be shooting and you need to keep out of the way of the bullets. But you also need to be close to us.'

'Good idea,' Ben murmured.

'You see those two trucks?'

Ben looked down the street. The vehicles were parked on the opposite side to the house, about thirty metres from where they were now standing. 'Yeah,' he said, 'I see them.'

'You need to use those for cover. You're going to go first, so you can be protected when the fire-fighting starts. Whatever you do, whatever you hear, don't come out from behind the protection of those vehicles unless one of us tells you to.'

'What if someone else finds me? What if they get out of the house and—'

'Nobody's leaving that house,' Ricki interrupted him, quietly but firmly. He turned to the rest of the unit. 'Toby, Matt, find a back way to the other end of the street. When you're in position, we'll cover Ben as he gets to the trucks. Then we'll go in.'

The men didn't need telling twice. Toby and Matt disappeared immediately, leaving Ben alone with Ricki and Jack, now both silent and concentrating. Ben looked around. Nobody else about – this was a quiet part of town. He didn't know if that made him feel better or worse. He thought about Aarya. What kind of state would she be in, if she was still in Amir's clutches? And then he thought about his mum, and his stomach knotted even tighter.

'Ricki?' he breathed.

'Yeah?'

'My mum. They'll get her out, won't they?'

Ricki gave him a serious look. 'I know this isn't easy, Ben, but you need to keep your mind on the job in hand. Amir's the only thing that matters right now. We'll deal with him first, then we'll deal with your mum.'

Ben nodded mutely. It was easier said than done.

Ricki looked at his watch, then peered round the corner of the street. 'They're in position,' he said. 'Ben, go.' He pulled out his M16 from under his robes and took up position at the street corner. 'Walk slowly and keep your head down. If you run, you'll attract attention to yourself; if they see your face, they'll realize you're not a local.'

'Right,' Ben said, stopping himself from adding: 'Thanks a lot.' He took a deep breath, nodded at the two SAS men, turned the corner, and walked.

He knew Ricki was covering him; he knew that the slightest sign of trouble would bring a burst of fire from the SAS man's weapon. That didn't make things any easier. The trucks were only thirty metres away, but each step felt like it took an hour. He looked at the ground as he went, scratching his head to obscure his face further. With every second that passed, he expected to hear the thunder of gunfire; with every step he took, the desire to break into a run increased.

Keep walking, he told himself. *Don't panic. They've got you covered.*

Fifteen metres to go. To his left, a motorbike parked in the street.

Ten metres. All the houses he passed were closed up. No light came from them. At the periphery of his vision he could see the man standing on the balcony up ahead.

Five metres.

When he reached the truck, he was sweating and breathing heavily. He crouched down and looked behind. Ricki was already following. There was no sign of his weapon, but Ben saw that his hand was delving into his dishdash, and he knew what that meant.

Everything seemed to happen so quickly. Ricki reached the trucks; by that time Jack was already following and Ben didn't doubt that at the other end of the street Toby and Matt were also advancing. Ricki passed the trucks, completely ignoring Ben. He pulled his M16 from underneath his dishdash.

A shout. It wasn't one of the SAS guys. They'd been clocked. Ben pressed himself against the body of the truck for protection. Ricki bent down on one knee. And then he fired. The suppressed gunshot made barely any noise, but it sounded all the more deadly for that.

Two shots. And then a thumping sound. Ben imagined the man on the balcony falling to the floor. Ricki and Jack started to run towards the house.

It was strangely silent. Ben knew he shouldn't, but he was unable to resist peering round the corner of the truck. Sure enough, two dead bodies lay on the ground. Toby and Matt stood on either side of the door to the house; Jack had taken up position on the other side of the road, covering the entrance with his M16; Ricki was in front of the door. The unit leader pulled something from his ops waistcoat, then aimed his weapon at the door.

One shot.

Two shots.

Ricki kicked the door and it fell open. He hurled the object he'd taken from his waistcoat inside.

Two seconds, then a blast of light and a huge bang. Smoke billowed from the house and the four men quickly slipped inside.

Ben pressed his back against the truck once more, breathing heavily. The SAS guys knew what they were doing, but he felt vulnerable stuck out in the street all alone. Ricki's instruction echoed in his head. *Whatever you do, whatever you hear, don't come out from behind the protection of those vehicles unless one of us tells you to.*

Muffled shouts from inside the house. Ben pictured the scene: smoke, guns blazing, the unit grim-faced and professional. And then . . .

'*Help!*'

A sudden scream. Close. Ben recognized it, of course. He'd know it anywhere.

'Aarya!' he whispered.

More shouts from inside the house.

Whatever you do, whatever you hear, don't come out from behind the protection of those vehicles unless one of us tells you to.

Ben's lip curled. He closed his eyes and took a deep breath, knowing it was now impossible to obey Ricki's instruction. He stood up.

Aarya and Amir had emerged from a house three doors down. Amir had the suitcase bomb on his back; in one hand he held the rifle, in the other he had Aarya's hair curled tightly in his fist. He was pushing her in the direction of the lone motorbike Ben had passed moments earlier. And for now, he hadn't seen Ben.

Ben looked up and down the road. There was

nobody, just the two corpses on the ground. Moving as silently as possible, he emerged from the protection of the trucks and started running towards Amir and Aarya. He might even have made it, had Aarya not looked over her shoulder and seen him.

'Ben!' she gasped, clearly unable to stop herself.

Ben winced. At the same time, Amir turned round. The minute he saw Ben, an incredulous look crossed his face, followed by a glare of anger. '*You!*' he hissed. Still holding Aarya's hair, he swung round his rifle and aimed it.

Without hesitation, he fired.

Ben threw himself to the ground, landing heavily on one side and rolling to the edge of the street. He half expected to feel the pain of a bullet wound, but there was nothing. Amir's round had missed him. He looked up. Aarya and her captor were running: they were still heading towards the motorbike.

Ben pushed himself up, but as he did so Amir turned and fired again, randomly. Ben hit the dirt and watched helplessly as Amir climbed onto the bike with Aarya in front of him. The suitcase bomb was still on his back, obscuring their bodies as Amir kicked down on the starting lever of the bike and the engine purred into motion.

'No!' Ben shouted. Scrambling to his feet again, he ran towards the bike, but it was already moving.

Above the sound of the engine, he heard Aarya's voice. Screaming. Terrified. 'The dam, Ben!' she yelled. 'He's taking me to the dam! *Tonight!*'

Ben continued to sprint towards the moving motorbike. If he could reach it, and just grab Amir from behind . . . He ran as fast as he could, but it was no good. The motorbike was accelerating, and at the last moment Amir managed to swing his rifle backwards and discharge another round in Ben's general direction. It whizzed past his cheek, sending him crashing to the ground for protection once more. He looked up helplessly, as Amir, Aarya and the bomb reached the end of the street, before turning a corner and disappearing from sight. 'Aarya!' he roared at the top of his voice. 'Aarya! We're coming after you!'

His voice echoed into the night as the sound of the motorbike ebbed away.

Ben was gasping for breath now. A surge of sickness hit him as he realized how close he'd come to being shot. Away from the protection of the trucks, he was suddenly aware that the sound of his encounter with Amir would have disturbed anyone in the vicinity. He needed to get back to cover and wait for the SAS men to reappear. Hauling himself to his feet, he ran back to the trucks. He was only halfway there, however, when the unit re-emerged from the house.

'*Ben! What are you doing?*' Ricki barked. He sprinted

up to where Ben was standing in the middle of the road. His robes, Ben noticed, were spattered with blood and he made no attempt now to hide his M16.

'Amir!' Ben shouted. 'He's got Aarya and the bomb. He's taking them to the dam. They're on a bike and they're going there tonight!'

Ricki's stern expression barely changed as he listened to this information. 'How do you know?'

'I told you. He's got Aarya – she shouted it out. We've got to follow them.'

As Ben spoke, a strange look passed over Ricki's face. He raised his M16 and for a moment Ben thought he was pointing it at him. Only when he saw the barrel being pointed over his shoulder, however, did he realize that Ricki's attention had been held by something else: a group of men at the end of the road. Maybe they had been attracted by the shouting and the noise of gunfire. Whatever, they were armed and looked lairy.

'Get to the trucks, Ben,' Ricki said quietly.

'But—'

'*Get to the trucks. Now.*'

Ben moved, just as Ricki fell to one knee, his M16 in the firing position. He heard the SAS man's voice, calling to the rest of the unit. 'Get the trucks started. Both of them.'

But the unit was already moving. Matt opened the driver's door of one of the trucks and urged Ben inside;

Toby got to work on the other vehicle and Jack joined Ricki in the firing position, ready to head off any potential aggro from the crowd building up at the head of the street.

'Get in the back, Ben,' Matt ordered tersely. 'This could kick off any second.'

Ben did as he was told, his mouth dry with nerves. From the back seat of the truck, he watched as Matt ripped a handful of wires from under the steering column, then started meticulously touching two of them together at a time. After about thirty seconds, he heard the other truck purr into life; moments later Matt found the right combination for hotwiring their truck. The engine coughed, then started turning over.

'Hold on,' said Matt. He yanked the gearstick into reverse and swung the truck round in a semicircle so that it was facing Ricki, Toby and the crowd. Toby's truck sped forward and Jack jumped in while Ricki, still aiming his weapon, stepped backwards until he was next to Ben's truck. He opened the door and got into the passenger seat, then rolled down the window and aimed his weapon out of it.

'Go,' he instructed.

The two trucks sped to the end of the road. A few members of the crowd dispersed, but not all of them. One man held up his rifle: he was just about to aim it in the direction of the moving trucks when Ricki discharged his weapon – a wicked-sounding burst of fire that skimmed over the crowd's head but did its job. The crowd finally dispersed, and just in time. The two trucks swung round the corner, screeching as they went. Ben felt the two wheels on the passenger's side lift off the ground and he grabbed the edge of the seat. Ricki, though, was leaning out of the window and facing backwards, ready to discharge his weapon should they attract any incoming fire. Only when the crowd was well out of view did he pull himself back in again.

They were travelling in single file now, and fast. Toby and Jack's truck was up front, with Ben, Ricki and Matt in the rear truck. Both engines screamed. Matt's face was a picture of concentration as he negotiated the complicated maze of streets; Ricki leaned back to Ben.

'*Get ready for a bumpy ride, mate,*' he shouted.

'Why?' Ben demanded. 'Where are we going?'

Ricki narrowed his eyes. 'Where do you think?' he asked. 'If your man's carrying out the operation tonight, we need to catch up with him. We're following him to the Kajaki dam.'

And with that, he faced the front again, clutching his gun and staring steely-eyed through the windscreen.

Chapter Twenty-one

Dr Bel Kelland had never been so scared.

She was surrounded by soldiers – eight of them, forming a protective semicircle around her as she cowered against the back wall of the compound. Their rifles were pointing forwards, but there was no light in the compound for them to see by; just the dusky glow of the still-burning Apache on the other side of the wall.

'Preserve your ammo!' one of the soldiers had called. 'Reduce your rate of fire!'

Private Mears had sidled back to where Bel was crouched. His face was bleeding and he had a harsh look.

'Why did he say that?' she asked him. Her voice was hoarse and dry – it sounded like someone else's.

'We don't know when we're going to get more air

support,' he said. 'We're firing towards the entrance of the compound to stop the enemy from trying to enter, but if our rate of fire is too high, we'll run out of ammo. And trust me, we *don't* want to do that.'

As if to highlight what Mears had just said, one of the soldiers fired a single shot. It didn't seem like much to fend off an advancing enemy as it pinged into the Afghan night.

'They've got to send someone soon,' Bel breathed. She wasn't sure if Mears heard what she said, because he didn't reply.

Time passed, punctuated only by the occasional firing of a round, which did nothing for Bel's shredded nerves. She had no idea what time it was when the sound of rotary blades drifted towards them. Half an hour later? An hour? Measurements like that had no meaning. The moment she heard the chopper, however, she felt a surge of hope.

'*Apache!*' Mears shouted. '*Apache approaching!*'

The flying machine appeared seemingly from nowhere, the thunder of its engines vibrating in Bel's ears. For a few seconds it hovered directly over the compound, its searchlights scouring the area like some kind of UFO in the darkness, then it moved on. Outside the front wall of the compound, the Apache dipped its nose slightly. Bel found herself holding her breath.

The chopper started to fire – loud, chugging rounds

coming in short, clinical bursts. The Apache turned ninety degrees so it was now facing away from the compound. It continued to pepper the surrounding ground with gunfire, and with each deafening burst, Bel felt just that little bit safer.

But not for long.

The ground-to-air rocket came from very close to the walls of the base. It looked to Bel almost as if it was moving in slow motion. As the rocket soared into the air, she almost couldn't bear to watch, couldn't bear a repeat performance, to see a second Apache crash and burn.

'*No!*' she gasped, clutching her dirty hair in panic.

It was almost a fluke that the chopper wasn't downed. The rocket sailed through the rotating blades, emerging unscathed on the other side and exploding in the air. Nuggets of shrapnel rained down on the Apache, which immediately rose higher into the air. It looked wobbly, and Bel heard one of the soldiers shout: 'The bird's been hit by shrapnel!'

Bel turned to Mears. 'Is that bad?' she breathed.

'Yeah,' Mears replied, sweat pouring from his moon-lit face. 'Yeah, you could say that's bad.'

'It's not . . . it's not going to crash, is it?'

Mears's face looked unbelievably grim. 'I don't know,' he said. 'I'm not a pilot. But I can tell you one thing – they're not going to risk another rocket strike like that. Not in the dark.'

'So what's going to happen?' Bel's voice was cracking up now as she tried to hold back tears of terror.

Mears's reply didn't give her much comfort.

'I don't know,' he said, returning his gun to the firing position and settling down once more to cover the entrance to the compound. 'I just don't know . . .'

'Do you know where you're going?'

The two-vehicle SAS unit had left the boundary wall of the town of Angoor and was now trundling through the desert. The trucks they had requisitioned were by no means comfortable: their suspension was shot and the ground underneath them was uneven and stony. It made for a bone-shaking ride.

'Toby has a GPS unit in his bergen,' Ricki replied. 'He'll be using that to navigate.' The unit leader didn't look at Ben as he spoke, but kept his eyes on the road ahead.

They travelled slowly. From the reflection in the rear-view mirror, Ben saw that Matt, who was driving, had a look of intense concentration on his face, examining the road ahead with fierce intensity. Ben remembered Amir, speeding off on his motorbike with Aarya and the bomb. He hadn't shown any desire to go slowly, and Ben felt sure he wasn't creeping through the desert now.

'Shouldn't we, er . . . shouldn't we hurry up?' he asked, a bit diffidently.

Ricki looked over his shoulder, one eyebrow raised. 'That all depends, Ben,' he said quietly, 'on whether you want to make it to the dam in one piece.'

Ben felt himself blushing and he was glad it was dark. 'What do you mean?' he asked.

'I mean,' said Ricki, 'just what I say. Of all the areas around Helmand Province, the bit near the Kajaki dam is the most heavily mined. Normally we'd be even slower, because we'd be sweeping for mines. As it is, we're driving slowly so that Matt can keep in the tracks of the truck ahead.'

Ben blinked. It was the same strategy that Amir had told him about, and he felt stupid for not recognizing what they were doing. Then the reality of what Toby and Jack were risking struck him. 'But whose tracks are *they* following?' he asked.

Ricki faced forward again. 'No one's,' he said grimly.

'But what if they . . . ?'

He didn't finish his sentence. He didn't need to. It was perfectly clear what would happen if Toby and Jack hit a landmine.

They trundled on in silence.

It was a clear night. The moon lit those parts of the desert not illuminated by the vehicles' headlamps and the sky was alight with stars. So much beauty, and so much danger. Ben dragged his eyes away from the canopy overhead and concentrated on their path through the desert, and still he could not get the image of Amir speeding along on his motorbike out of his head. 'Why don't we call for a helicopter?' he asked suddenly.

Ricki smiled. 'It isn't as simple as that, Ben,' he said. 'It's not like calling a cab, you know. Choppers are thin on the ground. Even if there's air support available, it can take an hour to arrive at the best of times, more if they have to scoop up extra personnel. The army has emergency procedures in place for all sorts of scenarios. I'm afraid this isn't one of them.'

Yet again, Ben felt a bit stupid. 'I'm sorry,' he said. 'It's just—'

'You haven't got anything to be sorry for,' Ricki interrupted him. 'There aren't many people who would do what you've done today.' He narrowed his eyes. 'And it's not over yet, Ben.'

Half an hour passed.

With every second, Ben half expected to hear the sickening boom of a landmine.

Forty-five minutes. Silence in the truck: just the noise of the wheels crunching over the sandy, stony earth. They started to climb, up and over undulating hills. Ricki pointed through the windscreen. 'Not far now,' he said. 'The British base is at the top of the dam. We're travelling up towards it—'

He was interrupted. The truck came to a sudden, juddering halt.

Ben didn't know whether he saw it first, or heard it; whether the red flash and sudden spray of metal burst into his senses before the deep boom of the explosion. All he knew was that one moment the truck ahead was there, and the next it wasn't. He heard shrapnel raining down on top of his own vehicle; the windscreen shattered as something thumped against it. *'Get down!'* Ricki shouted, and Ben quickly lay on the back seat, covering his head with his arms.

Suddenly the noise of the shrapnel on the roof stopped and they were surrounded by a thick, awful silence. Ben pushed himself up again just as a smell hit his nose. It was acrid and unpleasant. The smell of burning, of explosives. And of something else too. When he was younger, he had caught his hair in a candle. A few strands had fizzled and burned and the odour was horrible. It was that odour that he could smell now.

The SAS men were cursing under their breath. Ben looked through the window in shocked silence, but Ricki and Matt were already out of the truck. They ran towards the flaming shell of their mates' vehicle, holding their arms up to their faces to protect them from the heat of the fire. He watched, wide-eyed, as they ran around the inferno, shouting at each other and looking for a way into that devastated hunk of metal.

Looking for signs of life.

But it was clear, after a minute of searching, that there were no survivors.

Ben felt sick. He started to scramble out of the truck, to see what he could do to help, but at that moment Ricki and Matt started returning, so he took his place and waited for them to climb back into the vehicle. Their faces, glowing from the fire of the wreckage up ahead, were bleak as they took their seats.

'They're gone,' Ricki said. His face was dark and angry, his voice quiet. 'Nothing we can do.' Suddenly, out of the blue, he slammed his fist against the dashboard. The whole truck shook with his anger. Ben didn't know what to say.

Ricki turned to him, his eyes flashing. When he spoke, he sounded even more businesslike, more professional, and it was clear to Ben that he was hiding other emotions: shock, sorrow, anger. 'We have to keep going,' he said. 'We can't stop just because we're two men down.'

'Right,' Ben replied, his voice thick with emotion.

'We can't leave you here, Ben,' Ricki continued. 'You're going to have to stick with us. But you know the dangers. We won't now be following in Toby and Jack's tracks. If we hit a mine . . .' The three of them looked out at the wreckage of the vehicle up ahead.

'I know,' Ben said quietly. There was a bitter taste in his mouth and his skin tingled with nerves.

Ricki nodded curtly, then turned to Matt. 'All right, mate,' he said. 'Let's go.'

Matt nudged the truck into motion. They slowly drove around the wreckage, avoiding the hunks of metal that now littered the desert floor. As they passed the burning vehicle, Ben couldn't help twisting his head to look at it. There was no sign of the dead SAS men and he tried not to think about what state their bodies must be in now . . .

The wreckage slipped into the background. Matt accelerated – as there was nobody to follow, there was no need to travel slowly. The truck bumped and juddered up the hill as Ben felt a weird combination of numbness and fear: disbelief at what had just happened, and terror that history might be about to repeat itself. It seemed like madness, what they were doing. But they had no choice. He knew that.

Over the brow of the hill and up another one. In the distance he thought he saw lights.

'What's that?' he asked. His voice sounded very tense.

'British base,' Ricki replied. 'It's where we're headed.'

Ben couldn't tell how far away it was. Half a mile? A mile? As they sped up and down the undulating hills, the lights dipped out of sight and then reappeared.

They didn't seem to be getting closer at anything like the rate Ben would have wished. Nightmarish thoughts turned over in his mind. They were about to hit a mine. This vehicle was about to be shredded like the one they had just passed. They weren't going to make it . . .

You can't think like that, Ben, a little voice in his head told him. *Keep thinking those thoughts and you'll go mad . . .*

And so he tried to put all thoughts of landmines and burning vehicles from his mind, to concentrate on the only thing that was important: Amir and the bomb. Had he passed this way? Were they gaining on him? Were they, as the truck thundered bravely through the desert, any closer to stopping this bomb?

Ben had to believe they were. He set his jaw, faced fully forward and steeled himself for the struggle to come.

Chapter Twenty-two

Amir drove through the darkness.

The suitcase bomb was uncomfortable and weighed heavily on his back; the extra weight of the girl slowed the motorbike down. More than once, he considered throwing her from the bike and shooting her there in the desert. But he decided against it. He had brought her this far, and she could still be of use.

His rifle was slung to his side and he drove two-handed, his arms stopping the exhausted girl from slumping off the bike. He drove without his headlamp as that would act like a beacon to his enemies far and wide. Instead he relied on the light of the moon, so bright that it caused lumps of rock to cast shadows on the ground. Only when he came to the hills near the dam did the lack of artificial light become a problem as the upward slopes were in shadow. It didn't slow him down, though. It *couldn't* slow him down. He *had* to get to the dam tonight. His companions had fallen by the wayside: it was now up to Amir to complete their mission alone. And as the enemy were on to him, it had to be done tonight.

As he travelled, he found himself cursing under his breath. When he had seen that foolish boy outside the house, he had wanted to explode with anger. Why was *he* there? How could he have found them? And now, thanks to the girl's loose mouth, the boy knew where they were going, and why.

He did what he could to channel his anger, to turn it into something else. Into determination. Not that he wasn't determined before. No matter what happened, he *was* going to carry out his operation, and he was going to do it tonight.

They were at the brow of a hill now. The girl had started to slump. He pulled the motorbike to a stop. 'Sit up,' he barked.

The girl hauled herself up straight and Amir prepared to drive off again. But something stopped him. Something behind them.

An explosion.

He couldn't turn round quickly, not with the bomb on his back. 'Get off the motorbike,' he told the girl. She dismounted, then collapsed on the ground while Amir laid the still-purring bike on its side and looked back in the direction of the explosion.

It wasn't far away. Five hundred metres, maybe a little more. Amir saw a red glow. Flames flickering. He could even see, thanks to the light of the moon, a thick plume of smoke drifting up into the air. He squinted in order to see better. It was difficult from this distance, but he thought perhaps there were figures, silhouetted against the flames, running around the source of the explosion.

Amir smiled. It was clear to him what had happened: a vehicle had driven over the unseen pressure plate of a landmine. He was looking at the aftermath. He knew there were very few vehicles that would protect their occupants from a blast like that, which meant casualties. Deaths, probably. His smile became a smirk. Perhaps the boy was one of them. It was little more than he deserved.

He didn't allow himself to dwell on that attractive thought. If he was being followed, he needed to use his pursuers' delay to his best advantage. He pulled up the bike. 'Get back on,' he told the girl. She looked at him. Her eyes had rolled up in their sockets and he wondered if she'd even heard him. There was no time for threats, though. Holding the bike with one hand, he grabbed her hair and pulled her to her feet. She got the message and weakly climbed back onto the bike.

Within seconds, they were off again.

The motorbike bumped and growled over the hills. Amir had only been driving for another ten minutes when he came once more to a halt.

The view was spectacular. Far below him, the moon was reflected on the still waters of the Helmand River. On the far side of the river was the dark outline of a steep cliff, much like the one on top of which they now stood. To his right he saw the silhouetted outline of the dam. It was a massive structure, only a few hundred metres from where they were now standing. Impressive.

It wouldn't remain so for long, he told himself.

He needed to get closer. As close as possible. The bomb would be powerful enough to destroy the dam from a distance, but the less he left to chance, the better.

Amir dismounted, then pulled Aarya from the bike. The terrain ahead was too rough for a vehicle, so they had to advance on foot. He would have liked to hide the bike, but there was no cover here so he did the only thing he could, switching off the engine and leaving it there on its side.

There were mines here. He knew that well enough. If he stepped on one, he would die. So be it – he cared nothing for his own life. But he cared deeply for the success of his endeavour and so he turned to the girl.

'Walk,' he told her. 'You will go first, I will follow. My gun will be pointed at you all the time. You will go where I say. If you try to run, I will shoot you immediately. Do you understand what I am telling you?'

The girl nodded. 'I understand,' she said. Amir noted with satisfaction that her face was racked with terror. Fear, he knew, was a powerful incentive. It had served him well in the past, and it would do so again.

He pointed along the cliff. 'That way,' he said. 'Move. Now!'

They made slow progress. More than once, the girl stumbled and fell, her foot catching in one of the narrow indentations that covered the top of this cliff. Each time she hit the ground, Amir would pull her up by the hair and tell her to keep walking. And as she walked, he took care to follow her footsteps precisely with his own.

In the distance, a noise. They stopped. Moments later, a fluorescent light exploded above the dam like a firework, lighting up the surrounding area.

'Down!' Amir instructed. He knew what the light was: a lume sent up by the British base at the top of the dam. He sneered at the thought. It pleased him that the invading soldiers would be destroyed along with the dam. He caught up with the girl, who had not obeyed his instruction, and pushed on her thin, frail shoulders: it took no effort to force her to collapse. They remained crouched on the ground as the light faded away; then Amir stood again, tugged the girl up to her feet and they continued their slow, careful, stumbling walk.

The gradient of the cliff led downwards. They were close to the dam, now – no more than a hundred metres – and in the distance Amir thought he could hear the crashing sound of water. Ahead of them was a thin, V-shaped ravine, a crack in the cliff about as deep as Amir was high, but getting deeper the further it went towards the river. It bore left, down towards the edge of the cliff – a treacherous, narrow path, but wide enough for two people to clamber down. Just. It would serve two purposes: get them close to the dam, and give them cover from any lookout posts at the hated British base.

The going was treacherous. The floor of this small ravine was strewn with boulders and loose earth that caused them to slip as they carried on down towards the edge of the cliff. For Amir, it was doubly difficult: the suitcase bomb on his back grew heavier with each passing step. He felt sweat dripping down his face and veins bulging in his neck as he followed the girl. She too moved with great difficulty. Each time she stumbled and fell, however, she quickly scrambled back up to her feet, clearly terrified of Amir's reaction. That, at least, was good.

They had been hobbling down the ravine for several dark minutes when she fell and cried out. 'My foot!' she screamed. 'My foot!' Amir could tell it was a cry of real pain. He caught up with her. The girl's face was anguished, and her foot was twisted out from her body at an angle.

'Get up,' he hissed.

She tried, her whole body shaking. But the moment she put pressure on that twisted foot, she cried out again and collapsed to the ground once more.

'I . . . I think I have broken something.' Tears spilled from her eyes.

Amir spat. If this idiot girl was telling the truth, she was now a hindrance and not a help. 'Stay there,' he told her. 'If I hear a single noise, I will shoot you.'

She nodded vigorously. Amir did not mention that he intended to shoot her whether she made a noise or not.

Leaving the girl where she was, Amir continued down the ravine. He did not have to travel far – twenty metres, perhaps – before the river came into view once again. The path ahead of them stopped as it emerged onto the edge of the sheer side of the cliff face. He felt his stomach surge with the view of the sudden drop beneath him. He caught his breath, then looked out once more onto the sight of the moon shimmering on the water.

And to his right, the dam. It was close now. Very close.

He would plant the bomb here.

Amir eased the suitcase bomb from his back and laid

it gently on the ground. It was a relief to remove the weight from his body and he allowed himself a moment to appreciate it; and it was as he was rubbing his back that he noticed something. Just to the right of where the ravine opened out onto the cliff face, there was a narrow ledge. The cliff above was overhanging slightly, so it would be impossible to stand on the ledge, and it was not wide enough for him to venture onto on all fours, but it gave him an idea. To leave the bomb here would be to risk it being found. But if he could get it out of reach . . .

Maybe, he thought to himself, the girl had not entirely outlived her usefulness after all.

Leaving the bomb where it was, he returned up the ravine. The girl was still there, of course, whimpering with pain. He didn't speak to her; instead, he just pulled her up and carried her back towards the cliff face. Her body was shaking, but of course he ignored that.

'Stand,' he instructed.

He lowered the girl from his arms and she propped herself up against the side of the ravine, holding her bad foot up from the ground. 'Please . . .' she whimpered. 'My foot . . . the pain . . .'

Amir ignored her and turned to the bomb. It looked so innocent – just a khaki-coloured package that nobody would look at twice. He bent down and undid one of the straps that bound it together. It revealed a flap, which he raised. He smiled. Beneath the flap was a digital panel; and below it two very ordinary-looking batteries. Each battery was attached to a wire. Amir connected the free ends of each wire to two terminals just below the digital panel. The screen flickered into life: three red numbers.

00.00.00

Amir nodded with satisfaction. He turned a dial and watched the numbers rapidly increase.

0.20.00

Twenty minutes. Enough time for him to get away and do what he needed to; too little time for the bomb to be found. He pressed the dial inwards. It clicked, and immediately the digital display changed.

00.19.59

The countdown had begun. He replaced the flap and tightened the strap over it. Then he looked up at the girl. 'Turn,' he told her.

With difficulty, she did so.

Amir picked up the bomb and approached the girl. As he slung the suitcase over her back, she buckled under the weight. He lifted her up again and continued to fix the bomb to her body. Once he had finished, she was almost bent double.

'What is happening?' she gasped.

Amir didn't reply. He just guided her towards the

ledge – gently, not because he felt sympathy for her, but because she carried a precious load.

'Crawl,' he told her.

She started to gasp even more heavily. 'I can't,' she said. 'My foot . . .'

'*Crawl!*'

The girl whimpered again, but this time she did what she was told.

The first two metres of the ledge were narrowest, less than half a metre in depth. She moved slowly, shuffling along the ledge like a caterpillar on a leaf. Her bad foot dangled over the side, but Amir knew there was nothing she could do about that. Only when she stopped did he call out to her again.

'Further!'

No movement.

'Further, or I shoot you now!'

The girl continued. When she came to a halt again, she was nearly ten metres away from the ravine. Amir's eyes shone with triumph. With her broken foot, the weight of the bomb and the thinness of the ledge, there was no way she could turn round. The bomb was well hidden, out of reach. All he had to do now was make sure she couldn't crawl backwards.

He raised his gun. For a moment he considered shooting her, but he didn't dare: the force of the bullet could send her over the cliff, and he had no idea what effect the water down below would have on the bomb. Instead, he aimed it at the overhanging cliff.

He fired. Two clear shots rang through the air high above the river – each of them making the girl's body jump as though it had received an electric shot – and a hailstorm of rubble fell from the cliff. The girl screamed as a piece of debris struck her good leg; several other hunks of rock fell on the ledge behind her, blocking the way back.

Amir considered saying something to her. Letting her know that her death was very near. But in the end, he decided not to waste his breath. Leaving the whimpering, trembling girl on the ledge – immobile with the ticking bomb pressed down on her – he turned and started to make his way up the ravine.

Only minutes to go, he thought to himself. The very thought of it gave him extra energy as he hurried away from the very place where the blast was going to happen. *The bike*, he told himself. Get to the bike now and you might even be able to live. To watch it happen from a distance before making sure his group claimed responsibility for the explosion and the world knew what they had done – the hammer blow against the invaders. The very thought brought a smile to his face as he scrambled up the ravine, leaving the girl and the bomb far below.

Chapter Twenty-three

The British base at Kajaki.

'How many men can you spare?'

Ricki, Matt and Ben stood at the big metal gates to the base. They had left the truck a good distance away and continued on foot with their arms in the air in order to stop the British soldiers at the lookout posts from opening fire on them. Now, though, the two SAS men had their weapons firmly in their fists and Ricki was talking to the ranking officer at the base.

'Two platoons,' the OC replied. 'Maximum. Any more than that and the base is vulnerable to attack. But listen, the whole of this area is littered with mines. You can't just send men out there to scour the area – we need minesweeping units, the works—'

Ricki shook his head. 'Listen to me,' he said,

interrupting, 'and listen good. There's a nuclear suitcase bomb somewhere in this vicinity. If we don't find it, and soon, mine strikes are going to be the least of your worries. The whole dam's going to go up and everybody at the base with it. How long is it going to take to get your platoons ready?'

The OC – whose face had gone a distinct shade of white – stuttered, 'Er . . . twenty minutes, by the time we've sorted out the radios . . .'

'Get it done. What level of enemy activity can we expect?'

'Hard to tell,' the OC replied. 'We've had two patrols out each day this week and no contact. That suggests to me that the enemy are dispersed for the moment. Don't take my word for it, though . . .'

Ricki nodded. He turned round and indicated Ben. 'This is Ben. Take him into the camp and look after him. We're going out to try and find this guy.' He started to pull down his night-vision goggles.

'No!' Ben said.

Ricki, who had already started to turn away from the base, blinked. 'What do you mean?'

'I mean, I'm not staying here. I got Aarya into this mess in the first place, and I'm going to help get her out of it.' The SAS man started to shake his head, but Ben wasn't having it. 'You just said you need more people, Ricki. You've got no one for twenty minutes. You can't afford *not* to take me, and I don't want to hang around in the base waiting for the whole place to go up. I mean it, Ricki. I've come this far. I want to see it through. I'm coming with you.'

Silence from the SAS men.

'When Amir saw me,' Ben persisted, 'he was angry. If he sees me again, he'll be furious. It might force him into making a mistake. And anyway, Aarya knows me, trusts me. I could be useful . . .'

Ricki and Matt exchanged a glance. 'All right, Ben,' Ricki said. He sounded impatient. 'Stay close to me, don't get creative and keep your eyes peeled, OK?' He and Matt covered their faces with the NV goggles.

Ben nodded and the three of them set off from the camp. 'Where do we start looking?' Ben shouted as they ran over the brow of a low hill and saw the Helmand River come into view, far below. To his right was the dam; even though it was only lit up by the silvery light of the moon, he could tell how massive it was, and how devastating its destruction would be.

A shudder passed down his back.

The three of them came to a halt. 'We'll split up,' Ricki said. 'Matt, you search this area. Ben and I'll head south along the top of the cliff.'

'Roger that,' Matt replied, and without a second glance he disappeared into the darkness.

'Walk behind me, Ben,' Ricki instructed. 'You know why.'

Ben nodded.

Ricki moved swiftly, his head moving from left to right as he scanned the surrounding area through his night-vision goggles. Occasionally he would stop, holding up one hand to indicate that Ben should do the same. Ben would watch, holding his breath, as the SAS man raised his weapon. He always lowered it again, though, and kept moving.

Ben tried not to think about the threat of landmines; he tried to put from his mind the image of Toby and Jack's burning truck and instead concentrate on walking in the footsteps of his special forces chaperone. Behind them, he heard shouts in the distance: the two platoons of British army soldiers, he assumed, and he wondered if they would be picking their way through this minefield as bravely as Ricki was. Probably not, he decided, and he wouldn't blame them.

Suddenly, a noise.

'What's that?' Ben hissed.

Ricki had already heard it. He came to a halt and fell to one knee in the firing position. Ben peered into the darkness, squinting to try and see what it was. There was nothing, so he had to rely on his ears to identify the sound. An engine. A low hum. It sounded like a . . .

'Motorbike,' Ricki said, his voice taut. He raised his

NV goggles up onto his helmet and pressed one eye into the hologram sighting system of his weapon.

And then he fired. Once. Twice.

Up ahead there was a noise. A small explosion. Ricki pushed himself to his feet and ran in the direction of the sound. Ben followed close behind.

Ten seconds passed.

Twenty.

And then, in front of them, they saw it.

The motorbike was mangled. The rounds from Ricki's gun had burst one of the tyres and twisted the rest of the vehicle into a contorted hunk of metal. It was lost on neither of them, Ben realized, that the one thing they couldn't see was the driver.

'Wait there,' Ricki instructed. He moved his NV goggles down again and, weapon at the ready, prowled into the darkness.

Silence. Just the crunch of Ricki's footsteps on the unwelcoming earth. Ben held his breath. They were close. They had to be. Aarya was nearby. And the bomb . . .

'*If you say a word, I will kill you.*'

The voice hissed in his ear just as Ben felt a strong arm wrap its way around his throat and the butt of a gun press into the side of his ribcage.

'Amir,' he breathed. Ricki's footsteps grew quieter.

'You are foolish to come here.' Amir's mouth was

only a few centimetres from Ben's ear: he could feel the warmth of his breath and smell the sweat on his skin. 'More foolish, even, than the girl. Now you will die together. We will all die together.'

Ben's throat hurt: Amir was almost strangling him. But he managed to speak. 'Just tell me where the bomb is, Amir. You can't just kill all these people.'

Amir snorted. '*They* would kill *me* if they had the chance – which they won't.'

'But if the dam blows, the whole river will flood. Think about it, Amir. Think what will happen. You won't be killing British soldiers – you'll be killing innocent people.'

'Silence!' Amir whispered. 'We are going to move away from here. Walk. Now!'

He pushed Ben away from the wreck of the motor-bike. The gun dug deeper into his ribs. Ben didn't even stop to think. He knew the risk; he knew that he was just the squeeze of a trigger away from death.

But if the bomb exploded, they'd all be dead anyway.

'*Ricki!*' he shouted. '*Help!*'

The noise that came from Amir's throat was like a snake – a long, sibilant hiss of anger. He clenched Ben's throat harder – so hard that he found it difficult to breathe. But he didn't shoot, and within seconds the SAS man emerged from the darkness. He still had his NV goggles on and the extendable butt of his M16 was firmly pressed into his shoulder, ready to fire.

Ricki stopped ten metres from where Ben was held captive. '*Let him go or I shoot*,' he barked.

Ben sensed that Amir had lowered his head so that it was directly behind Ben's. 'Then shoot,' he said, 'if you want to kill the boy as well as me. Or if you don't, turn round and start walking.'

Ricki didn't move. He was like a statue. His gun was perfectly still and to Ben's eyes it looked as if it was trained directly at him.

Silence.

Stand-off.

An image flashed through Ben's mind, from just a couple of hours before – the town of Angoor. Two men lay dead in the street, killed by single shots from Ricki's gun. The SAS man wouldn't hesitate to shoot if he thought he could get a direct hit. The fact that he hadn't fired meant the target wasn't properly in his sights.

It was up to Ben to change that.

He drew a deep breath. It was difficult because his throat was constricted by Amir's arm. He would only get one chance at this, he knew. It had to go right.

He gathered his strength.

When he moved, it was with a swift, sudden jerk. Amir was taller and stronger, but Ben had the element of surprise. With all his force, he spun round in a semicircle, taking Amir with him. Now they were both facing away from Ricki, but Amir had his back to him.

The SAS man didn't hesitate. A single shot was all it required for Amir's vice-like grip to be released. Ben staggered forward, then turned round, fully expecting to see his captor on the floor. But Amir was still standing. Blood flowed from a massive wound that seemed to have taken away half his shoulder; his face was contorted with pain; but he was still on his feet. His milky eye glowing in the moonlight, he staggered away from both Ricki and Ben, towards the edge of the cliff.

Ricki kept his gun trained on the terrorist. 'Where's the bomb?' he demanded. 'Tell me now or I'll finish you off.'

Amir's head lolled. He kept walking backwards towards the edge of the cliff as blood continued to pump from his wounded shoulder. He said something in his own language: it was little more than a whisper, but it sounded strangely evil.

'The bomb,' Ricki repeated. 'Where is it?'

Amir's eyes flashed. He looked at Ben with a tooth-filled grin, but there was no pleasure or humour in that smile. None whatsoever. He continued to stagger backwards.

Ricki stepped forward. Amir was at the edge of the cliff now. He had stopped walking back because there was nowhere else to go. Only thin air, and it was clear where *that* would lead.

'Tell me where it is,' Ricki persisted. 'It's your only chance.' He continued to walk towards Amir, his gun pointed at the man's head.

'Chance?' Amir rasped. 'I do not believe in chance. Everything happens for a reason. That is why I am here. The bomb will explode any minute, and my rewards will be in paradise.'

His grin grew wider. More manic. His white eye bulged as he looked from Ben to Ricki and then back again. 'You will die now,' he announced. 'And so will your friend – if she has not done so already.'

'Where is she?' Ben yelled.

But too late.

Amir made no noise as he stepped backwards, his eyes shining with fervour. One minute he was there; the next he wasn't, like a magician who had made himself disappear.

Ricki and Ben ran to the edge of the cliff. Teetering on the brink, they stared down into the void below. Ben had no idea what Ricki could see with the aid of his night-vision; all he knew was that he himself could see nothing but darkness.

Seconds passed. Amir did not scream as he fell. He went to his death without a sound.

There was a moment of utter silence.

And then, from nowhere, Ben thought he heard the sound of a girl shouting.

Chapter Twenty-four

'Aarya!' he whispered.

Her voice was faint. Weak. It seemed to drift around them, floating in the night air like a ghost. Ben couldn't tell which direction it came from, nor could he tell what she was shouting.

'Get to the bike,' Ricki said, his voice clipped and urgent. 'We'll try and follow his footsteps back from there.'

They ran. All thoughts of landmines had disappeared from Ben's head with the new urgency of the situation. Aarya was nearby and she was their only hope – their only link to the bomb.

The twisted metal of the motorbike was still smoking from the impact of Ricki's rounds against the engine. The two of them stood by it and listened hard, trying to tune in their ears to the sound of Aarya's voice.

Nothing. Ben looked around, desperately trying to see where the shout might have come from; but he was just staring blindly into the night. Ricki had a different strategy. He was staring at the ground, his knees bent and his back arched, like someone on the trail of a wild animal.

'Over here,' he said suddenly.

'What?' Ben asked.

'The ground, it's been disturbed. Look: indentations. Footprints. He came from that way.' Ricky pointed away from the bike back towards the dam. 'Come on,' he instructed.

They moved swiftly. Occasionally Ricki stopped to examine the ground, searching for a displacement of the earth before carrying on. But he never stopped for long. Soon they came to what looked like a crack in the ground, a deep ravine that led downwards and towards the edge of the cliff.

'Quick,' Ricki said. They climbed down into the ravine and the SAS man took the lead. He clambered expertly down the V-shaped crack, stopping only to check that Ben was all right and still close behind him. Ben heard his own breath heavily in his ears. His heart was thumping, his senses on high alert.

'Stop!' he said suddenly. Ricki looked at him. Out of the silence, they heard the voice once more. Louder this time, but little more than a wail. 'It's her,' Ben said. 'It's Aarya. I know it is.'

They hurried down the ravine.

The river. There, below them. The ravine had emerged right on the cliff face, and Ben felt a moment of wooziness as he looked out over the water so far below. The dam itself was less than a hundred metres away. He and Ricki looked at each other, and as they did so, Ben felt a sudden sense of desolation. There was nothing here. No sign of—

Suddenly the air around them was shattered by the sound of a girl's voice. *Aarya's* voice. Wailing. Close. *Incredibly* close. Ben looked to his right. A tiny ledge. And at the end of the ledge . . .

'Aarya!'

There was a figure huddled in the darkness. Ben's eyes penetrated the gloom. It was her all right. He couldn't see her face, but he *could* see the outline of the suitcase bomb, cylindrical on her back as she was pressed down underneath it.

'Ben?' Her voice sounded impossibly weak. 'How did you find me?' And then, 'Amir, he's—'

'Don't worry about Amir,' Ben called. 'He's . . . he's been dealt with, OK?'

'But the bomb,' Aarya gasped. 'It is going to go off.'

Ben looked at Ricki in panic. The SAS man had removed his NV goggles and was now examining the entrance to the ledge. 'We need to get to her,' he said.

Ben followed his gaze. The cliff above the ledge was overhanging – it would be impossible to stand up there. Between them and Aarya was a large chunk of debris. It looked like it had fallen from the overhanging cliff, preventing her from shuffling backwards. The ledge itself was incredibly narrow. Too narrow, it was immediately obvious, for Ricki's bulk. But Ben was smaller. Thinner. 'I reckon I can get down there,' he said quietly.

Ricki's lips went thin. He clearly didn't like the idea.

'Come on, Ricki,' Ben said impatiently. 'It's obvious, isn't it? You'll never get down there. You're too big. And we can't just hang around, waiting for the bomb to go off.'

A short, tense silence.

'All right, Ben,' Ricki said quietly, so that Aarya wouldn't hear. 'When you get there, you'll have to defuse that thing. You need to listen to me carefully and not panic, all right?'

'All right.' He raised his voice. 'Aarya, I'm coming!' Quiet again. 'Wish me luck.'

'Luck doesn't come into it, Ben,' Ricki instructed. 'Be careful. Don't make any movement you're not sure of. It's a hell of a long way down . . .'

Ben nodded. He got down onto all fours and gingerly eased his way onto the ledge.

The first few metres were the most difficult and he had to twist his body onto his side in order to keep firmly on the ledge. He knocked a few stones over the edge, but never heard them hit the bottom. It was too far down. The moon shimmered on the water down below; the distance made his stomach turn. He crept slowly along the ledge, not wanting to make large sudden movements that might cause him to lose his balance.

'You're doing good, Ben,' Ricki called.

Ben was out of breath already. It was a huge relief when the ledge widened out slightly, but now there was another obstacle: the boulder. It wasn't all that big, but as Ben curled his fingers underneath it, he could tell that it was very heavy. 'I'm nearly there, Aarya,' he called.

'Be careful, Ben!'

He heaved at the boulder once more. It toppled slightly, but not enough to roll it over the edge. He was going to have to use every bit of force he could muster.

Ricki's voice. 'Stay in control, Ben. Use just the strength in your arms. If you put your whole body behind it, you'll go over with the rock.'

'Great,' Ben muttered to himself. 'Thanks.'

He gripped the boulder again, took a deep breath, then strained as hard as he could. The muscles in his arms burned; his face contorted into a grimace and he heard a groan of exertion escape his throat.

The rock moved; but as it did, Ben felt his balance go. He pressed himself up against the wall of the cliff, caught his breath again and continued pushing the rock.

That final surge was what it needed. The rock teetered on the edge for a moment, then fell into the darkness below. Again, no sound as it hit the bottom. Ben's breath came in short bursts, but he knew this was no time to take a breather. Doing what he could to master his fear, he continued to shuffle along the ledge until he came to Aarya. She was lying on her front, with one foot hanging precariously over the edge. It pointed out at an angle and looked to Ben as if it was broken. Her whole body trembled.

'Aarya, I'm here.'

'Ben,' she breathed. 'I cannot move.'

'Don't even try,' Ben warned her. He raised his voice. 'Ricki!' he called. 'I'm there. What do I do?'

'Can you get to the bomb?' Ricki's voice sounded unnervingly distant.

Ben looked up. 'Yeah,' he called. 'I think so.' Slowly, carefully, he pushed himself up to his knees, doing his best not to think about the drop below. Manoeuvring himself along Aarya's good leg, he got his hands on the suitcase.

Ricki's voice: 'You need to find the detonator.'

'What does that look like?' he called back.

'I can't tell you. But you'll know it when you see it. There'll be some kind of timer mechanism . . .'

Ben frowned. It wasn't a whole lot to go on.

Aarya spoke. Her voice was thin and terrified. 'Hurry, Ben. I saw him do it. He set the clock for twenty minutes. There isn't much time left.'

'Where's the timer?'

'You need to . . . you need to unstrap the back,' she whispered. 'You will see . . .'

Taking deep breaths and being careful to keep his balance, Ben examined the bomb. There was indeed one big strap, tightly buckled. He worked away at the buckle with his fingertips. It was tight and difficult to loosen, especially as his hands were now trembling with nerves; but after what seemed like ages, he managed it.

A flap of material. He lifted it. And then he saw the panel. The very sight made him sick to his core.

00.01.01

00.01.00

00.00.59

'RICKI!' he roared. 'I'VE GOT THE TIMER. THERE'S LESS THAN A MINUTE LEFT!' He heard his voice echo across the river.

Less than a minute left . . .

Less than a minute left . . .

'Tell me what you see,' Ricki barked.

Ben could barely get the words out. 'A panel,' he shouted. 'Red numbers, counting down.'

00.00.48

'Some kind of dial. And underneath the numbers there's what looks like ... like two batteries. Wires coming from the batteries leading to two terminals on the timer.'

00.00.41

'I think that's what's powering the detonator,' he screamed. 'Shall I pull them?'

'*No!*' Ricki's voice was firm with just a hint of panic. 'These things are sometimes booby-trapped. If you pull the wires, it could make the whole thing blow . . .'

'*Then what am I going to do?*'

00.00.32

00.00.31

'Can you see anything else?'

'Nothing.'

'Can you get to the underside of the bomb?'

'No!' Ben shouted. 'It's strapped to Aarya. She can't move. If I try to roll them, they'll both go over the side. Ricki, there's less than twenty seconds to go!'

00.00.19

00.00.18

Silence from the SAS man.

'Ricki, what am I going to do?'

00.00.11

He felt his fingers twitching towards the wires. '*What am I going to do?*' he repeated.

'OK, Ben. You haven't got any choice. Pull the wires. Now!'

00.00.07

00.00.06

Ben's blood ran cold. *If you pull the wires, it could make the whole thing blow* . . . His fingers and thumbs felt thick and unwieldy. Clumsy. He tried to grab the wires, but his hands were shaking.

'Ben!' Aarya wept. 'What is happening.'

00.00.03

There was no time to reply. His fumbling fingers managed to grab the wires. He closed his eyes, thoughts of booby traps, explosions and mushroom clouds flashing through his mind.

And then he pulled, his eyes clenched shut, his breath held.

Ben didn't know if it would be the last thing he ever did.

Chapter Twenty-five

Silence.

Ben unclenched his eyes. The bomb was still there. Aarya was still there. *He* was still there. And the timer panel was blank. He felt a surge of relief. 'It's OK, Aarya,' he whispered. 'We've done it.' He was almost laughing with relief.

She didn't reply.

Ricki shouted. *'Ben, what's happening!'*

'The timer's stopped,' Ben yelled back. 'I think it's de-fused. I think we've done it.'

'Can you crawl back?'

Ben turned his attention back to Aarya. 'Can you hear me?' He shook her gently. 'Aarya, can you hear me?'

No response.

'Something's wrong with Aarya,' he shouted. 'She's

not responding. I can see she's breathing, but . . . I think she's passed out.'

'*Can you crawl back?*' The SAS man repeated his question.

'I'm not leaving her. What if she gains consciousness and doesn't realize where she is? What if she topples over the edge?'

A pause.

'All right, Ben. Stay there. We need air support to winch the bomb up. I'm going back up to where I can get radio contact with Matt, see what we can sort out.'

Ben nodded, even though there was nobody to see him do it.

'Don't let the bomb fall, Ben. The impact could . . . just don't let it fall, OK?'

'Right,' Ben breathed. He clutched Aarya and the bomb firmly. 'Hurry up,' he shouted. 'Aarya needs help.'

Ricki didn't reply. Ben heard him scrambling away from the cliff edge, and then all was silent once more.

Time stood still. Ben's whole body had started to shiver – not through cold, but through fear. The bomb might have been de-fused, but he felt that even if he was prepared to leave Aarya, he could never get back along this ledge. Shuffling backwards was too precarious and there was simply not enough room to turn round.

Every now and then he called Aarya's name. There was still no response and so he held her and the bomb firmly on the ledge. And then he simply waited, trying not to think about the danger he was in.

Ben was alone with his thoughts. He remembered the distress call when they were in the Black Hawk and his blood ran cold. He didn't know if he was more sickened by the thought of his mother in danger, or by the uncomfortable truth that he had all but forgotten about her in the frenzy of the past few hours. Now the gravity of her situation came crashing in on him again. Every cell in his body wanted to go to her rescue; he wanted to howl with frustration and helplessness that he couldn't.

'Come on,' he whispered to himself. '*Come on . . .*'

Ben had no idea how long he had been on that ledge when he heard it – the distant beating of a helicopter's blades. He turned his head and looked down at the river. Sure enough, flying high over the water he saw the silhouette of a chopper pass in front of the moon. The noise grew louder and louder – Ben couldn't see the outline of the helicopter now, but could sense its bulk as it passed. He restrained the urge to shout, knowing how useless that would be; but then the sound of the rotary blades passed and grew quieter, and he found himself yelling into the void. 'Here! Over here!'

The helicopter carried on, over the dam and out of

sight. Ben cursed. How could they just pass him by? Taking deep breaths, he tried to get a hold of his anger. Losing it wouldn't serve any purpose up here.

And it was just as he reached that decision that he heard the noise of the chopper once more.

It was returning over the dam, slower this time, and with searchlights beaming from its side. Ben could barely look at them for fear of dazzling himself, but he could see that the beams were focused on the cliff tops and he could well imagine side gunners with their heavy weaponry keeping watch for enemy combatants on the ground. The chopper drew closer; one of the searchlights was moving over the cliff face. It picked out Ben and Aarya, and he had to cover his eyes with one arm as they adjusted to the sudden brightness. He raised his free arm and started to wave.

Suddenly he was aware of movement from Aarya. 'Stay still,' he screamed, moving his arms so that he could hold her firmly. His voice was almost lost under the sound of the chopper. '*Stay still!*'

The helicopter performed a couple of fly-pasts, then rose up above the cliff until it was almost directly on top of Ben and Aarya and the two of them were plunged once more into darkness. Thirty seconds passed. A minute. And then, almost magically, Ben saw a figure appear in mid-air by the ledge, suspended only by what looked like a treacherously thin rope.

It was Ricki.

He had something in his hands, a bundle of fabric, rope and metal. Holding them out towards Ben, he yelled, 'Take these. Don't drop them.'

Ben stretched out his arm. His fingertips barely reached, but he managed to get some kind of hold on the bundle and pull it towards him. 'What is it?' he shouted.

'Harnesses,' Ricki replied, his voice hoarse over the noise of the chopper. 'You both need to wear them. Put them on like pants, then tighten them up. Quickly, Ben – we need to get you out of here.'

Ben untangled the harnesses. He rested one on top of the bomb, using it like a table; the other he slid up Aarya's legs. She shouted in pain when he moved her broken foot, but Ben didn't have time to be gentle. It was difficult attaching Aarya's harness while keeping himself pressed against the wall. Awkward. His fingers felt clumsy as he tightened the straps between the bomb and her body, but eventually he felt confident that it was on properly. Only then did he turn his attention to his own harness.

He held his breath as he wriggled to get it on. There was barely any room to move; when he did, it was with great care. Pulling the harness up his legs, he tightened it as firmly round his own waist as he had round Aarya's. Then he turned to Ricki, who was still suspended in mid-air, watching them.

'What now?' he called.

'There's a rope leading from each harness,' Ricki shouted, 'with a metal link at the end. Throw them to me, one at a time.'

Ben located the ropes – the sturdy links had levers on one side that only moved inwards – and did as he was told. The SAS man caught them with ease. Sweat pouring down his face, Ben saw that at the end of the winch rope there were two loops, each with similar metal links. Ricki attached Ben's rope to one loop and Aarya's to another. Then he turned his attention back to the two of them.

'Is she awake?' he shouted.

'Kind of,' Ben replied. 'But not really aware.'

'All right, Ben. Listen carefully. You're both firmly attached. You need to roll her off the ledge, and yourself at the same time. Can you do that?'

Ben felt himself going white, but he knew he didn't really have a choice. 'I'll try,' he said.

'Don't think about it too much,' Ricki advised. 'Just do it.'

Ben clenched his teeth together. He put his arms around Aarya and the suitcase bomb, holding them firmly. He drew a deep breath, counted to three.

And then he rolled.

In his mind, the fall happened in slow motion. They

fell towards the earth as the rope remained slack; when it tightened it was like a jolt going through Ben's whole body, followed by a sinking, spongy feeling as the extra weight pulled the chopper downwards slightly. But then he felt them being lifted up, and he saw Ricki grabbing Aarya and the suitcase bomb, making sure it didn't slip from her back.

They rose higher, above the level of the cliff and then over firm ground. The rope was winched up – slowly, it seemed to Ben – until finally they were just a metre away from the side door of the chopper.

'Ben!' It was Matt's voice. 'Give me your hand!'

Ben stretched his arm up and a firm grip seized him. He felt himself being pulled up into the chopper. There were other men here as well as Matt, and a good deal of confusion as Aarya and Ricki were also pulled up into the body of the aircraft, and to safety.

Numb with exhaustion, it was all Ben could do to sit up. Aarya was lying on the floor of the chopper while Matt and Ricki removed the bomb from her back. Her eyes were open, but her face was racked with pain.

'Her foot,' Ben shouted over the noise of the aircraft. 'I think she's broken it. Be careful.'

Ricki nodded to show that he had heard as he stowed the suitcase bomb at the back of the chopper.

'We should get her to a doctor,' Ben insisted.

'Roger that,' Ricki replied. 'We're going to take her

back to the base at Kajaki – there's a medic on stand-by and we can offload the bomb. And then I think we've got something else to attend to, haven't we?'

And with that, Ben felt the chopper perform a sharp turn and speed back over the dam, accompanied by a group of grim-faced but determined soldiers . . .

Chapter Twenty-six

It had been the longest night of Dr Bel Kelland's life. No question.

The noise of the attack on the base – the brutal sounds of war – had been bad enough. But she was beginning to think the silence was even worse. The quiet was only occasionally shattered by the noise of a round from the weapons of one of the soldiers who still stood in a protective semicircle around her. All night they had continued firing towards the blown-open gates of the base, single shots that made it clear to the enemy that they were still armed and protected, even if it was only just.

Bel was optimistic by nature. She tried to look for the positives in everything, even in a dreadful situation like this. She was glad of the cover of darkness. It meant she couldn't see the dead bodies that she knew littered the floor of the base; and Private Mears had told her that if the enemy were going to attack again, they were more likely to wait until dawn.

Dawn, however, had never been so fast coming. It was just round the corner now and still they were here. Dug in. Surrounded by enemy. Half expecting an attacking surge and desperate for someone to get them out of this mess. But no one came. The red glow of the burning Apache outside the walls of the base had long since faded away. Now the air was still. Empty.

'How long till dawn?' Bel asked. It was the only thing she'd said for ages.

Private Mears's lips were thin and nervous. 'It gets light early,' he said. 'Less than an hour, I'd say.'

'How much ammo do we have?' Bel couldn't believe the way she'd slipped into military slang.

Mears avoided her question. 'We'll be all right.' He sounded like he was trying to persuade himself as well as her.

Silence again.

It was cold. Very cold. A different place to the one that only hours ago had been so burning hot. She shivered as a round whizzed through the air.

Voices outside the base. Shouting.

Alarmed, Bel's eyes searched for Private Mears. He'd heard them too – they all had. 'What was that?' she breathed.

More shouting. Bel couldn't tell what they were saying, but she knew this: they weren't speaking English. And as that thought hit her, there was a loud bang. A whizzing sound over the walls of the compound, and then an explosion.

'RPG!' someone yelled, and everyone hit the ground as a burst of shrapnel kicked up.

'*Don't stop your fire!*' It was Mears shouting. He scrambled to his feet and pointed his rifle at the entrance to the compound. '*If we stop covering the gates, they'll be in here like flies!*'

He fired, but as he did so a second RPG flew over the compound walls out of the darkness.

'They're attacking!' Bel screamed. She just couldn't control herself any more. '*They're attacking!*'

But the soldiers knew that. Once the shrapnel threat of the second RPG had disappeared, they got to their feet again. To a man, they were white-faced and their eyes bulged with a strange mixture of fear and numbness. They took up their firing positions once more while Bel retreated hard against the protection of the back wall.

As she looked at the young men protecting her, she couldn't help thinking that they had the aura of a group of soldiers preparing themselves to fight to the very end . . .

* * *

There were only five of them in the chopper now: Ben, Ricki, Matt and the two pilots. Ricki and Matt were talking to the pilots in shouted military jargon Ben could barely understand; which left Ben, almost deafened by the noise of the chopper, his brain racing. Aarya had been safely off-loaded and was even now being treated by an army medic; the suitcase bomb had been carefully carried off the helicopter and taken to the safety of the British base. 'You need to stay with her, Ben,' Ricki had said, but Ben had refused to get out of the chopper.

'They'll take care of her,' he'd shouted. 'I'm coming with you.'

Ben's insistence almost appeared to amuse the SAS man, who seemed intuitively to know that nothing was going to stop him from going to help his mum, no matter how dangerous it was. More than that, he seemed to understand it. 'You're getting obstinate in your old age,' he had shouted.

'Just part of my charm,' Ben replied, his face totally serious.

The chopper had barely been on the ground for two minutes – just time to offload – before they had taken off again. It was now mostly empty, to leave plenty of space for the evacuation they anticipated making.

Ben looked out from one of the side-gunners' positions. They were flying high, following the course of the river. The moon still sparkled on the water, making the ground below them as beautiful as it was perilous. Adrenaline surged through him, replacing his exhaustion with a new sense of purpose. His mum *was* going to be all right.

Ricki turned to him.

'We'll be at FOB Jackson in about two minutes,' he yelled over the noise of the chopper. 'That's where your mum is, Ben.'

Ben clenched his jaw and nodded.

'I'm not going to lie to you. The soldiers defending the base have taken casualties. Deaths. There's no confirmation who. It's possible your mum is one of them, we just can't say.' Ben's blood ran cold, but he did his best to concentrate on what Ricki was telling him. 'The base is surrounded by enemy combatants. They've already brought down one attack helicopter and nearly downed another.'

'What's going to stop them doing the same thing again?' Ben asked.

'The pilots are going to switch off all the lights and use night vision to approach. The enemy will be able to hear us, but they won't be able to see us until we're right on top of them. We'll have the element of surprise, but that doesn't mean we won't take incoming fire, and the enemy might just get lucky.' He handed Ben his weapon. 'I meant what I said before, Ben. This isn't a toy. But if you need it, use it. Me and Matt are going to provide covering fire from the side-gunners' positions.'

Ben nodded, his face serious, and he took the gun. If he'd expected to feel better with that weapon in his hands, he was wrong. He checked the safety catch was on, then put it to one side, doing his best to pretend that it wasn't there, but at the same time running through the instructions Ricki had given him on the weapon's use earlier that night.

They started to lose height. Ben felt his stomach churning as Ricki and Matt attached their night-vision goggles and approached the side-gunners' positions. He edged towards the back of the chopper, taking the weapon with him, nervous sweat pouring from his body.

Ben took a deep breath and closed his eyes. He only opened them again when he heard the sound of firing. It was like thunder inside the chopper. Ricki and Matt were firing in short bursts, one followed by another. Ben watched the links of ammo chug into the guns as the chopper continued to lose height. He tried not to think about what would happen if they attracted enemy fire.

The aircraft wobbled. Heavier bursts of fire from the SAS men. Ben grabbed hold of the M16 to stop it sliding along the floor.

A change in the sound of the engines. Higher-pitched.

From the side of the chopper Ben saw compound walls. The SAS men left the side guns and Ricki grabbed his M16 from Ben. 'We're landing in the middle of the base,' he shouted. 'You're going to need to help people up.' He handed Ben a torch. 'Use this to guide them in.'

Ben jumped into action just as he felt the chopper touch down. Ricki and Matt hurled themselves from the side of the aircraft as Ben looked out. Through the darkness he saw scenes of devastation. To his right, a boundary wall with a huge hole blown into it and just beyond it, barely visible, the tangled remains of a downed helicopter. Ricki and Matt had positioned themselves between their Black Hawk and that hole and had started to discharge their M16s in the direction of the destroyed wall. The noise of the weapons, on top of the roar of the chopper, was almost deafening. Ben switched on the torch Ricki had given him. It was small but powerful. Almost immediately it illuminated a terrible sight: figures lying on the ground, entirely still. The sight sent a shiver down his spine.

He turned and looked through the other side of the aircraft, shining his torch out into the base. All he saw was confusion – people running towards him. In the light of his torch he saw flashes of camouflage gear; and beyond that, a body lying on the ground. 'This way!' he shouted. 'Follow the light!'

Ben tried to pick out the faces of the people running to the chopper. He knew what he was looking for, but with each face that was not his mum, he felt a sickness growing in his stomach.

'This way!' he shouted again. '*This way!*' Ricki and Matt's M16s continued to fire in the background.

The first of the soldiers reached him. He didn't look surprised to see someone of Ben's age, but then Ben realized that he was hidden behind the light of the torch. He held out one hand to help the soldier up into the helicopter, but at the last moment the soldier stepped aside. The beam of light from the torch lit up three more figures. Two of them were armed, flanking the third figure, which they quickly manoeuvred up towards the side of the helicopter. And the sight of that figure made a wave of total relief crash over Ben.

He barely recognized his mum. Her face was dirty, her clothes torn and her eyes wide with fright. She stumbled as her chaperones hustled her towards the chopper. 'Help her up!' one of them shouted at him.

Ben didn't need telling twice. He held out his arm and grabbed his mother's hand firmly. 'It's OK,' he shouted. 'We're going to get you out of here.'

Bel stopped. A look of confusion crossed her face as she peered towards him, trying to see past the glare of the torch. '*Ben?*' she whispered.

He tugged on her arm. 'Get up, Mum,' he shouted. 'We can't stay on the ground for long.' Behind her a small crowd of soldiers had congregated, waiting for her to get in. She clambered into the chopper, her face still a picture of astonishment.

'What are you *doing* here, Ben?' she said as she scurried to the back of the chopper.

'It's, er . . . it's kind of a long story,' he bellowed as he helped the soldiers up.

'Then you'd better start talking, young man!' she shrieked. Ben couldn't tell if she was angry or relieved.

'Actually, Mum,' he shouted back, 'I think I might wait until we're out of here.' He helped the last of the soldiers onto the chopper. 'Are there any more?' he demanded of the man.

The soldier shook his head. 'We'll have to come back for the bodies,' he said grimly.

Quickly, Ben moved to the other side of the chopper. Ricki and Matt still had their backs to the helicopter and were keeping up the covering fire. He raised his torch to illuminate them, but at the last moment stopped himself. The SAS men wouldn't thank him for lighting them up like a Christmas tree, he realized. Instead he called out to them. 'Guys!' he yelled. 'Everyone's on. *Everyone's on!*'

Ricki raised one hand – a thumbs-up – and the two of them started to walk backwards, firing their M16s as they went, their backs slightly arched to protect them from the force of the helicopter's rotary blades. The chopper's engines changed pitch again: the aircraft was preparing to take off. Matt turned and jumped up into the body of the helicopter while Ricki continued the covering fire. Then he too joined them. He had barely set foot inside the aircraft when it lifted off the ground. Within seconds the SAS men had taken their side-gunners' positions again: their weapons pounded above the noise of the rotary blades as the pilots gained height with a speedy, sickening lurch before swinging the chopper round and roaring away from the base.

Only then did Ben turn to his mum. Her mouth was open, agog. Her eyes were darting around and one of her hands clutched her hair in an expression of terrified bewilderment.

'Will someone tell me what's going on?' she shouted.

The thunder of the side guns stopped. Ricki turned to Ben, and even in the darkness he could see that the SAS man had a smile on his face.

'Looks to me,' he said, 'like you might have a bit of explaining to do.'

Ben looked from the SAS man to his mum, then back again. 'You know what,' he said, nodding his head sagely, 'I think you might be right.'

Outside the helicopter, the sky was beginning to lighten. Thursday had been the longest day of Ben's life;

Friday, finally, had come. The early morning sun glimmered above the craggy peaks of the mountaintops as the Black Hawk, laden with soldiers and two exhausted civilians, continued its way southwards along the Helmand River, towards the main British base at Camp Bastion.

Towards safety, at last.

Epilogue

Camp Bastion. The following day.

In a place as dangerous as Afghanistan, Ben had come to realize, you take your pleasures wherever you can find them. To most people, the stark canvas pod in which he was sitting would be far from luxurious; it was hardly where Ben would have chosen to spend his Saturday morning. But it had air-conditioning, so it was blissfully cool; more importantly, it was safe. And safety was something Ben had been hankering after for quite a while now.

Aarya sat by his side. The doctors at Camp Bastion had given her painkillers and put her foot in a cast. When Ben first saw his friend being carried off the Chinook that had evacuated her from Kajaki, even he had been shocked by the way she looked after the ravages of her ordeal. A couple of days of medical treatment, however, alongside plenty of water and some half-decent food, had put her well on the road to recovery. Within the next hour, a military transport would be taking her back to her village, while Ben and his mum were to be flown to Kandahar air base, and from there back to the UK.

They sat in silence, feeling awkward on account of the goodbyes that they both knew were just round the corner. He suddenly found himself talking. 'You should come and live in England,' he blurted out. 'There's no wars there. No Taliban, or terrorists, or, you know, all that stuff . . .'

Aarya smiled at him. 'Why would I want to go anywhere other than home?' she asked. 'My parents are waiting for me. You would not want to come and live in my village, even if it was the safest place in the world, would you?'

Ben thought about that. He thought about the small house in Macclesfield he shared with his mum and dad, and how he would feel about not going back there. And he realized that Aarya was right.

'But I will visit you,' she continued, still smiling. 'After all, we still have the second part of our exchange programme. I hope you haven't forgotten about that.'

'I'm sorry I got us into so much trouble,' Ben replied.

Aarya shot him a quizzical look.

'Well,' he continued, aware that he was gabbling slightly, 'if I hadn't insisted on us going to get your books back . . .' He gave her an apologetic smile. All that seemed like a very, very long time ago.

His friend shook her head. 'Ben,' she said, her voice very quiet, 'I owe you my life. If you had not made it onto that ledge . . .' Her voice trailed off, as though she couldn't bear the thought of such a thing. Ben too felt himself shuddering at the memory.

They fell into silence once more.

The door opened and they both looked round quickly. Ricki walked in. It was the first time Ben had seen the SAS man without his weapon and ops waist-coat. He smiled at the two of them – a slightly strained smile, and Ben had to remind himself that the soldier had not long lost two of his friends in the field.

'Ben, Aarya,' he greeted them.

'Hi, Ricki,' Ben said. 'We're, er . . . we're leaving soon.'

'Yeah, I heard. Just bumped into your mum.' He winked. 'I think she's calmed down,' he said. 'A little bit, anyway.' He turned to Aarya. 'How's the foot?'

She shrugged. 'Things could be worse,' she said.

Ricki nodded. 'They could be,' he agreed. 'Especially if Ben hadn't been around.'

Ben felt himself blushing.

'Got a minute?' Ricki asked him. 'Thought we might take a bit of a stroll before you go.'

Ben looked at Aarya. 'I'll be fine,' she said. 'You go.'

It was hot and arid outside the air-conditioned pod. The air was filled with dust and Camp Bastion was busy. Ben and Ricki walked in silence for a while.

'I'm sorry about Toby and Jack,' Ben said. He had wanted to say it, but it still seemed rather inadequate.

'Thanks, Ben,' Ricki replied. 'They were good friends. Good soldiers. When I get back to the UK, the first thing I'll do is visit their families. Tell them that the guys died . . . bravely.'

Ben nodded and they continued to walk.

'You were brave too, Ben,' Ricki said after a moment. 'Very brave. If it wasn't for you, things would have turned out very differently.'

Ben shrugged, uncomfortable with the praise. 'I just did what seemed right at the time,' he said.

'A lot of people wouldn't have. A lot of people would have been too scared to act.'

'Oh, I was scared all right,' Ben replied.

'I'm sure you were. But some people know how to manage their fear. That's quite a skill, Ben. Not many people have it. And I meant what I said – if that bomb had gone off, the consequences would have been unthinkable.'

Ben took a deep breath and tried to push away the

images in his mind of that night above the Kajaki dam. 'What's happened to it now?' he asked. 'The bomb, I mean.'

Ricki smiled. 'I'm afraid we'll never find out. It's been delivered up to military intelligence. Those guys give a new meaning to the phrase hush-hush. At a guess, it's being dismantled as we speak. They're really not the kind of objects you want lying around.'

'No,' Ben said. 'I guess not.'

'So I suppose things will seem a bit quiet when you get back home.'

'Maybe,' Ben observed. 'Me and peace and quiet don't seem to get together very often.'

'What do you mean?'

'Nothing.'

'Well, if you want a bit of excitement, maybe you could think about joining up.'

Ben stopped. 'About what?'

'Joining up. The army, I mean. A couple of years and you'll be ready for SAS selection. You've more than proved you've got the guts for it, after all. And there's never a shortage of places in the world where guys like you can do a lot of good.'

Ben sniffed. He looked around at the bustling military base. He thought that maybe he liked the idea. 'I've heard people talking,' he said. 'About the war, here in Afghanistan. They say it's unwinnable.'

Ricki inclined his head. 'Maybe,' he said. 'Maybe not. You can never really tell if a fight is unwinnable. And anyway, sometimes you don't fight because you know you're going to win; you fight because you know it's the right thing to do.' He gave Ben a piercing look. 'But I reckon you know that as well as anyone.'

Ben looked at the ground. He didn't know quite what to say.

Ricki spared him from having to respond. 'You'd better get back,' he said. 'Say your goodbyes to Aarya – she'll be leaving any minute.' He shook Ben's hand firmly. 'Think about what I've said, won't you?'

'Yeah,' Ben replied. 'Yeah, I will.'

And with that he turned and started walking back to the air-conditioned pod where his friend was waiting.

The time truly had arrived for both of them to go home.

Author's note

In August 2008, 3,000 British troops and a convoy of
vehicles spent five days moving a new turbine across
Helmand Province to the Kajaki dam. It was one of the
biggest operations of the current war effort in
Afghanistan and is testament to the importance of
Kajaki. British forces continue to guard the dam
diligently. It remains a principal target for the enemy
insurgents in the area, who would like to see it
destroyed. If this happened, it would be an untold
disaster for southern Afghanistan.

BATTLEGROUND GLOSSARY

Apache – A type of attack helicopter with twin engines and four blades. Can take a crew of two.

Bandolier – A pocketed belt for soldiers to hold their ammunition in.

Bergen – A large military rucksack.

Black Hawk – A type of utility helicopter with twin engines and four blades.

Brize Norton – The largest airbase of the Royal Air Force, in Oxfordshire, UK.

Chinook – A type of cargo helicopter that can be operated in many different environments, ranging from Arctic conditions to desert warfare operations.

Civvies – Civilian, or ordinary, clothes, not uniform.

Dishdash – An ankle-length long-sleeved garment like a robe.

Forward Operating Base/FOB – A secured forward position or site used by forces to support operations. The base may or may not contain an airfield, hospital or other facilities.

Helmand Province – A province (division) in the south-west of Afghanistan.

Hercules C-130 – A type of military transport aircraft.

ISAF – International Security Assistant Force. A NATO-led security and development mission in Afghanistan.

Islamabad – The capital of Pakistan.

Kajaki – A village in the Helmand Province of Afghanistan close to the Kajaki Dam.

Kandahar – The second largest city in Afghanistan.

Ku Klux Klan – A series of secret organizations in the US who wanted to restore white supremacy through violence and intimidation.

LZ – Landing Zone.

Mujahideen – An Arabic word which refers to Islamic terrorists.

NV – Night Vision.

OC – Officer Commanding.

Ops Sergeant – Operations Sergeant. The senior member of a special-forces team.

Pashtun – An eastern-Iranian group with many populations in Afghanistan.

Platoon – A military unit that tends to be made up of two to four squads, and containing about 30 soldiers.

Platoon Commander – The officer in command of a platoon.

Pressure plate – A pressure-activated detonator on a landmine.

POW – A prisoner of war. Somebody kept in custody by the enemy during armed conflict.

Quetta – The largest city of the Balochistan province of Pakistan. An important marketing and communications centre with Iran and Afghanistan.

RV – A military term for 'rendezvous' or meet.

Sangin – A town in the Helmand Province of Afghanistan in the valley of the Helmand River.

Tailgate – A door or hatch at the back of a vehicle.

Taliban – A fundamentalist religious and political movement that ruled Afghanistan from 1996 to 2001.